ISBN 978-1-7391387-0-7

Prologue

March 1999

This house believes that British imperialistic policy of the nineteenth century cannot be blamed for Africa's problems of today.

Simon Nkaba read the poster for the evening debate over the shoulders of his two friends. Jason Korrundi looked round with a smile.

'Ready for tonight's battle?' he asked.

'Sure,' replied Simon. 'Bring it on.'

Simon had been looking forward to this evening from the moment the list of debates had been pinned up outside the debating chamber of the Oxford Union.

'He's been ready for the last month,' chipped in Peter Achebe.

Jason, Simon, and Peter were inseparable. They had been ever since they first met as wide-eyed five-year-olds on their first day in Mr Pomeroy's Private Institute for Education, a very select school on the outskirts of their nation's capital New Devon. Born into the new elite that emerged after West Africa Free State gained independence from Great Britain in 1970, they were the first scholars from their country to study at Oxford.

'And even better, your kid sister is here to watch your performance,' continued Jason.

Right on cue, the door opened and down the corridor burst a whirlwind of energy.

'Hi bro, hi guys,' called Afia as she bounced towards them. Simon hugged his sibling. He had hardly seen Afia during his three years at Oxford, and here she was all grown up. Simon adored her.

'I still can't believe you persuaded papa to let you come over and visit.'

Afia flashed a mischievous smile.

'You know I always get what I want.'

Jason and Peter looked on grinning. Afia's personality was infectious.

'You need to go find your guest speaker,' said Jason.

Simon reluctantly let his sister go.

'Don't worry about Afia,' said Peter. 'She can come to the bar with us.'

'Okay,' agreed Simon still looking at his sister. 'But only the one drink for you.' Afia pouted, but Simon was serious.

'You may be old enough to drink, but papa would never forgive me if I let you get drunk.' He gave his friends a look. 'Just one drink.'

Jason and Peter nodded, and Simon headed off to find his partner for the evening's debate.

A few minutes later, another undergraduate stopped in front of the notice board and casually scanned the same poster. Tall and dark, he rocked gently forward on the balls of his feet. In his mind, a young Richard Gere. He subconsciously flicked at a fop of brown hair and couldn't help nodding in approval as his reflection appeared in the long mirror next to the president's office. The bespoke suit and handmade shoes cost more than most student loans. Just the image he wanted.

The door opened.

'Oh Anthony, there you are.'

The young man turned to see the president of the Oxford Union standing in the doorway.

'Good evening, Hilary,' he said. 'How are you?'

Hilary Blythe moved to one side, leaving room for an older version of Anthony to step out of her office. Similar suit; identical shoes.

'Sir Hugh Anderson, may I present Anthony Brownlow, your lead student speaker for tonight's debate.'

The permanent secretary at the Foreign and Commonwealth Office extended his hand.

'Hello Anthony, very nice to meet you.'

'Good evening, Sir Hugh. Nice to meet you too. I told father you were my guest speaker for tonight. He sends his regards.'

'Of course,' said Sir Hugh with a nod of recognition. 'You're a dead spit. Not seen your father for ages. Assume he's still running the family business?'

'He is,' confirmed Anthony. 'I think he leaves most of the day-to-day work to the CEO, but he still makes all the important decisions.'

Hilary cut in.

'Anthony, perhaps I could leave you to look after Sir Hugh until dinner. I still have a bit of last-minute admin to sort for the debate.'

'I'd be delighted,' said Anthony. 'Perhaps a pre-dinner drink Sir Hugh?' He gestured to the bar. 'I'm sure you remember the way.'

The president of the Oxford Union opened the debate at half past eight and Anthony Brownlow was first to speak. He was eloquent, confident and didn't use any notes. After nine minutes, he started to sum up. Exactly one minute later, he sat down to a prolonged and well-deserved round of applause.

With a nod of encouragement from his guest speaker, Simon got to his feet, deliberately leaving his notes on his chair.

If Brownlow can do without them, so can I.

As he approached the dispatch box, his throat began to dry, and his legs began to shake. He stumbled into his opening remarks without conviction, forgetting the key points he had so painstakingly researched that now lay three feet away.

Three feet, he thought. *May as well be three miles.* Pride overruled the simple logic of returning to his chair and things went from bad to worse.

Simon became less and less coherent. He started rambling and couldn't stop. After fifteen minutes, Hilary waved desperately to the secretary who had to move Simon forcibly from the despatch box.

From then on, the result of the debate was never in any doubt. In fairness, Sir Hugh was quite gentle, and Simon's guest speaker was excellent. But even his oration could not repair the damage. Questions from the floor only prolonged the agony. Brownlow could sense victory and was going for the jugular. He savagely rammed his points home, like a deranged serial killer, plunging the knife in again and again. Simon had no answers. Tears of frustration welled up and he struggled to keep control.

'The "ayes" two hundred and ten, the "noes" fourteen.' The final vote was crushing.

Back in the bar, Simon was inconsolable.

'Don't worry about it,' said Peter sympathetically. 'After all, it's only a debate.'

'It was so much more than a debate,' replied Simon. 'It was my chance to stand up for our country. What we've achieved. I've just let everyone down.'

'You didn't let me down, big brother,' said Afia. 'I was proud just to see you up there in front of all those people.' She reached over and squeezed his hand.

Simon managed a weak smile in response, but still felt wretched.

'Hey guys, how are you all doing?'

Simon looked up to see Anthony Brownlow standing over him, flanked by a couple of his cronies. He groaned inwardly. Brownlow was the last person he wanted to see right now.

'No hard feelings, eh?' said Anthony. 'Great debate, I thought. We really got to the nub of the issue.'

Simon was struggling for a response. Then Afia came to his aid.

'Of course not,' she said with her trademark smile. 'You and your guest speaker did really well. You should be delighted.'

Anthony looked hard at Afia, trying to detect some malice in her words. But it was obvious there wasn't any. Afia smiled again and he was captivated.

'That's very kind,' he said. 'Let me buy you all a drink. Barman!' he called, 'champagne all round.'

Half an hour later, Simon's mood was easing slightly, but he was still far from good company.

'Look,' he said eventually, 'I've had enough for one night.'

Jason nodded. 'Me too.'

Anthony was still generously handing out champagne when he heard the exchange between the two friends.

'We're heading off into town. Are you guys going to join us?'

Simon shook his head.

'What about me?' said Afia. 'It's still early and it is my last night in Oxford.

Simon started to object, but he could see the disappointment on his sister's face.

'Hey,' said Peter. 'I'm up for a some more fun.' He turned to Simon. 'I'll look after Afia. You know she'll be fine with me.'

Afia gave Simon a pleading look and his face softened.

'Okay,' he said. 'But stick with Peter and don't stay out too late. The taxi's booked for nine tomorrow. I'll be waiting in the hotel lobby at quarter to.'

Afia beamed.

'Thanks bro. You're the best.'

'Great.' said Anthony grabbing a half-full bottle of champagne from the bar. 'Let's go and have some fun.'

1.

May 2022

Sarah squinted up at the midday sun. Its glare easily defeated the cheap lenses in her anti-ballistic goggles. She tutted to herself. Should've spent the money on a decent pair, rather than rely on the army-issue ones. They were rubbish. Humidity levels were off the charts, and deep in the West Africa Free State hinterland, it was getting like the inside of a pressure cooker. The river of sweat down her back had dried up long ago as the sun tried its hardest to bake the life out of her. The crusty salt stains on her camouflage shirt were already rubbing at her skin, especially beneath her large pack. The assault rifle was heavy in her hands, and she could feel a blister nagging at the heel of her right foot. Sarah caught the eye of Lieutenant Tommy Ele, the Free State army officer leading the patrol, and grinned. Right now, there was nothing else in the world she would rather be doing.

Major Sarah Grey was in West Africa Free State training new members of the UK's high-readiness military headquarters. After a few days of planning exercises, the ab-initio staff officers had been let loose on a series of unsupervised reconnaissance tasks in and around New Devon. With time on her hands, a restless Sarah sought out a British mentoring team working with the Free State army headquarters. Captain Terry Willis, a former colleague from Sandhurst, was the team leader. It took Sarah no time at all to persuade him to include her on an upcoming Free State patrol. At 0600 the following morning, she was in Joseph Khalli barracks, just outside the capitol, for the patrol briefing. Half an hour later, she was in the back of a three-ton truck, heading deep into the West Africa Free State hinterland.

As the patrol continued, the open savanna plains gave way to woodland, lightly forested with acacia trees. Sarah was grateful for the protection the treetops provided from the relentless sun, but also concerned about the tactical implications of the reduced visibility.

'Close up,' ordered Lieutenant Ele.

Sarah was impressed. The patrol commander had clearly picked up on that as well. Half an hour later, they came across a small clearing. Ele ordered a halt and posted sentries. The rest of the patrol sought what little shade there was and took a well-earned breather.

Sarah slipped off her pack and reached inside for a small gas stove. Her father had commanded a squadron of Challenger tanks in the first Gulf War and swore that a cup of tea was the best thirst quencher in very hot weather.

If it's good enough for dad, Sarah thought to herself as she heated up a mess tin of water to boiling and dropped in a tea bag. Carefully pouring two cups, she carried them over to where Lieutenant Ele was finishing up with his sergeant. She held one out for him.

'Ma-am,' Ele braced up smartly and saluted.

'It's Sarah, and there's definitely no need for that.'

'Understood, ma-am.'

Sarah smiled. The tea was good, and her father was right.

'How often do you patrol this far into the hinterland?'

Ele unfolded his map on the ground in front of him. It was old and faded and had been on many more missions than its present owner.

'We'll keep heading northeast until we reach the Demba Mari region.' He traced a line on the map with his finger and circled what looked like a cluster of small villages. Sarah looked. The nearest one was about twenty kilometres away. Close enough to reach by nightfall.

'We never used to come this far out,' continued Ele. 'Then last year the kiniun began attacking villages in the hinterland.'

'The what?'

'They're rebel soldiers. No-one knows where they came from, but they're very ferocious. The local people call them *kiniun* … lions. They take food and women. Sometimes they attack the larger villages where police are based. They kill them and burn down the police houses.'

Sarah shook her head. None of this was in the country briefing pack that the intelligence section had put together.

'What's your government doing about it?

Lieutenant Ele gestured at his men.

'We do our best, but our equipment is poor, and my soldiers have very little training.'

Sarah had to agree. A British patrol this size would have all manner of tech. GPS trackers, up-to-date comms kit, maybe even hand-held drones. It would have been able to call up close air support and a CASEVAC helicopter would always be no more than an hour away. She looked around. None of the soldiers carried a weapon heavier than an AK47 assault rifle and the only piece of tech was an enormous valve radio on the back of the unluckiest soldier in the group. And that hadn't worked since they'd got off the truck.

Lieutenant Ele called his sergeant. Time to get moving.

Then, some way off but clearly audible, Sarah heard the distinctive pop-pop of small arms fire. She wasn't the only one. The soldiers hurriedly gathered their weapons and looked to Lieutenant Ele.

'Sergeant, defensive positions.' Ele had the map out again. 'Ma'am?'

Sarah cocked her head to one side and listened carefully. The gunfire was less intense, but she could still hear it. Then, as she tried to orientate herself towards the sound, there was a muffled boom. Some type of grenade. Definitely. Coming from her right. A quick look up at the sun confirmed that was east.

'What's due east of here?'

Ele looked down at the map.

'Batanto. About two klicks. It's got to be coming from there.'

He looked up at Sarah expectantly.

'You're in command here,' said Sarah.

'I know ma'am. But what would you do?'

Sarah didn't have to think.

'A good soldier always marches to the sound of the guns.'

Lieutenant Ele had a difficult choice to make. He wanted to reach Batanto as quickly as possible, but the patrol couldn't afford to abandon all tactical discipline. After all, he had no idea who or what had attacked the village, or where they were now. If he wasn't careful, his soldiers could be next. In the end, he compromised. The patrol covered the first kilometre at a fast jog. They then moved into an arrowhead formation with weapons ready and approached the village at a slower, more guarded pace. Ele advanced at the point of the arrowhead, with his sergeant to his left and Sarah to his right.

The patrol broke clear of the woodland approximately two hundred metres to the west of the village. Ele signalled his soldiers to stop, and they sank down into a crouch. To their front, a single dirt road ran from left to right. The village of Batanto was strung out along it. They could see about fifty dwellings, most with timber walls and corrugated iron roofs. Here and there were slightly larger buildings, a mix of packed mud and stone. What looked like a convenience store and probably a couple of bars. The biggest structure by far was right in the centre. Sarah thought it had to be a church or a mosque. It was impossible to pick out any distinguishing features because it was engulfed in flame.

Lieutenant Ele waved them forward cautiously. Sarah walked slowly with her eyes focused ahead, scanning for any signs of danger. There were none.

It was a church. Sarah could now make out the wooden spire burning fiercely. It looked like one of the low buildings beyond the church was also on fire. The patrol reached the edge of the village and stopped again. The church was directly in front of them, and Sarah could feel the heat from the blaze above the baking afternoon sun. The cracking and sputtering of the dying building was loud in her ears, but the sound of gunfire had disappeared. Whoever had brought death and destruction to Batanto was long gone.

They skirted around the church and spread out along the dirt road. A low moan caught Sarah's attention, and she turned back. On the ground in front of the church were two bodies, horribly twisted and burned black like charcoal. A clawed hand reached upward grotesquely. Thin whisps of smoke rose slowly from the charred remains before being sucked towards the burning church. Next to them was a third body. The priest. He had been spared the agony of burning. Instead, he had been repeatedly hacked with a heavy machete. His once-white cassock was now soaked black with blood. His face was smashed, and his skull had been cleaved open. He lay there helpless to stop the flies that were already beginning to feast on his open wounds.

Sarah ran to him, grabbing a field dressing from her webbing belt as she did so. The stench from the blackened bodies was unimaginable. It invaded her nostrils, forcing bile into her throat. Her head began to spin, and she retched violently.

The priest opened his eyes and moaned again. More weakly. Trembling, Sarah knelt at his side and gently lifted his head. The flies buzzed loudly, angry at the interruption as she applied the dressing. It barely covered the largest wound and Sarah knew immediately that there was nothing to be gained from any further attempts at first aid.

Cradling the priest's head in her lap, Sarah willed the end to come quickly.

'Don't talk,' she whispered, as he agonizingly tried to work his shattered jaw. 'You don't need to say anything.'

But the priest was determined.

'*Kin … kiniun*,' he croaked, almost wordlessly. '*Funfun … kiniun*.'

Sarah blinked hard but couldn't prevent her eyes from welling up. Angrily she shook her head, forcing her vision to return. When she looked back down, the priest was dead.

For Sarah, the rest of the day was little more than a blur. She was no stranger to death. Two tours in Afghanistan had made sure of that. But this was on an unimaginable scale. The village had been devastated. Free State soldiers collected over thirty bodies for burial. Most had been shot at close range, but here and there the work of the machete was also evident. A grenade had been thrown into one of the bars. No-one survived. The other building set alight was a small police station. Five policemen had been inside. It was impossible to tell if they'd been killed before the fire. Sarah prayed that they had.

Lieutenant Ele set up a command post in the schoolhouse opposite the church. He stood in the doorway with Sarah. Like his men, he had a makeshift shemagh wrapped tightly round his nose and mouth. The smell of death was everywhere.

'Nobody's talking.'

'Sorry?' said Sarah looking up. Her mind was still with the priest.

'The villagers. Nobody's talking,' repeated Ele.

'I'm not surprised,' said Sarah. 'They must be scared to death.'

'No. It's the children.'

Sarah didn't understand.

'They've taken the children,' said Ele.

Sarah looked around. Suddenly it dawned on her. Apart from a single baby in its mother's arms and a couple of frightened toddlers peeking out from one of the houses, she hadn't spotted any children in the village. The schoolhouse had over a dozen desks. But there were no pupils to be seen.

'Who knows,' said Ele. 'Child soldiers or brides. Either way, it's an easy way to spread terror.'

Sarah shuddered. She thought immediately of her ten-year-old niece and the bile started to rise again.

'But why spread terror here?' She gazed across at the church, now just a smouldering ruin. 'Who could possibly gain from doing that?'

Her thoughts went back to the dying priest, and the final words he had tried so hard to speak.

'What's *funfun*?' she asked quietly.
'What's what?'
'*Funfun*. It's not English.'
Ele scratched his head.
'In Yoruba, *funfun* means white. Why?'
'In his dying breath. I'm sure the priest said *funfun kiniun*.'
They stared at each other, without a clue.
'Why would the priest's last words be white lions?

2.

Exactly one week after Batanto, Sarah was ready to leave West Africa Free State. The training was over, and she was the last member of the Joint Force Headquarters left in country. Someone had to square away the last-minute admin and Sarah had no immediate family to return home to. Besides, she'd promised to take Terry out for a thank-you dinner.

Terry chose a local restaurant on the waterfront. He tipped the head waiter for a table discretely located on the edge of a large stone patio with a wonderful view out over the Atlantic Ocean.

Sarah walked into the restaurant just as the sun was disappearing over the horizon. The simple white cotton dress and coral cardigan were the prefect combination for a late spring African evening. Her shoulder-length hair shone golden in the last rays of sunlight and her blue eyes sparkled. Heads turned as the waiter led her to their table.

'You look fabulous.'

'Thank you, Terry,' she said, her eyes still smiling. 'Sometimes it's nice to leave the soldier at home.'

The restaurant's speciality was seafood, and it was excellent. They both avoided talking about work during dinner, but once the waiter had cleared Sarah was eager to steer the conversation towards her experience at Batanto.

'So just what exactly is going on out in the hinterland?'

'Good question. Not sure anyone in New Devon really knows.'

'Well Lieutenant Ele seemed pretty sure.'

Terry leaned back in his chair and looked up at the night sky. Its blackness punctuated by a million stars, all so much brighter than he was used to back home.

'You've been out here for a while,' Sarah persisted. 'You must have some idea.'

'It's complicated,' Terry said finally.

Sarah leaned forward.

'No-one in the army headquarters is too keen to talk about it, but we do know that sometime last year attacks on small, unprotected government facilities started happening in the hinterland. Police stations and court houses were a favourite target. Unrest was also being stoked elsewhere. In the remotest parts of the country. There have been issues with the government allowing foreign contractors to re-start diamond mining on land some of the locals believe is sacred.'

Sarah thought for a moment.

'That doesn't make sense. Is it an insurgency or a terror campaign? It can't be both.'

'That's the issue,' said Terry. 'Some stuff looks like it's aimed at alienating the government, but other stuff is just random killing.'

'Well, what I saw in Batanto wasn't about winning hearts and minds.' Even the warmth of the evening couldn't stop Sarah from shivering as she recalled the horror she had witnessed. 'That's for sure.'

For the longest time, neither of them said anything. The muted conversations and clinking cutlery from the other diners were the only sound. Then, far out to sea, a ship's horn blasted. Sarah jumped. She was in danger of ruining the evening but needed to know more. The waiter hovered nearby but Sarah waved him away.

'What do you know about the *kiniun*?'

'*Kiniun* as in lions?' said Terry.

'Yes, *kiniun* as in lions.'

'It's what the locals are calling the terrorists in the hinterland.'

'I know,' said Sarah. 'What about white lions. Have you heard that?'

Terry shook his head.

'Where did that come from?'

'The priest whose brains are all over my combat trousers. It was the last thing he said.'

'No idea,' said Terry. 'I did see a J2 briefing that talked about the insurgents being led by someone called *Kiniun Nba*.'

'Don't tell me. The Lion King.'

Terry risked a smile.

'Not quite. A better translation is Great Lion.'

'And he is ...'

'No idea. I guess the intelligence boys' crystal ball wasn't working that day!'

Sarah sighed, exasperated.

'Surely someone knows what's going on. I mean, there must be a plan.'

'You need to understand how fragile things are here,' said Terry. 'President Korrundi has been in power for less than eighteen months. Before him it was just a free for all. All the good work that Joseph Khalli did after independence was ruined by the guy who came next ...'

'Is that Joseph Khalli as in the army barracks?' interrupted Sarah, embarrassed by her lack of local knowledge.

'Exactly. He was West Africa Free State's first president. Lasted almost forty years and did a lot of good. The next bloke was useless. And corrupt. Korrundi is much better. He's more like Khalli, but his fight against corruption has pissed off a lot of powerful people. The politics here is unbelievable.'

'So why doesn't Korrundi just ask us for more help. I mean you guys are out here, so he must already have asked for some.'

'That's complicated too. We're here as part of a wider ECOWAS initiative. It's all about getting armed forces across Western Africa working together. It's got nothing to do with this country's insurgency problem.'

Sarah understood, but that didn't make it any less frustrating.

'The Foreign Secretary's out here right now, as part of his big Africa trip, but I bet he doesn't even know there's an SAS training team in country.'

'I know,' said Sarah. 'My flight home tomorrow's been delayed because of him.'

'Not surprised,' replied Terry. 'We've been providing a bit of unofficial overwatch for his visit. Once he's gone, I can give you a lift to the airport if you like.'

Sarah smiled her thanks. She had learned all she was going to for one night.

'Time to get the bill. It's getting late and I've still got a bergen to pack.'

Sarah strode out of her hotel at exactly nine o'clock. Parked right in front of the entrance was a stripped-down land rover. Terry waved from the passenger seat. Sarah heaved the bergen off her shoulder and threw it over the tailgate. It landed on the load deck with a thud. Nimbly she jumped up after it and chose a spot on the bench seat behind the driver.

'You must be Staff Sergeant Hayes,' she held out her hand. 'Sarah Grey.'

The driver twisted in his seat.

'Morning boss,' he said, using the SAS's informal greeting for officers.

'Here, you'd better take this,' said Terry, handing over a Glock pistol in a flat, pancake holster.

'You think I'm going to need that?' asked Sarah.

'Probably not. But we are supposed to be the back-up security. And you know what they say. Hope for the best; plan for the worst.'

Sarah reached behind her and clipped the holster to her belt. She pulled down her shirt to hide it.

'Good to go?' asked Hayes. Without waiting for an answer, he slipped the land rover into gear and pulled away.

Morning rush hour in New Devon was a nightmare. Sarah shook her head in astonishment as a taxi driver pulled out directly in front of them, horn blaring to signal his right of way. Mopeds and scooters were everywhere, darting in and out of the traffic, like fireflies over a pond. Impossibly overladen trucks wobbled along slowly, threatening to shed their loads at every turn. And at each major intersection a traffic officer stood on a low concrete pedestal, blowing loudly on a whistle. Their hand signals only adding to the chaos.

Staff Sergeant Hayes had seen it all before. He negotiated his way calmly through the maelstrom of noise and disorder, like a veteran commuter strolling across the concourse at Waterloo station on his way to catch the five-fifty to Surbiton. It may have taken over an hour to cover the five miles to the airport, but he'd planned for that and when they arrived, he was as relaxed as if they'd spent the whole time lounging by the pool.

Hayes parked the land rover in a drop-off bay, approximately one hundred metres from the entrance to the departure hall. New Devon international airport was small and uninviting. Apart from a couple of daily flights to Europe, it mostly catered for short hop routes around Africa. A single terminal served both departures and arrivals. Its architecture was a bad copy of Eastern European Communist. The façade was incredibly ugly, a mix of concrete slabs and heavy rectangular panes of glass, baked into a dull shade of brown over time by the unrelenting sun. There was no shade in front of the terminal and Sarah pulled her ball cap down low to protect her face.

'What time's the foreign secretary due?'

'1100 hours,' said Hayes. 'Goodbyes in the terminal from the deputy president, then onto the pan for 1115. Flight plan has the departure time as 1130.'

As usual, the senior non-commissioned officer knew everything.

Before long they began to see signs of activity. Two truckloads of soldiers arrived and started to deploy around the terminal building. Local taxi drivers were directed away from stands in front of the building and curious New Devonians were herded behind some ancient wooden barriers that had appeared from the back of a third truck. In front of the terminal, a large and obviously senior officer was pacing around, gesticulating with a short, swagger stick, while the soldiers ran around trying to carry out his orders. At one point, a young officer approached the land rover to move it on. A withering look from Staff Sergeant Hayes was enough to convince him he was better employed doing something else.

'Have you noticed anything strange?' asked Hayes.

Sarah considered the efforts of the local military. It wasn't exactly how the Guards would have done it, but all the bases seemed to have been covered.

'Nothing obvious. What are you getting at?'

'What about the uniforms?'

'What about them? They're just bog-standard jungle-cam. Same as we used to wear.'

'Exactly,' said Hayes. 'These guys are regular soldiers. I've been following Harknall since he arrived, and everywhere he's gone the border force has been on protection duty. They wear that god-awful blue tiger-pattern stuff. How come for the very last event, it's all change?'

'Could just be sharing things out between the army and the border force. You know, a prestige thing,' suggested Terry.

'Maybe,' said Hayes. 'But it's still a bit strange.'

'Heads up,' called Sarah from the back seat. A small convoy of vehicles was approaching.

Like most airports, New Devon International was served by its own dedicated access road. It came off the country's only dual-lane highway, looped round in front of the terminal and then made its way back to the main road. The convoy moved slowly onto the access road where a pair of soldiers raised a single-pole barrier. There were six vehicles. First was an army land rover filled with soldiers. Next came three old, black Mercedes limousines. A small panel van followed, and another land rover brought up the rear. The barrier was lowered after the second land rover had passed and the convoy continued its way towards the terminal building. It finally came to a halt with the middle Mercedes directly in front of the departure hall entrance.

There was a short pause as a reception party emerged from the terminal building, the tall figure of the West Africa Free State finance minister, and de facto deputy president, at its head. Reginald Harknall stepped out of the middle Mercedes. This was the fifth stop on his Africa trip, and it showed. His lightweight suit was badly crumpled, and his balding head had seen far too much sun. Four more British officials emerged from the other two limousines, blinking in the bright sunlight. The deputy president strode forward.

As Sarah watched the two men shake hands, her eyes were drawn to a commotion at the top of the access road. A motorbike approached the barrier and then swerved off the road to avoid it. In a billowing cloud of dust, the young rider almost came to grief on the adjacent scrubland. Revving the engine hard, he regained control and accelerated towards the terminal. On the back of the bike was a passenger, his baggy shorts billowing wildly in the bike's slipstream. Sarah could see a brown canvas bag slung over one shoulder. Across his bare chest was an AK47 assault rifle.

'Shit!'

Without another word, Sarah leapt out of the land rover and raced towards the danger. As she ran, she reached behind for her pistol.

The motorbike skidded to a halt, spitting up stones that hammered into the paintwork of the nearest Mercedes. A second later, the passenger let loose with the AK47 on full automatic. The noise of the gunfire echoed deafeningly off the face of the terminal. Bullets sprayed everywhere, sending hosts and visitors diving for cover, like falling pins in a bowling alley.

Sarah was still thirty metres from the motorbike when the rifle finally fell silent. The passenger made no effort to reload. Instead, he reached into the bag and pulled out a hand grenade. The new threat registered in a rush of adrenalin. Still running flat out, Sarah raised the Glock and began pulling the trigger.

Her first two rounds missed, giving the passenger time to rip the pin from the grenade. Before he could toss it, rounds three and four hit him squarely in the chest. He was thrown from the bike and landed right on top of his own grenade.

It exploded.

The already lifeless body jerked up off the ground, as if it were a puppet on a string. The force of the blast ripped the torso open. Its severed head trundled grotesquely into the road, coming to rest against the front wheel of the panel van.

The blast checked Sarah's run. She was suddenly aware of the motorbike accelerating towards her, as the rider tried to make good his escape. She threw herself to one side as he roared past.

'I don't think so pal.'

As usual, Staff Sergeant Hayes was one step ahead of the game. He already had the land rover moving forward and a quick turn of the wheel was enough to put it directly into the biker's path. The bike smashed into the near side front wing and the rider flew clean over the bonnet. His unprotected skull smashed into the concrete kerb with a sickening crunch, and he came to rest, lolling half on and half off the pavement, like a discarded rag doll.

Sarah picked herself up as quickly as she could. She tucked the Glock back into its holster, wincing at the sharp pain in her side as she did so. Above the doorway, the concrete façade was peppered with bullet holes, like a giant join the dots puzzle from a child's activity book.

Below them, the cluster of dignitaries were slowly getting to their feet. The babble of nervous chatter increasing dramatically as the realisation dawned that they were safe and unhurt.

All except one.

To the left of the deputy president, a single body lay face down, unmoving. A crimson stain rapidly expanding across the back of his crumpled linen jacket. As Sarah had expected, the automatic fire was wildly inaccurate. In fact, twenty-nine of the rounds fired had gone high. But that was no consolation to the Secretary of State for Foreign, Commonwealth and Development Affairs. The thirtieth had struck Reginald Harknall right between his shoulder blades and he was as dead as his two assassins.

3.

Anthony Brownlow was incandescent with rage. He smashed his first down on the cabinet room table. The China teacup in front of him jumped wildly, its contents slopping out over the saucer onto the expensive green baize.

'It's been two days since Reginald Harknall was murdered. How come we still don't have a bloody clue who's to blame?' Brownlow's voice was so loud it seemed to rattle the window blinds.

The small group of officials eyed each other nervously, none wanting to be first to speak. The government had enjoyed a fairly easy ride in the ten months since its re-election victory. This was fast becoming its first real crisis of its second term in office. Across the table, Tom Fletcher, the defence secretary kept his mouth firmly shut. It was left to the deputy foreign secretary to speak up.

'Well prime minister, as you know, from an intelligence perspective, West Africa Free State is a tier four country, so we have virtually no dedicated resource allocated to it. Even the defence attaché is split across two other countries. Our best source for information right now is a small SAS training team that's currently in country, but so far they've not managed to turn up anything useful either.'

'Stop telling me what we don't know,' Brownlow thundered. A second smash of his fist spilled more tea. 'I want to hear what we do know.'

The hapless minister retreated from the firing line. The prime minister's senior advisor, Cedric Ratley, exchanged glances with the chief of the Secret Intelligence Service. Against her better judgement, Hilary Blythe stepped up.

'Sir,' she began, 'the minister is correct about the paucity of intelligence assets we have in that part of the world. The defence attaché does have a couple of sources, but they're quite low level. We do know that West Africa Free State is currently experiencing a growing spate of unrest that's threatening to develop into a full-blown insurgency. While we have very little information on who's behind it, there is evidence they are well organised and well armed. Whoever they are, they're spreading a great deal terror in the country's hinterland. Their ultimate goal remains unknown. It may well be the overthrow of President Kirrundi's democratically elected government. The foreign secretary's assassination was probably an escalatory step towards that.'

'So not a terrorist act against us?' said Brownlow.

'No sir, there is no evidence to support that.'

'Finally. Someone with at least some idea of what the bloody hell is going on.'

Hilary shuffled her briefing papers together and made a mental note to pass on a huge well done to the Africa department at Vauxhall Cross.

'From now on, SIS has the lead in tracking down the foreign secretary's killers,' proclaimed the prime minister. He glared across the cabinet table, daring someone to question his direction.

Hilary wasn't sure she wanted that poisoned chalice.

'Nevertheless,' he continued. 'The whole world is watching. We have to do something.' He turned to the defence secretary.

'Tom, I want military response options and I want them quickly. Your department sucks up forty billion pounds of taxpayers' money every year, it's time they started doing something to earn it.'

The defence secretary nodded sycophantically.

'Of course, prime minister, I'll get onto it right away.'

Brownlow pushed his chair back and stood up abruptly. The meeting was over.

'Prime minister,' interjected his senior advisor hurriedly. 'President Kirrundi has been seeking a call with you since Friday. I really think now's the time to take it. One to one, you may learn more of the internal problems he's facing, and that can only improve our overall situational awareness.'

Ratley had the reputation for being a hard-talking firebrand, but his advice was always measured and well thought through. The prime minister frowned, unconvinced. Ratley pressed on.

'I may not be a military expert, but I do know any intervention in this part of the world will be fraught with difficulties. We must be strong in the eyes of the international community, but the last thing we can afford is British soldiers coming home in body bags. Kirrundi isn't the enemy and early engagement with him is vital if we're to get this right.'

'Very well,' conceded Brownlow. 'Set it up. But if we're going in, Kirrundi needs to know it won't be a partnership of equals. I want a swift outcome that's good for us. I don't give a damn about his problems.'

Jason Kirrundi walked quickly from the presidential office to the main conference room. There were never enough hours in the day, and the British foreign secretary's murder hadn't exactly helped.

The president didn't like the conference room. It was small and pokey. The oak panelled walls kept all the heat in, and the matching table was far too large. What's more, there hadn't been enough money to install air conditioning during the last refurbishment. He squeezed passed the tiny secretaries' desk and took his seat.

There were only two other attendees. The commander of the West Africa Free State army, General Samuel Karrick, sat to the president's left. He was an immense man with a round, pugnacious face. At one time his dress uniform had fitted him comfortably. Now it strained at every seam. Karrick had served in the army for more years than anyone could remember and ruled with a rod of iron.

Opposite him was Simon Nkaba. The president's life-long friend was now the interior minister. He was almost as large as the general but looked more composed in an expensive silk suit and open-neck shirt. The interior ministry was by far the most corrupt, having traditionally exercised most of the power within the country. The jury was still out on whether Simon's appointment had made things better or worse.

There was only one subject on the agenda, and it took less than a minute for the two heavyweights to start arguing.

'I've said it before, and I'll say it again. It was all the army's fault. Security at the airport on Friday was atrocious.' Simon was quick to distance himself from the failure. 'The border force handled the rest of the visit faultlessly. We give one task to the army, and this is the result.'

Although visibly angry, General Karrick kept his emotions in check.

'You waited until Friday morning before you told my headquarters they needed to secure the airport for the British departure. It's almost as if you wanted us to be ill prepared.'

'And what's that supposed to mean?' replied Simon, his voice rising quickly. 'The president instructed my ministry to co-ordinate the visit. He also made it clear that border force and the army both had to provide troops for security. It's not my fault if your soldiers weren't up to the task.'

Jason closed his eyes and sighed. It was like watching two bull elephants squaring up against each other.

'General ... Simon,' he began. 'Arguing amongst ourselves is not helping. The enemy is outside this meeting room. There'll be time to learn lessons from last week, but right now we must concentrate on the real threat. It's clear that the problem in the hinterland is growing. If the insurgents are not stopped quickly, they will become bolder. And woe betide us if the fighting reaches the streets of our capital.'

The president paused, letting the seriousness of the situation sink in. The sound of the secretary, tapping on her stenotype machine, filled the room.

'Prime Minister Brownlow has finally agreed to take my call, but I don't expect it will be pleasant. He'll be angry we were unable to protect his foreign secretary and we can hardly blame him. I also think he will push to deploy troops here to help tackle the insurgency. The media in London are screaming for action, and he needs to look strong. The question is, how should we respond?'

General Karrick was first to offer an opinion.

'The improvements the British special forces team has made are obvious. We should ask for more of that.'

'It makes sense, but I'm not sure that'll be enough for Brownlow. And the British special forces are limited. I'm not sure we'd get any more support from them even if we asked.'

The president stared hard at the general.

'While no-one doubts their bravery, our army is small. If the British want to send combat troops to help us, why shouldn't we just accept them?'

Before General Karrick could respond, Simon intervened.

'That's the last thing we should agree to. Many of our people still remember British rule. Under the boot of the British army. And you want to invite them back?'

'Come on Simon,' said the president. 'That was over fifty years ago. Surely we've moved on?'

General Karrick was less concerned.

'As long as we keep control over operations in the hinterland, we can work with the British.'

'No, no, no!' interrupted Simon again. 'Brownlow will never accept operating under Free State command. And if our people start dying at the hands of the British, we'll get the blame.'

'My friend, I understand your concerns, but these are difficult times. There must be a compromise here.'

It was Simon who eventually spoke next.

'All right,' he said. 'You want a compromise; I'll give you one. We accept support from the British, more training teams, maybe some helicopters and logistics. What we don't accept are combat troops. We make it clear that taking the fight to the insurgents is a job for us. Their generals will understand that. And Brownlow will see it as an opportunity to intervene without any of his precious soldiers getting in harm's way. He gets to look like a strong and decisive leader.'

The president thought for a minute.

'You know what Simon, that's a really good idea. If we play our cards right, we could leverage all sorts of help from the British. But we'd still be calling the shots. And when the insurgency is defeated, we'll get all the credit. What do you think general?'

'If I could move our forces around the hinterland by helicopter, that would be a game-changer. We'd defeat them in a month.'

General Karrick and Simon were suddenly friends again. Like children in a sweet shop, they started picking out what support they might get from the British. President Kirrundi tuned them out. He was already rehearsing the conversation he must have with Prime Minister Brownlow to make it all happen.

4.

The squally shower retreated eastwards just as Tom Fletcher began his walk across Whitehall. By the time he reached the heavy black security gates, the sun was busy drying out the pavement and a watery rainbow had appeared high above Horse Guards. Fletcher loved strolling up Downing Street. It reminded him just how important he was. He cast a superior eye towards the journalists and photographers penned in on the other side of the road, and then deliberately ignored their shouted questions.

Fletcher was from the most recent generation of politicians and was very much one of Anthony Brownlow's men. Suave and confident, his Oxbridge degree had been his steppingstone into politics and his rise within the government had been nothing short of meteoric. A short stint as a junior minister in the treasury and unswerving loyalty to Brownlow had proved sufficient to elevate him to the full cabinet with the defence portfolio as part of the prime minister's last re-shuffle. A total lack of knowledge of the military had not made him popular with the service chiefs, but Fletcher didn't care. Defence was small beer compared to what his sights were set on.

Cedric Ratley met Fletcher in the hallway of 10 Downing Street, and together they climbed the stairs to the prime minister's office.

'Come in, Tom.' Anthony Brownlow was putting the phone down as Fletcher entered. 'I've just finished talking with President Kirrundi. We were at Oxford together, you know.'

'No, prime minister, I didn't. What did he have to say for himself?'

'Well, as you might expect, he was full of apologies about what happened to Reginald.'

'So he bloody should be. What about sending our troops?

'Well, he was obviously expecting it, but his response was surprising. He said he was happy to accommodate whatever I thought appropriate, but when I mentioned the spearhead battalion, he pushed back. Apparently, he's concerned about how that will go down with his people, especially the older generation. Thought it might re-ignite imperialist fears.'

'What utter bollocks,' retorted Fletcher. 'He's hardly in a position to start imposing conditions.'

But Ratley was already thinking ahead.

'Maybe so,' he said. 'But think it through. 'We increase training and maybe provide some logistical support, but we leave all the fighting to Kirrundi. No British casualties. And once the insurgency is defeated, we can spin it that it was all our doing.'

'Always assuming Kirrundi's men can actually defeat the insurgents,' interjected Fletcher.

But Brownlow was warming to the idea.

'Well, yes of course,' he said. 'But with our help, that shouldn't be too difficult. Surely?'

'No, prime minister,' replied Fletcher, changing his tune immediately he sensed where his boss was heading. 'It should not. I'll have that fed back to the army, so they can start reverse engineering their planning to fit.'

'Good,' said Brownlow. 'Make sure the loose ends are tied up with Kirrundi.' He turned to Ratley. 'Right, Cedric. What's next?'

'The Chancellor and the Business Secretary are waiting to talk about the Indian trade delegation visit in July.'

'Well, let's have them.' Military intervention in West Africa Free State was already disappearing from the prime minister's radar scope.

The chief of the defence staff was not impressed with the new planning direction. Admiral George Bellis knew a bad deal when he saw it and wasn't afraid to say so.

'Minister, we have very little intelligence regarding the current threat in West Africa Free State. Increasing our training and logistics footprint, without considering force protection, would be extremely foolhardy.'

'What do you mean? Are you suggesting our people can't look after themselves?' replied Fletcher. The admiral sighed. It really was like teaching a kindergarten class.

'It's not a case of them not being able to look after themselves, minister. They will simply be fully employed on their primary duties. Let me give an example. We are considering deploying support helicopters – Chinooks – to support the Free State army. They can be based offshore on an aircraft carrier, but they'll need somewhere in country to refuel. That will mean establishing a forward base close to where the Free State army will be operating. We would want to man that base as leanly as possible, but without any force protection, it would be extremely vulnerable.'

'Why couldn't the locals guard it?' demanded Fletcher.

'Well, they could. But how will that look? British forces having to be protected by West Africa Free State soldiers. Not quite the impression we would want to portray, don't you agree?'

Fletcher gave in angrily.

'Well bloody hell, if you must. But you'll have to justify every single force protection soldier. The PM's orders are to only send support troops. And that's what we're going to do. Understood?'

'Yes, minister,' answered Bellis. 'Completely.'

Two days later, Admiral Bellis was stood in front of the National Security Council, ready to brief on deployment options.

'Prime minister, ladies and gentlemen. Based on your guidance we have concluded our planning. You all have in front of you a copy of my draft directive. I recommend three separate, but interrelated initiatives. First, we expand the support currently provided by our small special forces team, through a dedicated British military assistance and training team, or BMATT. Second, we deploy a Royal Engineer squadron to the capital, New Devon, to assist the Free State army in improving its defences for the city. Finally, we send Chinook helicopters to provide aviation support to the Free State army. The Chinooks will operate from HMS Prince of Wales, positioned off the coast. To support aviation operations, we will need to establish a forward base in the country's hinterland. It will provide essential maintenance and refuelling for the Chinooks. The whole operation will be commanded by the Joint Force Headquarters from on board the carrier. Our footprint ashore will be limited to two locations: the forward base and the Joseph Khalli barracks, on the eastern edge of New Devon, where the BMATT and the engineers will be based.'

Bellis paused.

'Thank you, admiral,' said the prime minister. 'Talk to us about numbers and timings. And what sort of risk would we be taking on?'

'The forward base would be no more than two hundred personnel, which includes two flights from the RAF Regiment to provide force protection. The engineer squadron and training team together total approximately one hundred and fifty, so boots on the ground will not exceed three fifty. The carrier will be accompanied by a frigate and a support ship, so Royal Navy numbers will be quite high, but they'll be out of sight, so out of mind too. All forces are currently at very high readiness so can begin deploying within a few days. Personnel to deploy by air, but the engineer and refuelling equipment will need to go by sea. With loading and transit that'll take approximately three weeks. From when you give the go-ahead, we can be operational within thirty days.'

'And risk?'

'Low,' replied Bellis. 'There have been no reports of insurgent activity anywhere close to the capital, so the threat to the BMATT and engineers is minimal. Locating the forward base in the country's hinterland is necessary to ensure the Chinooks can operate effectively and that will bring some risk. We have identified a disused airstrip that was built to support diamond mining. It's a suitable size and self-contained. The primary role of the RAF Regiment is airfield protection, so I think they'll be up to the task of safeguarding the base.'

'What sort of contingency would we have available if something were to go wrong?' pressed Brownlow.

'We've considered that,' responded Bellis. 'By deploying the carrier, we would be impacting the work-up schedule of our new F-35 force. However, we could embark the aircraft, in addition to the Chinooks, and continue the training off the African coast. It would increase our support costs, but if the Treasury is prepared to cover them, it's doable. Even though the F-35s would primarily be training, we'd have enough combat ready pilots on board to provide air cover for our forces in country should we need to.'

Bellis stopped to let the National Security Council debate his proposals, but it was clear from the outset that the prime minister liked them so there were few dissenters.

'It's a good plan,' said Brownlow after the discussion died down. 'Thank you, admiral, you have our approval to proceed.'

At the same time Admiral Bellis was briefing the National Security Council, Wing Commander Rob Salmon was sat in his brigadier's outer office. It was small and the desks for the brigade commander's staff officer and personal assistant filled most of the available floor space. Filing cabinets lined two walls, together with a bulky security container complete with a heavy front panel and combination lock. The rest of the space was taken up with a tiny coffee table, and a couple of easy chairs.

Rob glanced at the clock above the filing cabinets. Five to nine. Always good to be a few minutes early, even if the whole set up reminded him of being in the headmaster's office at school.

The intercom on the PA's desk buzzed.

'The brigadier will see you now.' Rob grabbed his tea and stepped into his boss' office.

'Rob, good to see we've finally managed to get you down to brigade HQ. How long have you been in post now?

'Still not a month,' replied Rob a little guiltily. Like all commanding officers, he did all he could to keep out of his boss's office.

'And how's your new command shaping up?' Rob had recently been appointed commanding officer of Number One Joint Logistics Regiment, or 1JLR as it was universally known. It was a brand-new unit and part of a fresh idea to bring together army and RAF support capabilities. The job was the busiest he'd had in his twenty-odd years of service and the first few weeks had gone by in a flash. Still, since his recent divorce, he had plenty of time to give, he thought wryly.

'A few teething problems, but nothing we can't work through,' Rob answered honestly. 'Our first real test will be Exercise Joint Warrior up in Scotland next month ...'

The brigadier cut him off.

'Yes, I've had a look through the presentation slides you emailed yesterday, and it looks like you have all the bases covered. Well done.'

Not what Rob was expecting.

'Well, yes sir, that's the bottom line, but there's still a stack of detail I need to brief you on.'

'I'm sure there is,' replied the brigadier. 'But right now, we've more important things to think about. How up to speed are you with the situation in West Africa Free State?'

'To be honest sir, not massively. I've discussed it with my command group, but our view was it's likely to be more special forces and training, rather than boots on the ground.'

'Well, you're not completely wrong,' said the brigadier. 'CDS is briefing the NSC as we speak. I was on the Higher Command and Staff Course last year with his military assistant, and she's given me a sneak preview of what's being proposed. If the prime minister approves, it will be an enabling operation to increase the ability of local forces to take the fight to the insurgents. It will also include a large Chinook detachment operating from HMS Prince of Wales.'

'If they're operating from the carrier, the Chinooks will need a forward base somewhere ashore,' thought Rob out loud, unable to keep the excitement from his voice.

'Exactly. And whose job is it to provide that?'

'Ours,' confirmed Rob.

'That's why Joint Warrior is no longer the highest priority,' said the brigadier. 'I have a feeling this will move very quickly. Get back to Stafford and start planning. I'll get my staff to push out a warning order before close of play to give you some guidance. Focus on the detail. And Rob ...'

'Yes, sir.'

'You're a lucky bugger. Opportunities like this don't come along very often. Be sure to make the most of it.'

5.

The High Rocks Country Club sat on a low hill a few miles north of New Devon. Its single-story club house overlooked a wide, sandy beach that was strictly for members only. The long drive up to the club house skirted a tall granite outcrop that gave the club its name. The club house was flanked by a large outdoor swimming pool on one side and grass tennis courts on the other. The croquet lawn in front of the main entrance was meticulously cut and rolled every day. Beyond the tennis courts, half a dozen rifle ranges were laid out facing towards the ocean. Although High Rocks had been built a century and a half ago, there was no pre-1970 memorabilia anywhere to be seen. Its current members only celebrated post-colonial achievements.

That suited Simon Nkaba just fine. It was only nine o'clock, but he had already finished his thrice-weekly swim, had a hearty breakfast, and caught up on the daily news. He left his paper on the table and strolled out past the tennis courts towards the sound of rifle fire. It was coming from the 800-metre range.

Simon took a seat in the small viewing stand behind the firing point. The morning sunshine was just beginning to warm the rough wooden benches. By lunchtime, they would be baked too hot to sit on. On the range a solitary marksman was practising his skills, under the watchful eye of an old and wizened instructor.

Simon recognised the instructor as Paul Knowles. Knowles had been teaching at the club since well before his pupil was born. Although still technically a British citizen, he had lived and worked in Free State all his adult life and no-one in the country could match his knowledge of target shooting. The pupil was in his early twenties. He wore the blue tiger-pattern camouflage of the border force. On his shoulder were the two pips of a lieutenant.

The shooting stopped and Simon climbed down from the viewing stand.

'How was that?' he asked.

'Uncle,' said the marksman. 'I didn't know you were watching.' He dragged his ear defenders back over his brown, buzz cut hair.

'Double off down to the butts and get the targets, lieutenant.' Knowles ordered. His pupil ran to a waiting push-bike and cycled away.

'Well?' asked Simon again. 'How was that?'

'The kid's good, very good.'

'I know that,' responded Simon not bothering to hide his impatience. 'I know he's very good. But is he good enough?'

'What? Good enough to shoot at Bisley? Yes sir, he's good enough.'

'Good enough to seriously compete for the Queen's Prize?' pressed Simon.

'Well, he'll need to practise solid from now until July, and then get lucky on the day. But I'd put a wager on him being placed at the end of the Imperial Meeting.'

Simon knew enough to recognise the high praise that the old instructor was handing down.

The squeal of worn-out brakes signalled the return of Simon's nephew. Breathing hard, Jelani Achebe jumped off the bike with two large wooden targets tucked under one arm. Each target had four white painted blobs painted in the centre, set as corners of a square. Jelani held up the targets for inspection. Within each blob were five bullet holes. The best grouping was no larger than a mobile phone. Simon was impressed.

'Not bad, lieutenant,' said Knowles gruffly. 'But room for improvement. We'll take a break, then you can try again. I take it you put up fresh targets while you were down there?'

'Of course.' Jelani gave Knowles a piercing look. His hazel eyes and slim nose were almost angelic. But Simon knew his nephew was no angel.

'Mr Knowles thinks you have a chance at Bisley this year. What do you think about that?'

'Of course. I'm the best marksman in the whole country,' shot back Jelani. The air of superiority was impossible to miss.

'I know,' replied Simon. 'And I'll make sure the president of the National Shooting Association knows it too.'

Simon paused, making sure Knowles was out of earshot.

'But if you go, you can't lose. If you go, I expect you to come home with the Queen's Prize.'

Jelani's confidence was supreme.

'I won't lose. I guarantee that.'

Soon after Simon left High Rocks, another meeting began in a far less salubrious part of New Devon. It took place in a seedy, all-night bar on the waterfront. One half of the meeting entered the bar, together with a huge, muscle-bound bodyguard. He was in his mid-forties, with dark hair and a moustache. His clothes were nondescript, grey military-style trousers and a black polo-shirt. His expensive sunglasses were pushed high up on his head, doing nothing to hide the violence in his eyes.

The aftermath of the previous night's drinking was everywhere. Empty bottles littered the tables and the stink of stale beer seeped from the sawdust-strewn floor. The visitor ignored it all and headed for a small backroom.

'Stay here, he ordered his bodyguard. 'And no interruptions.'

The backroom was as dark as the bar. A naked lightbulb hanging from a dirty black cord produced only marginally more light than a small window high in the room's only external wall. The other half of the meeting was an apologetically thin man in a lightweight business suit. His round horn-rimmed glasses had incredibly thick lenses and he held a brown, imitation-leather briefcase close to his chest. It was clear he'd much rather be somewhere else.

'Mr Smith,' opened the visitor in a heavy South African accent.

'Good morning, Mr Black.'

'Meeting face to face again is a bad idea,' said Black. 'What's so important that we couldn't use normal comms channels?'

Smith blanched. He hated military jargon.

'My client wants to be sure that you understand completely the importance of the next phase of the mission.'

'Which is?'

'Up until now, your job has been training volunteers in basic military skills and generally stirring things up in the hinterland. Tell me about that.'

'What's there to tell that you don't already know?' said Black. 'We've trained over one thousand fighters to a basic standard, meaning they know which end of an AK-47 is the dangerous end and can take orders. We've also identified a bunch who've already had some previous military experience and would make half-decent NCOs. We're giving them a bit more instruction. The problem is these men have no officers to lead them. They're also untested in combat. All the missions to date have been carried out by my people. And they've all been one hundred per cent successful.'

'Yes, we know,' said Smith tetchily. It was clear the two men had no fondness for each other. 'But it's time to raise the stakes. The British are coming, and my client wants them greeted with violence. Lots of violence. He also wants you to plan something spectacular. Something that causes maximum casualties.'

'Hold on a minute,' responded the South African. 'That's a big step up in a short space of time. Didn't you hear what I just said? Your men are good for basic work. Nothing more. You've got no leaders worth a damn, and if you go up against the Brits, you'll get ripped to shreds.'

'Well, your people will have to provide the leadership. Because this will happen.'

'Okay, but that's going to cost you. If you want my men to help fight the Brits, they get double what we agreed. And my price goes up by another hundred thousand.'

Smith detested haggling, but he knew his client would expect him to drive the hardest bargain he could. After a few minutes' toing and froing, they agreed an uplift to the contract price, and he was ready to hand over the standard half up front.

'You know that taking on the British army will cost you a lot of men. Even if the spectacular you want goes well, it could still wipe you out.'

'Yes, thank you Mr Black. I'm sure that's none of your concern. You just keep to your part of the deal. We'll worry about the rest.'

Black accepted the advice with a shake of the head.

'Sure. You call the shots,' he said, heading for the door and deliberately ignoring Smith's outstretched hand.

Mr Smith waited until he heard the main door of the bar slam shut before he reached into his jacket pocket. The number he dialled was answered after only one ring.

'The contract has been amended as you requested, *Kiniun Nba*.'

At the other end, the information was acknowledged with a grunt.

6.

It was Monday morning and Rob Salmon had been called to the Joint Force Headquarters for a deployment planning conference.

'How long 'til we get to Northwood?' he asked his driver. Normally Rob would have driven himself, but it had been an early start from his regiment's base in Stafford and he still needed time to get his presentation squared away. As the car stop-started its way round the M25, he was grateful for his foresight. Northwood was a busy military establishment sat atop a large hill in northwest London. Despite the heavy commuter traffic, they arrived in good time. The site was already teaming with people. Military personnel and civil servants all hurrying about, like hundreds of worker ants all focused on their own business but working to a common goal.

Rob knew Northwood well, having served back-to-back tours there earlier in his career. No electronic devices were permitted in the headquarters building, so he handed over his mobile phone and laptop at reception before making his way to the main conference room. The Joint Force Headquarters commander, Major General Sam Wilkinson, was stood at the door to the conference room greeting the attendees as they arrived.

'Good morning general, Wing Commander Salmon, CO 1JLR.'

'Morning Rob, glad you could make it down from Stafford this morning,' responded the general. 'The staff have been keeping me up to date with your regiment's progress. It's shame that you're no longer going on Joint Warrior, but this operation will be far better for you.'

'Absolutely sir, said Rob. 'Our exercise work-up was going really well and that's helped planning for this op. I'm giving an update later in the conference, but I think we're in good shape.'

'Good to know,' said the general. 'I look forward to hearing all the detail.'

Rob had expected the Joint Force Headquarters to run an extremely professional planning conference, and he was not disappointed. Alongside his nameplate were a pile of maps and diagrams, the joint commander's planning directive and a draft deployment order. Rob looked around the table. At the head was a seat for the general with his chief of staff and deputy chief of staff to his left and right. Arranged down both sides were the headquarters' department heads and its legal and policy advisors. Then came the commanding officers from the units that would be deploying. Directly across from Rob was the captain of HMS Prince of Wales and next to him were two army majors. Rob didn't recognise either but assumed one was from the BMATT and the other commanded the Royal Engineer squadron. The final seat on the opposite side was taken by a wing commander from 617 Squadron, the RAF's recently formed F-35 Lightning squadron. To Rob's immediate right was Squadron Leader Jim Farmer, who Rob had known for years. Jim was third generation British, his grandparents having emigrated from Antigua and Barbuda in the 1950s. He was the nominated Chinook helicopter detachment commander. Next to him was the commander of 15 Squadron, RAF Regiment who Rob had met over email the previous week. His name was Dan Scrivener. At the far end of the table from the general was a podium. Next to it was a large screen waiting to be attacked by power point slides.

General Wilkinson kicked off the planning conference.

'Welcome everyone and thank you for coming. We've a lot to do so no long opening speech from me. We'll get straight into the country brief. JFHQ has just finished a training exercise in West Africa Free State. It was run by Major Grey, who's our country lead. Sarah, over to you.'

Sarah stepped up to the podium.

'West Africa Free State is a small country situated on Africa's Atlantic coast. With an approximate total land mass of thirty thousand square kilometres, it is about one and a half times the size of Wales. It lies at a low altitude, with its highest point only three hundred metres above sea level. Terrain is mostly coastal plains in the west rising to a hinterland of interlaced forest, savanna, and grassland in the east. Time zone is the same as UK, so they're currently on Alpha, or British Summer Time. The climate is warm to hot all year round with only mild temperature fluctuations. Average temperature is twenty-eight degrees Celsius; average rainfall is two thousand one hundred millimetres per annum. Rainy season is between June and September, so make sure you pack your waterproofs.

'Normally referred to simply as Free State, the country is a former British colony. It declared independence in 1970. Population is just under one million, according to the most recent census, which was taken last year. Almost half live in or around the capital, New Devon, with the remainder in small villages stretching back into the hinterland. As you'd expect, English is the first language, but many people speak Yoruba – especially in the hinterland. Its current GDP is estimated at three and a half billion US dollars and its economy is centred on mining, mainly diamonds, agriculture, and a growing tourism sector.

'Free State is a republic. Its current president is Jason Kirrundi, elected in 2018. The elections were overseen by the EU and the process was declared fundamentally fraud free and credible. The country is a secular state, although Islam and Christianity are the two main and dominant religions.

'Turning to the armed forces, Free State has an army of approximately six thousand. It's divided into four infantry battalions and one artillery battalion. No combat service support to speak of. The infantry relies on land rovers and three-ton trucks for manoeuvre. They have no armour, and their heaviest weapons are fifty-calibre machine guns. The artillery battalion has a couple of batteries of towed one-oh-five-millimetre light guns and a mix of eighty-one- and eighty-two-millimetre mortars. The standard of training is generally low but has improved recently following the deployment of a UK special forces training team. The army seldom operates above company level with platoon-sized ops being the default. In addition to the army, Free State also has a border force of around three thousand troops, which is better funded and better trained. It has its own officer cadre and comes under the control of the interior ministry. Free State has no fixed wing assets, and its aviation is limited to a small number of second-hand Bell Hueys, all operated by the border force. We don't have reliable information regarding numbers, but it's unlikely that they are able to have more than one or two serviceable on any given day.

'General, that concludes the background brief. Before I take any questions, I have one final piece of information. We now have a formal codename assigned to the operation. Operation *Weybourn*.'

Sarah fielded a few follow-up questions before handing back to the general for the next item on the agenda – the commander's outline of his intent for the operation.

'This operation is going to present some distinct challenges,' began General Wilkinson. 'On the ground, we will be supporting the Free State army as it takes the fight to the insurgents. That means our primary focus will be the delivery of combat support, in the shape of the Royal Engineers, and combat service support, from the Chinooks of 7 Squadron and 1JLR. The BMATT will also be up-gunning our delivery of basic infantry training, which we expect to be focused on improving the Free State army's ability to conduct unit-level operations. At the same time, the maritime element of the deployed force will be concentrating on the continued development of the UK's carrier strike capability. Don't forget that the plan was for HMS Prince of Wales not to deploy operationally until 2023.'

After the general finished, there was a short break. Then it was time for updates from all the commanding officers. The captain of HMS Prince of Wales went first. Rob was next.

'General, ladies and gentlemen,' he began. 'The scheme of manoeuvre for the forward base is reasonably simple. Its primary role will be the provision of twenty-four hours a day refuelling support for the Chinook force. Its secondary role will be to provide a safe location for any onshore aviation maintenance activity. We expect the Chinooks to provide six task lines from the eight helicopters deployed, including a standby for medical evacuations. There's no information yet on the Free State army's concept of operations, so it's difficult to predict sortie rates. Based on worst case, we plan on providing four simultaneous rotors-turning refuel points. Using imagery from google earth, we can confirm that the disused airstrip identified in the joint commander's planning directive has more than enough real estate to support four refuelling points, although one of my critical commander's information requirements is to get actual eyes on as soon as possible. Google reckons the airstrip is called 'Harris Field', so our planning designation for the forward base is Hotel Foxtrot.

'We will ground dump fuel in pillow tanks. Max sortie rates will empty a tank a day and our standard operating procedure is to hold seven days' stock. Aviation fuel is available at New Devon International Airport, which is a three-hundred-and-sixty-kilometre round trip from Hotel Foxtrot. That's a twelve-hour task. We've planned on road bridging using our own TTFs, which have a twenty-two cubic metre capacity. So, on average, a two-TTF run every day. There are six TTFs on the force element table.'

'What's a TTF?' asked the 617 Squadron wing commander.

'Oh, sorry,' said Rob. 'Truck tanker fuel. A bowser to you and me. Any other questions?'

There were none.

'As always, there's been a lot of pressure to keep the manpower footprint as low as possible. Our standard laydown for four refuelling points supported by a six TTF road bridge is one hundred and eighteen personnel. That includes all our life support, but not medical cover. Add in the medics, a helicopter engineering detachment and the two force protection flights from the RAF Regiment and we expect to come in all up at one hundred and ninety.'

'Thanks Rob, good brief,' said the general. 'What are your most pressing issues going forward?'

'I guess there are two sir. All our work has been done without any on-site reconnaissance. I'd be much more comfortable if I could get someone from my team in country to confirm our assumptions. What's even more pressing is the lack of up-to-date intelligence. It's been impossible to do force protection planning with any degree of certainty.'

'Well, what do we know?' asked General Wilkinson looking squarely at his intelligence officer.

'Well sir, it's confusing to say the least. There have been widespread attacks on villages, mainly targeting state-owned infrastructure. But elsewhere it seems to be more about stirring up unrest amongst the rural population.'

'So, we don't know if this is traditional insurgency, or subjugation through a campaign of terror,' interrupted the HMS Prince of Wales's captain.

'No sir, we don't,' replied the intelligence officer. 'There are some indications that whoever is behind this is trying to get the local population on side. But there's also evidence that it's aimed at terrorising the people into submission.'

The captain turned to General Wilkinson.

'That's pretty strange, general,' he said. 'You'd think the two approaches were mutually exclusive. I mean, why bother about hearts and minds, if you've already decided on the iron-fist approach?'

'But why commit atrocities if you can take the population with you?' interjected the BMATT major. 'It doesn't make sense.'

'Perhaps there's disagreement within the insurgency's leadership as to the best way to proceed,' offered the legal advisor.

'There could be more than one group involved,' said the intelligence officer.

'Or maybe we're just not seeing the bigger picture,' said the general. 'We don't have enough information to make an informed judgement right now, so let's not get too wrapped around the axle.' He turned to his chief of staff. 'We need to elevate this. Encourage Northwood to get an intelligence meeting together. They'll need to bring in defence intelligence and SIS and perhaps lean on our five-eyes partners as well.'

'Got it, general,' replied the chief of staff.

'And your other point is noted too,' said the general, turning back to Rob.

'We're deploying an operational liaison and reconnaissance team into the High Commission in New Devon first thing tomorrow. They'll get you all the in-country information you need.'

'Ack sir. Thanks,' said Rob.

Shortly afterwards, the conference broke for lunch. As Rob stood up, someone lightly touched his arm.

'Hello sir, I'm Sarah Grey.'

Rob found himself looking into the bluest and most inquisitive eyes he had ever seen. He had to be staring, but Sarah just smiled.

'Pleased to meet you, I'm Rob Salmon,' he managed.

'You too sir. I'll be commanding the OLRT. If you have some time later, I'd be happy to add your questions to our to-do list.'

'Great,' said Rob. 'I doubt we'll get time this afternoon, but I'm staying in the mess tonight. Perhaps we could meet up after dinner and I'll take you through what we've got.'

'Sounds like a plan,' said Sarah. 'I'll look out for you later.'

7.

Ever since the SIS had been handed the role of lead investigator for the murder of the foreign secretary, Rebecca Salmon had been working even longer hours than usual. Head of section for Africa was not the highest profile role within the organisation, but right now it was certainly the busiest.

It was not yet seven in the morning and Rebecca was surprised by a knock on her office door. At that time, the floorplate was usually deserted.

'Oh, good morning Noah, come on in.'

'Sorry, I'm not disturbing anything am I?' Fresh-faced and keen, Noah Wilson was the newest member of the Africa department.

'Of course not. Sit down. What can I do for you?'

'Well …' began Noah cautiously. 'The deputy head said you wanted to know about anything out of the ordinary to do with West Africa Free State.'

'Uh-huh.'

'So, I was just reviewing the latest persons of interest movements file and noticed this man was flagged flying into New Devon airport last Wednesday and then flying out again the very next day.'

Noah handed over his iPad. The grainy picture looked familiar to Rebecca, but she couldn't place him.

'I think it's Max Kruger,' said Noah.

Of course, thought Rebecca. He was only the best-known mercenary in the whole of Africa. He owned Lion Pack Incorporated, a private security company reportedly worth millions. Although Lion Pack was a legitimate business, the SIS was sure Kruger still engaged in a considerable number of illegal, off-the-books activities.

'He used a South African passport in the name of Johan Black, which is one of Kruger's suspected aliases.'

'Any idea what he was doing there?' asked Rebecca.

'None, whatsoever.' Two months in, Noah was smart enough to know what he didn't know.

'No problem. And thanks. You did exactly the right thing.'

Noah stood to leave.

'Ma'am?'

'No ma'ams in this department. It's Rebecca.'

'Sorry … Rebecca. Are we any nearer finding out who killed Mister Harknell? I mean, I know I haven't worked here for very long, but for someone to murder the foreign secretary …' Noah trailed off.

'To be honest,' said Rebecca. 'No. But we will. Our role is to find answers through careful analysis. It might not be as glamorous as some of the jobs in this place, but it's just as important.'

Rebecca thought about what Noah had discovered. It could be nothing, but it could be something. Flying in and out on successive days almost certainly meant Kruger had been in the country for a meeting. Everyone knew that with encrypted communications, most lawful business activity can now be done over the phone or by video link. Only the most sensitive discussions warranted a face-to-face meet. Rebecca reached for her mobile phone.

'Hi darling, sorry to call you so early. Is Terry Willis still out on the ECOWAS mission?' Rebecca's boyfriend, Major James Wilberforce, was second in command of 22 SAS regiment. Her twin brother, Rob, had introduced them during a summer ball at the Defence Academy the previous year.

'He is? That's marvellous. I wonder if you could get him to do me a small favour?'

Terry Willis was very happy with his short-notice task. The sun was shining brightly over Joseph Khalli barracks, and even being woken early by the crack of small-arms fire from the nearby range couldn't dampen his mood. As he stepped out of the officers' mess, a battered old green SUV pulled up alongside him.

'Morning boss,' the broad smile of Corporal Faz Farrell greeted Terry from the wide-open driver's window.

Corporal Farrell was originally from Sierra Leone, just a couple of countries down the coast from West Africa Free State. His father had died in a car accident when Faz was just seven and his mother emigrated to London soon after. She re-married, a plumber from Putney who treated her son very badly. As soon as he was old enough, Farrell ran away from home and joined the army. The recruiting sergeant quickly realised that young Farrell was much brighter than the average volunteer and pointed him towards a technical trade. Farrell opted for the Royal Corps of Signals. Almost ten years on, he was an experienced corporal, providing communications and information systems support to UK special forces.

'Morning Faz,' replied Terry. 'Are you up for a bit of informal detective work?'

'Sure thing boss. Teaching the local crap-hats is okay, but it gets bloody boring after a while.'

Terry couldn't agree more. When he got the call from Major Wilberforce, he jumped at the chance to do something different. And taking Corporal Farrell along was a smart move. In his loud shirt, dirty ripped jeans and knock-off designer sunglasses, Farrell looked every inch the local. With Farrell, and a large roll of US dollars in his back pocket, Terry was confident he could track down the information SIS was after.

'Right. There are only three hotels in New Devon that are decent enough for someone with a mercenary's ego to stay in. The Imperial, The Country Lodge, and The Radisson Blu. Where do we start?'

'The Country Lodge,' was Farrell's immediate reply. 'It's locally owned and not in the centre of town. Bound to be less security there. If I was a soldier of fortune on a secret mission, that's where I'd stay.'

'Okay, Country Lodge it is,' said Terry. 'Let's get cracking.'

It took almost an hour to get from the barracks to the Country Lodge hotel. Farrell bullied his way into the smallest of parking spaces, completely queue-jumping a Toyota hybrid that had been aiming for the same spot.

Who says size doesn't matter? thought Terry. 'Right Faz, you know the drill,' Terry pulled several dollar bills from his money roll and handed them over. 'Keep it relaxed and no indication this is the Brits asking. If anyone questions your story, just back off and we'll try something else.'

'No problem boss, I'm all over this!'

Farrell jumped out of the SUV and headed for the hotel entrance.

Terry was busy watching an argument developing between the Toyota driver and a beefy security guard. Although at least a foot shorter, Toyota driver wasn't backing down. Just as the dispute looked certain to descend into a fist fight, a knock on the window announced Farrell's return.

'Shame. That was just getting interesting,' said Terry as Farrell climbed in behind the steering wheel.

'Maybe, boss. But not as interesting as what I just learned. Kruger did stay here last week, but only for one night. He checked in as Mr Black. The bellboy said he was a right stroppy bastard. Didn't tip no one neither. Anyway, next morning, he took a taxi early, and for twenty bucks the concierge coughed up the license number of the driver.'

Terry was straight on his phone.

'There's only one daily flight to South Africa, and it doesn't leave until 1330. It's unlikely he went straight to the airport.'

'The concierge also said the taxi driver our guy used did the night shift last night and won't be back until about midday,' said Farrell.

'Excellent,' replied Terry. 'Time for a mid-morning wet then.'

The coffee served in the Country Lodge was passable, but the pastries were a bit plastic.

Still, better than a ration pack breakfast, thought Terry. And a little people watching out on the veranda was an easy way to while away an hour or so. It was soon clear that the security guard saw himself as a bit of a king-of-the-hill, strutting around the hotel concourse like a drill sergeant on the parade square. He was just wading in to his third altercation of the morning when Farrell pointed out a shabby yellow Prius joining the back of the taxi rank.

'Forty-seven, twenty. That's his number. How do you want to play this boss?'

'Same as before,' said Terry. 'Act like a local and keep it low key.'

Farrell waved away the offer of more cash and headed for the taxi rank, while Terry settled their bill and strode back to the SUV. After a minute head down by the driver's window, Farrell straightened up, gave his ear a quick scratch, and got into the back seat. Completely ignoring the truck coming the other way, the taxi driver pulled an expansive U-turn and sped off. Terry had been closely watching his corporal and immediately picked up the "all good" signal. Sliding across into the driver's seat, he started up the SUV and set off in hot pursuit.

The taxi driver's approach to his profession was part formula one racer, part kamikaze pilot. He hurtled through the New Devon traffic without a thought for his own safety, or anyone else's. The only way for Terry to keep up was to drive the same way. But where the Prius was small and nimble, the SUV was a bulldozer. Terry ran three successive red lights. Every time, he clipped, scrapped, or banged another vehicle. It was like driving inside a pinball machine. The taxi's journey eventually ended down at the docks. Terry followed him, exhausted. By the time he'd safely parked the SUV, Farrell had paid the taxi driver and was waiting in front of a squat, single-storey bar. Its exterior had been neglected for years, and what paint remained was bleached a dull grey by a mix of sunshine and sea spray. The gaudy green neon sign outside proclaimed it "The O-Bar".

Like every African bar Terry had ever been in, it was darkly lit with bare wood furnishings everywhere. It stank of stale beer and fried food. They made their way to the bar past a handful of sorry-looking customers all of whom had eyes only for the drink in front of them. It wasn't even one o'clock, but they looked like they'd been there for hours.

'Are we drinking?' asked Farrell.

'Guess we should.' Terry knew African beers. There wasn't a local brew; most New Devonians drank either Star Beer from Sierra Leone or Nile Special from Uganda.

'Two bottles of Star,' Farrell handed over a ten-dollar bill. Although Free State was a member of the West African Economic and Monetary Union, the US dollar was accepted almost everywhere in place of the Free State shilling. Farrell waved away the change, and the two soldiers took their beers to a table in the far corner of the room, where they could talk without being overheard.

'Seems like a strange place for a business meeting,' began Farrell. 'Wonder why he didn't just do it in the hotel.'

'Perhaps whoever he was meeting needed to keep a low profile. Or perhaps they couldn't risk being overheard. See how quiet it is now. When Kruger was here, I bet there weren't any other customers at all. Let's see how helpful the owner wants to be.'

For the third time that day, Farrell went to trade money for information. Soon he was back at the table with the owner in tow.

'Mr Bacchi. This is my boss, Mr Green.' The owner was old, and very weather beaten. He looked like he'd spent his life at sea, rather than running a bar next to it.

'Very pleased to meet you Mr Bacchi,' said Terry. 'I'm sure my colleague has explained why we're here.' The owner had no qualms about telling what he knew. There's no such thing as a secret in Africa, providing the price was right.

'The man you're looking for came here one day last week. In the morning. Must have been Thursday. Wednesday nights are always long because that's the day the fishermen pay the boat boys. Fatou and me were still clearing up when he arrived.'

Terry nodded patiently. Mr Bacchi clearly liked a story.

'Anyway, he came in with a very big man. Like a bodyguard. The big man stayed in the bar, but your man went into the backroom,' he pointed to a door at the far end of the bar.

'Who else was in the backroom?' asked Terry.

'Don't know his name.'

'But you must know something about him. I'm sure you don't just let anyone use that room.'

'Of course,' confirmed Bacchi. 'He was a lawyer and he paid me fifty dollars.'

'How do you know he was a lawyer?'

'They're all the same. Same expensive clothes, same fancy talk. He was a lawyer for sure.'

'And was this the only time you've seen him?'

'Oh no, he's been here before. Last year sometime. He met the same man.'

The two soldiers exchanged glances. That was interesting.

'Thank you, Mr Bacchi, said Terry. 'You've been really helpful. One last thing. Could we have a quick look in your backroom?'

'Well … I'm not sure.'

Farrell reached into his pocket and pulled out another twenty.

'Well, okay. But be quick.'

The backroom was small and as dark as the bar. There was a desk and two high-backed chairs. An old bureau sat beneath the window. No computer and no phone.

'Wonder what they talked about,' said Terry.

'No way of knowing boss, but I can change that for next time.' Farrell reached into his daysack and pulled out a small black electronic device. It was cylindrical and no more than a centimetre in length.

'This looker-listener is bloody brilliant,' he said. 'Miniature HD camera with wide-angle lens at the front. Battery behind. There's a microphone built in too. In low-power mode it's good for a couple of months. It fires up automatically when it detects movement and starts recording. Broadcast range isn't great, but we should be able to pick it up at the barracks.'

Farrell dragged one of the chairs over to the bureau and climbed up. The window frame must have been repaired and repainted a dozen times and was as much putty as wood. Using a small penknife, he gouged out a hole just large enough to squeeze the device into. He then reached for his mobile phone.

'There's an app for everything.'

A few taps later, he was satisfied the device was fully up and running.

'One last thing,' he dialled a number, which was quickly answered. 'Alan, it's Faz. You should be getting a feed from looker-listener serial zero two one.'

'Stand by .... coming through now. Move around a bit Faz.'

Farrell walked round the table waving his arms.

'Visual's good. Now say something.'

'Testing, testing, testing. Signaller Talbot is a virgin.'

'Fuck off Faz!'

'Guess the sound's good too,' laughed Farrell.

'All right Faz,' said Terry. 'Time to thin out before old man Bacchi finds out what we're up to.'

Five minutes later they were back in the SUV heading to the barracks.

'I reckon that was a pretty good morning's work,' said Terry. 'Thanks for leaning in, Faz.'

'No problem. Everyone loves a bit of variety.'

'Good stuff,' replied Terry. 'Just the boring report to write and send off to Hereford now.' Farrell grinned.

'You're on your own there boss.'

8.

'Don't forget you've got Senior Aircraftman Marsden at 1600, sir.' the adjutant's reminder was timely. Rob had forgotten. He looked up at the clock. Twenty minutes away.

'Can we wrap this up by then?'

Rob's question was directed at his deputy Major Pete Thurlow and Dan Jones, the regimental sergeant major. They both nodded.

Major Thurlow was a Royal Logistics Corps officer. He had more time on operations than any other officer in the regiment, with six tours in Iraq and Afghanistan under his belt. Quiet and thoughtful, his voice was rarely the loudest in any discussion, but his experience meant he was always listened to.

Mr Jones was 1JLR's senior non-commissioned officer and Rob's right-hand man. Nothing escaped his attention, anywhere in the regiment. He was scrupulously honest and, with over thirty years military service behind him, thoroughly professional.

'The final part of the briefing is the timeline for establishing the forward base,' said Pete. 'Our advance party flies out on the first C-17 tomorrow. They'll step through theatre reception that the OLRT has put together at Joseph Khalli barracks and then deploy to Hotel Foxtrot on Monday. If the rest of the outload goes to plan, flights two, three and four will leave Monday through Wednesday. We fly out with the main party on Wednesday. Twenty-four hours for theatre reception and move down to Hotel Foxtrot on Friday.'

'Okay,' said Rob. 'How soon after that can refuelling ops start?'

Mr Jones answered.

'It'll take up to four days to get all the pillow tanks laid. But the TTFs can pick up fuel from the airport on their way down, so we'll have wheeled fuel on site a couple of days early. We can always conduct rotors-turning refuelling direct from the bowsers if we have to.'

'Let's make sure that information is fed back to JFHQ,' said Rob. 'The latest I've seen is that the carrier will be on station by the tenth of June. I'm sure they'll have heli-ops planned as soon as possible after that.'

'Got it,' replied Pete. 'While we're talking about JFHQ, the information that Major Grey sent back from New Devon has been invaluable.'

'Have you worked with her before?' asked Rob. 'I mean, you're the same cap badge, have your paths crossed at all?'

'No, never. I went through Sandhurst a good few years before her and we're a large corps, so that's not a surprise. But I do know of her. She's considered a real rising star, in the army not just the RLC. Very smart, very ambitious and by all accounts, thoroughly pleasant too. Not a combination you see very often in my service.'

'Okay, thanks,' said Rob. 'Sorry, I interrupted you mid flow.'

'No problem, sir. Unless Mr Jones has anything, we're done.'

Rob went back to his emails. Bureaucracy in the military was like the Hydra, generating two emails for every one he opened.

And I'm no Hercules, he thought ruefully. He managed to chop off half a dozen heads before a light knock told him it must be 1600. He looked up and saw the adjutant stood in the doorway with a young airman behind him.

'Sir, Senior Aircraftman Marsden.'

Rob stood and gestured for Marsden to enter.

'Have a seat,' he said pointing to the comfy chairs directly in front of his desk. Marsden was short, no more than five foot eight, and stocky. Rob knew from Mr Jones that he was good at his job and popular with his colleagues. Marsden had a younger brother, Tony, who had joined the army straight from school. During a drunken leaving-home party, they'd bet each other who could reach the rank of sergeant first. Tony became a petroleum operator and had been promoted to lance corporal a day after his twenty-fifth birthday. He was also one of the first from the army to be posted onto 1JLR. Steve and Tony were now members of the same close support squadron, and both would be on the C-17 to New Devon in the morning.

'How are you feeling about the deployment?' asked Rob.

Marsden was animated.

'Great, sir. Can't wait to get out there. It's my first op and I'm buzzing.'

'How about the rest of your team?'

'We all are. Our troop's a really close bunch. We trained really hard for Joint Warrior. But getting on the op is much better. We're gonna smash it!'

Rob was pleased to see Marsden's enthusiasm, but a bit concerned about his gung-ho attitude.

'Confidence is a good thing Marsden, but don't get too carried away. Ops are dangerous and this one is no different. 1JLR will be the only unit operating outside the capitol. If anyone wants to pick a fight with the Brits, we'll be first in line.'

'No, yes sir. I get it,' said Marsden. 'The RSM has told us what to expect. We know we've got to stay focused and we're ready for it.'

'Good,' said Rob. 'Well, there's just one more thing, Marsden. I have to tell you that you're incorrectly dressed!'

'What? I mean … Sir?' Marsden didn't know what to say. Rob was now looking sternly at him. 'I don't understand.'

Rob held his stare for another couple of seconds and then relaxed into a smile.

'It's okay Marsden. You're incorrectly dressed because you're wearing SAC rank. As of now, you are *Corporal* Marsden. Congratulations.' Rob held out his hand.

'Bloody hell! I mean, sorry sir, that's bloody brilliant. Sorry sir.' Marsden was even more flustered. But now he had a good reason.

Seeing that his newest junior non-commissioned officer was a bit too discombobulated to shake his hand, Rob withdrew it and reached for the corporal rank slides instead.

'Here,' he said. 'Put these on.'

'Thanks sir.' Marsden removed his old badges of rank and quickly slid on his new corporal chevrons.

'I assume you'll be wanting to go find your brother and share your good news with him,' said Rob.

'Absolutely sir. Can't wait to see the look on his face.'

'Well off you go, but Corporal Marsden ...'

'Yes sir.'

'Don't forget the transport leaves for Brize Norton at 0530 tomorrow morning. I expect you to be there, on time and not hung over. There'll be plenty of time to celebrate your promotion after the op.'

'Got it sir!' Marsden all but ran from Rob's office in his haste to find his brother.

As Marsden disappeared, the secure phone on Rob's desk rang. Its synthetic, tinny ring reminded Rob of the awful sound effects from the 1970s sci-fi re-runs his son loved to watch on Netflix. The LCD display told him the call was from Vauxhall Cross.

'Hi Becca.'

'Hi Rob, how was your planning conference?'

'Good, thanks. Not quite the standard when I was in JFHQ,' he joked. 'But they did okay.'

'I'm glad they met with your approval. Look, just a quick one,' said Rebecca. 'There's an intelligence-wide meeting at Northwood tomorrow to discuss the Free State insurgency situation. Before I go, I'd be keen to hear your views on the threat level and force protection issues.'

'Of course,' responded Rob. 'But I doubt I've got much to add.' He flipped open his notebook. 'My biggest concern is the mixed messages we're getting. On the one hand, you've got the classic approach of getting the population behind the insurgency. The diamond mining thing is an obvious example of that. But we also know of whole villages being terrorised. Homes burned, men and women murdered, and children dragged away and never seen again. The two approaches just don't go together.'

'So, what do you conclude from that?' asked Rebecca.

'I'm not sure. It could be that there is no clear leader of the insurgency, or whoever is in charge can't control his men. The JFHQ intelligence officer suggested there could be more than one insurgency, but I don't buy that. It may just be that they don't know what they're doing.'

'And I don't buy that,' said Rebecca. 'We know that a high-profile South African mercenary has had at least two secret meetings in Free State, the first of which was just before the trouble started. If he's being paid to stir up unrest, that's not a cheap way to start an insurgency.'

'But it is a good way to guarantee results,' said Rob.

'Yes. But what results? I mean, if you think about this strategically, there are no obvious ends and the ways and means seem to be working against each other.'

'Maybe there's a bigger picture we're not seeing,' said Rob.

'What do you mean?'

'Well, what if the insurgent activity is just one line of development in a larger plan. Or what if it's just a diversion to take our eye off something more significant?'

'Like what?' asked Rebecca.

'I have no idea. But deception is a key part of operational planning. Someone could be deliberately trying to keep us focused on the Free State hinterland, when their real objective is somewhere or something completely different.'

'Yes, but there's no-one in the region with the resources to do that, even if they wanted to.'

'Who said anything about countries? What about non-state actors? Terrorist organisations like Boko Haram or Al Qaeda? Or what about an individual? Someone with stacks of money and their own agenda?'

Rebecca thought for a moment.

'Al Qaeda in the Islamic Maghreb just don't have the resources anymore. Five years ago, maybe, but not today. And what would Boko Haram gain by sucking the UK into a confrontation in western Africa? Besides, using mercenaries is hardly their MO. As for a lone wolf, it's a bit James Bond, isn't it?

'Then we must be missing something,' said Rob. 'Because I can't believe anyone goes to all this trouble and expense without having a very clear picture of what they're trying to achieve.'

'Good point. We need to keep working the intelligence problem.'

'Well, you do,' said Rob. 'I just do the tactical stuff. One more thing. When did the mercenary's second meeting take place?'

'A week ago.'

'So, after the decision to deploy UK forces was announced. That's not great. It suggests whoever is behind all this is upping the ante, ready for our arrival.'

'Then you'd better be extra careful out there.'

With planning and preparations going on at various levels beneath him, Admiral Bellis' focus was on maintaining political interest in Operation *Weybourn*. And that was not proving easy. His military assistant soon learned that getting into the prime minister's calendar was harder than breaking into Fort Knox. She called in every outstanding favour she could think of and finally managed to secure fifteen minutes.

Anthony Brownlow was in an extremely irritable mood, which wasn't helped when he realised his next meeting was with the chief of the defence staff.

'He's had my direction,' Brownlow complained to Cedric Ratley. 'Why can't he just get on with it?'

'I know,' replied his chief advisor. 'I'll make sure that this briefing is the only one.' Together, the two men headed for the cabinet office room where Admiral Bellis and Tom Fletcher were waiting.

'Admiral Bellis, so good of you to find the time to come over. I'm sure it must be unbelievably busy in the MoD right now.' The admiral detected more than a hint of sarcasm in the greeting, which he ignored.

'Prime minister, thank you for seeing me,' he responded neutrally. 'I'll be brief but with force elements already en route to the JOA, it's vital that you're up to speed on our activities.'

Brownlow gave the admiral a withering look. He hated all the acronyms the military used and never remembered what they stood for.

'The JOA?'

'Joint operational area, prime minister,' replied Bellis.

'Right, fine.'

For the next quarter of an hour, the admiral stepped through the latest military preparations, including deployment timings and in-theatre work-up plans.

'Two key dates to remember prime minister. HMS Prince of Wales arrives off the Free State coast next Wednesday. And the force reaches full operating capability two days later, on Friday the twelfth of June. Do you have any questions?'

Brownlow had none, and Tom Fletcher certainly wasn't going to prolong the meeting. Then Cedric Ratley spoke up.

'Admiral that was a very helpful update, but when can we expect to actually make some progress in defeating the Free State's insurgency?'

'That's a good question,' replied Bellis. 'We still have very little information regarding potential enemy forces and their intentions. That'll change once we get more boots on the ground. There's also a cross-Whitehall intelligence meeting underway right now, which will also increase our understanding. I'm sure I'll be able to provide a more complete answer for you in my next update,'

Right, that's enough, thought Brownlow. *And there isn't going to be a next bloody update.* Without a word of thanks, he got up and left the room.

9.

Sarah was in her element. She had been a member of the Joint Force Headquarters for almost two years and was easily the most experienced staff officer on the operational liaison and reconnaissance team. She had driven the team relentlessly from the day they arrived, but the hard graft had paid off. A day ahead of schedule, they were ready for the deployment of the main force.

The team was working out of a tiny office on the top floor of the British High Commission. Six staff officers crammed into a space big enough for two. They'd had to shift a ton of old files just to get in the door. Even with the windows permanently open, the place felt musty and stank like an old library stockroom. As always, the day began with a short team meeting.

'Main activity today is the 1JLR advance party move to the forward base, and the arrival of the second C-17. Are we all squared away for that?' asked Sarah.

'All good with the C-17, ma'am,' answered the team's movements specialist. 'It's due to leave Brize at 1045. ETA here is 1700. Local customs are happy, but I'll be at the airport to meet it with the air movements team anyway.'

'Thanks Mr Martin,' said Sarah. 'And the road move?'

Jamie Phillips, the ops officer, took over.

'All good there too. We ran theatre reception for the advance party yesterday. There's a Free State army convoy heading east today, so we've arranged for our guys to travel with them. My only concern is comms – the Free State army's kit belongs in a museum.'

'Tell me about it.' said Sarah. 'What's the solution?'

'I've given them one of our sat phones. They can keep it down at the forward base until the rest of 1JLR pitches up at the end of the week.'

'Good work,' said Sarah. 'I'm off to the Free State army HQ this morning. Terry Willis has arranged a meeting with the chief of staff. We also need to talk to their staff about heli-ops. I doubt anyone out here has been in anything bigger than a Huey. We'll need to arrange some familiarisation training before their soldiers can be let loose in the back of a Chinook. Dai, that's your department.'

Squadron Leader Dai Evans nodded. He was the team's plans officer, and a qualified helicopter instructor.

'Terry's sending a driver to pick us up at half eight. Jamie, might be worth you coming too.'

The Free State Army Headquarters consisted of several single-story prefabs tucked away in a corner of Joseph Khalli barracks. The buildings were connected by a series of narrow, wooden boardwalks. At the centre was an operations room, which co-ordinated all the army's day-to-day activities. In front of the headquarters was a large parade square marked out by dozens of small, white-washed stones. Outside the main entrance a national flag hung limply from a sorry-looking wooden flagpole.

As they approached, Sarah watched a squad of soldiers being manoeuvred around the parade square. Their marching was appalling. She could clearly hear the abuse being hurled at them by the drill sergeant, even over the rumble of the land rover's diesel engine and the crash of Corporal Farrell's hopeless gear changing.

They pulled up next to the flagpole.

'The ops room is directly behind this building,' said Farrell. 'I'm pretty sure the chief of staff's office is in there.'

'Thanks, corp. I'm sure we'll find it,' replied Sarah. 'Are you hanging around?'

'No, ma'am. I've got to be on the range in a bit, but we're working out of that crappy old hut next to the parade square.' He pointed to a small unpainted building that looked so decrepit a strong wind could blow it over. 'One of the team is bound to be around and can give you a lift back into town if you need it.'

'Great, we'll wander over when we're done.'

Sarah followed Farrell's directions to the operations room. A weather-worn sign confirmed they were in the right place. The main door opened into a short central corridor, with a small guard post on one side, an even smaller kitchen and two toilets on the other. The corridor opened out onto an open plan room that stretched the width of the building. At the far end, another corridor disappeared towards the rear of the building.

What immediately caught Sarah's eye was the complete lack of technology. No plasma screens on the walls and no computers on the desks. Instead, the room was dominated by a huge table. On it was pinned a large-scale country map. The table sat in the centre of the room, flanked on two sides by trestle tables manned by busy staff officers. Suspended from the ceiling was a huge, double-faced analogue clock with a large second hand that ticked noisily. At the far end of the room was a heavy wooden desk. On it was a large ink blotter and two ancient Bakelite telephones. Next to it was a chalkboard. Written on the chalkboard were a series of timings, under the heading "Battle Rhythm." Ancient communications racks were stacked untidily down both walls, their bare-metal fronts covered with heavy black switches and frequency dials. Thick leads snaked from them to field telephones located on the trestle tables and heavy cables disappeared out of the open windows towards a large aerial farm just visible in the distance. None of the leads had been secured to the floor and Sarah smiled to herself. The Joint Force Headquarters quartermaster would have had kittens at the potential trip hazard.

A tall, straight-backed officer got up from behind the desk. He walked forward to greet the new arrivals.

'Good morning, I am Lieutenant Colonel Koffi, senior staff officer at army headquarters.'

'Good morning colonel. I'm Major Grey. This is Major Phillips and Squadron Leader Evans.'

Koffi acknowledged the British officers with a nod.

'Colonel Ele is expecting you.' He turned towards the far corridor.

'No need for us to go in mob-handed,' Sarah said to Jamie and Dai. 'You guys are better off doing introductions here and getting to work on the helicopter familiarisation plan.'

Colonel Ele had a corner office at the far end of the building. At best it could be considered functional, but at least its large windows guaranteed plenty of natural light and a good view of the aerial farm. Colonel Ele was an older version of Lieutenant Colonel Koffi. He offered his hand with a welcoming smile.

'Very pleased to meet you, Major Grey. Please take a seat.'

'Thank you, colonel.'

'I believe you've met my son.'

Of course, thought Sarah.

'Yes, Lieutenant Tommy. He's a very impressive young officer.'

'Thank you,' said Ele. 'He speaks very highly of you too.'

For a second, Sarah was back in Batanto. The putrefying stench and the blackened corpses.

'Forgive me but I'm surprised your male colleagues have not joined us. You are all the same rank, are you not?'

Sarah forced the nightmare from her mind.

'Yes colonel, we are. But I am the team's commander.'

'I see,' acknowledged Colonel Ele. 'Having a female in command is very forward thinking. I'm afraid you may not always find the same attitude here in Free State. In some ways we still have much progress to make.'

'I understand,' said Sarah. 'And I must pass on my general's compliments. He'll be arriving next week. I know he will want to come here as soon as possible to discuss your operations in response to the insurgency.'

'Ah, yes. The insurgency,' said Ele. 'You know I attended your Royal College of Defence Studies last year. While I was there, I studied post-colonial insurgencies in Africa. During my thirty-five years in the army, I have witnessed many. Mostly as an African Union peacekeeper. I can tell you with certainty that what we are dealing with here is not an insurgency.'

'I'm sorry?' remarked Sarah. That was not what she had expected. 'What do you mean?'

'An insurgency is a political effort with a specific aim. An uprising if you will. Usually, it starts from within a disaffected part of a country's populace and spreads like an ink blot on paper. As it gains momentum, its followers grow in number and conviction, until it becomes an unstoppable force.'

'So, what's different here?'

'Everything.' said Ele. 'For a start, our people are not disaffected. Some are unhappy of course and many are poor, but that's true in every country in Africa. The villagers in the hinterland have been forced to be disaffected. Those that needed encouragement have seen their homes burned and their women violated. The anger that they now have is fuelling unrest, but it did not start it.'

'How do you know?'

'Everyone thinks we are simple, and all of our soldiers are good for nothing. We are given the worst equipment, while the police and the border force get fancy uniforms and modern weapons. But our soldiers come from the villages in the hinterland. They know what's happening, and some of us are smart enough to listen to them.'

'But if there's no insurgency, then what is going on?'

'That is a harder question to answer,' conceded Ele. 'Why was your foreign secretary attacked at the airport? Whoever arranged it must have known your country would seek retribution. It's almost as if they wanted British soldiers back on Free State soil.'

'But if you're so sure of this, why haven't you passed it up the chain of command to your president?'

Ele laughed.

'You are a very smart officer Major Grey, but I think you know little about Africa. I am just a lowly colonel. No-one would give me the time of day, let alone consider my point of view. I know my place.' Sarah shook her head, struggling to believe what she was hearing.

'Well, your chain of command may not be interested in good intelligence, but I know mine will be. With your permission, I'd like to include this in my daily situation report.'

'Of course. Now please forgive me major, my general is due to visit this afternoon and I still have a lot of preparation to do.' Colonel Ele stood up.

'Of course,' said Sarah, standing as well. 'It has been a pleasure to meet you colonel.' She saluted smartly and headed for the door.

Jelani Achebe made no effort to hide his anger as he stomped into the operations room. He hated his role as border force liaison officer to the army headquarters. He had much more important things to do. The Imperial Meeting at Bisley was less than a month away and he needed to spend every spare minute practicing.

Jelani ignored everyone around the map table and headed straight for Colonel Ele's office. He got there just as an unfamiliar face in an unfamiliar uniform was leaving.

'Who are you?' he demanded.

'I'm sorry?' replied Sarah, confused.

'I said Who-Are-You!' he repeated, only louder.

Sarah was blunt.

'I think you mean "who are you, major".'

'What?' It was Jelani's turn to be confused.

'I think you mean "who are you, major",' Sarah repeated, pointing to the two pips on the shoulder of Jelani's multi-blue, camouflage jacket. 'You're a lieutenant and I'm a major. A little professional courtesy wouldn't go amiss.'

'Why don't you just fuck off!'

Jelani pushed past Sarah, barged open the door to Colonel Ele's office without knocking and slammed it behind him. Sarah stepped into the operations room to see everyone staring.

'Wow,' she said simply.

Lieutenant Colonel Koffi hurried over.

'Major Grey, please forgive us,' he said apologetically. 'Border force officers are a law unto themselves. They treat regular army officers like we were something they stepped in.'

'And he's the worst,' added one of the staff officers from behind a trestle table.

'Yes, that was Lieutenant Achebe,' continued Koffi. 'His uncle is Simon Nkaba.'

'What? Your interior minister?' said Sarah.

'Yes. The second most powerful man in the country.'

'Well, that's as may be,' replied Sarah. 'But his nephew is clearly a total wanker.' Sarah's profanity prompted laughter throughout the room.

'Come on you two,' she called to Jamie and Dai. 'We should be getting back to the high commission.' Turning to Koffi she said. 'Thank you for your time, colonel. We look forward to working more closely with you as soon as the rest of the British forces arrive in theatre.'

'Us too,' replied Koffi, still smiling. 'I think it is going to be very interesting.'

10.

Rob's first view of Free State was from a small portside window of an RAF Voyager air transport aircraft. With space for almost three hundred passengers, it was only two-thirds full, so he had a bank of three seats all to himself. During the descent into New Devon, Rob had seen the heavily forested hinterland give way to low coastal plains and eventually the squat, ramshackle buildings that sat on the outskirts of the capital. A low, chain-link fence marking the airport perimeter rushed into and out of view, and the landing was confirmed with the screech of tyres on concrete.

The airport wasn't large and within a few minutes of landing the Voyager had taxied onto the hardstanding in front of the terminal building. There was the inevitable delay when the local ground crew realised they had wheeled out the wrong sized steps, but the mistake was rectified as soon as the British air movements team appeared on the scene. A minute later, the loadmaster nodded to Rob that he could deplane.

Rob had been to Africa a few times during his career, and it was a continent he had grown to love. It had an air of excitement that Rob hadn't experienced anywhere else, like stepping into a giant adventure novel. Although he'd never been to Free State, the sights and sounds that greeted him as he descended the steps were wonderfully familiar. Equally wonderful was the smiling face of Sarah Grey who was standing on the tarmac.

'Afternoon sir, welcome to New Devon.'

'Major Grey, super to see you.'

Although it was barely a week since the planning conference at Northwood, it felt like much longer. They had worked long into the evening sorting through the planning information, but for Rob that certainly hadn't been a chore. The chemistry between them was obvious and in the days that followed, Sarah had never been far from his thoughts.

'How are things?'

Sarah's reply was predictably positive.

'All good. Your advance party is cracking on down at the forward base. Yesterday's C-17 came in late, so we had a bit of a faff with the local transport. That's all sorted now. The final C-17 is about one hour out. It's got all the DAC on it, so we may have a few issues with the local customs. Not something they deal with regularly, I suspect.'

'What dangerous air cargo are we talking about?' Pete Thurlow joined Rob and Sarah at the foot of the aircraft steps. 'We hardly sent any.'

'It's all the 15 Squadron stuff. Without a clear understanding of the threat picture, Squadron Leader Scrivener wanted to bring as much weapons and ammunition as he could.'

'Smart move,' said Rob. 'Given the unknowns, I'm much happier being over rather than under prepared. Aren't you?'

'Right, sir,' said Sarah taking charge. 'If you're happy, we need to get you through immigration. Can you believe it, they still stamp passports here. Then we'll get you bussed over to JK barracks, and you can start theatre reception.'

Rob waited patiently in the queue that had formed in front of the immigration counter, which barred the way to the tiny baggage reclaim hall beyond. Perched on a high swivel chair was a rotund immigration officer who should have been wearing a uniform jacket at least one size larger. The line was moving very slowly as she seemed intent on quizzing every passenger.

Rob looked up at the bark of a klaxon and saw the single baggage carousel reluctantly shake itself into life. A moment later, the first Bergens began to make their way slowly into the hall.

'Passport.' Rob's attention was brought back to the immigration counter.

'Are you here on business or pleasure?' Not what Rob was expecting.

'I'm sorry?'

'Are you here on business or pleasure?' the immigration officer asked again, a little less patiently. Rob looked up and down the line of uniforms and shook his head.

'Er, business I guess,' he answered, keeping the sarcasm out of his voice with difficulty.

'And are you bringing any foodstuffs into the country?'

'No, definitely not!' he replied, trying hard not to laugh. The officer stamped his passport and handed it back to him.

Rob strode toward the carrousel.

'Passport. Are you here on business or pleasure?' The metronomic questioning faded away behind him, but it had clearly caused some mirth amongst his troops.

'Are you bringing any foodstuffs into the country?' he heard one of his young soldiers mimic. 'I was so close to saying "Why ... are you hungry?"' His mates laughed.

Although he had to admit it was a bit funny, Rob kept a straight face as he hauled his Bergen off the carousel. Even though he could never condone it, Rob knew that kind of politically incorrect humour was never far away among his troops. On the plus side, its presence was a good indicator of high morale. Slinging the heavy backpack over his shoulder, Rob stepped out of the hall and into the bright afternoon sunshine. Looking up, he couldn't help noticing the pockmarks climbing up the wall above the doors to the departures hall. As he got closer, he could also see the dull stain on the pavement where a poor job had been made of cleaning up after the foreign secretary's assassination. A land rover pulled up alongside him.

'Hey sir, can I give you a lift to the barracks?' Sarah called.

'Thanks a lot,' replied Rob. 'Just let me tell the RSM I'm going with you.'

Mr Jones had been first through immigration and was already bringing order to the transition of troops from aircraft to bus. A wave, a point to the land rover and a thumbs up was all it took, and Rob jumped into the passenger seat.

Sarah swiftly negotiated the airport slip road and then took the land rover up to fifty on New Devon's only piece of dual carriageway. With the wind howling, Rob had to shout to be heard.

'Where did you get the wagon?'

'What?' Sarah still couldn't hear.

'The land rover?'

'Oh. We blagged some space on yesterday's C-17 for a couple of our own vehicles. The standard of the local hire SUVs is shocking, and Terry's boys are getting a bit fed up acting as a taxi service for us.'

'Makes sense,' said Rob, lowering his voice as the dual carriageway ended and Sarah was forced to brake heavily as they raced up behind a slow-moving tractor.

'What's the plan for the OLRT when the carrier gets here?'

'Normally we'd close it down and move everyone back into the main headquarters. But as that's going to be a hundred miles offshore, I suspect the general will want to keep some presence in the high commission. We've also agreed to put a liaison officer in the Free State Army HQ. Think I'll volunteer for one of those jobs. After all, who wants to spend the whole op on a ship?'

'Not me,' said Rob. 'The job with the Free State army would be the better choice.' Sarah nodded. 'What happens to you once the op is over? You'll have done two years in post, so you must be due a move soon.'

'I am,' confirmed Sarah. 'I'll be part of the summer staff turnover. So even if the op's still going, I'll leave at the end of August. I start my new job on the army staff in Whitehall in September.'

'How does that suit?' asked Rob.

'The job's half power point monkey, half brew bitch. Can't say I'm looking forward to that very much. Not quite the responsibility I've had here. On the plus side, I'll get to see how things work at the top of the army and that's experience you can't buy.'

'And staff course after that?'

'Unlikely,' said Sarah. 'This is my first job in rank, so I still need to do sub-unit command. Also, the army's stopped sending majors to the Defence Academy. You need to be a lieutenant colonel now.'

'You say that, but I was on staff course with James Wilberforce a couple of years ago and he's only a major.'

'True, but he's special forces, isn't he?' Rob nodded. 'They're a law unto themselves. Anyway, I'm only thirty-one, so I've still got loads of time.'

'Well, from what I hear, staff course can only be a matter of time.'

The conversation stopped as Sarah pulled off the main road.

'Good afternoon Corporal Bawinda,' she called to the non-commissioned officer standing guard at the entrance to Joseph Khalli barracks. The corporal beamed at being recognised. He leaped to attention and threw up the most immaculate salute. As they drove through the barracks, Sarah pointed out the various buildings she thought would be useful for Rob to know. They finally stopped outside a large hangar.

'This is where we're running the theatre reception briefings.' As they got out of the land rover, a towering Free State soldier marched up to them.

'Good afternoon, ma'am,' another huge smile and another immaculate salute.

'Good afternoon, sergeant major,' replied Sarah. 'Sir, this is Sergeant Major Owuso. He's the Free State Army's Command Sergeant Major.'

'Very pleased to meet you sah,' said the sergeant major with another salute.

'Pleased to meet you too, sergeant major,' replied Rob. 'And I'm very much looking forward to working with the Free State army in the coming weeks.'

Sergeant Major Owuso turned to Sarah.

'Ma'am, the hangar is all prepared as you requested.'

'Thank you very much Mr Owuso,' replied Sarah. 'The coaches should be here shortly, and we'll get started as soon as they arrive.'

The sergeant major gave a final salute, performed a perfect parade ground about turn and marched away.

'Wow. You've been out for less than a week,' exclaimed Rob. 'Is there anyone here you don't know?'

Wednesday afternoon at the High Rocks Country Club was always quiet. The taxi brought Mr Smith all the way up the approach road without passing another vehicle. As he walked into the foyer, he was immediately approached by a white-coated attendant.

'Mr Smith, welcome to High Rocks. Please come this way.'

The attendant led his charge into a large anteroom. The late afternoon sun had still to penetrate the ocean-facing windows and the room was quite dark. Leather armchairs of all shapes and sizes were arranged around the room in tight groups. All were empty. Mr Smith was directed to a snug in the furthest corner of the room. In it were two high-backed chairs facing inwards. A large figure occupied one and the attendant gestured Mr Smith to the other. He then left without a word.

Mr Smith waited for his client to speak first.

'What's the news from Mr Black?'

'All positive, *Kiniun Nba.*'

'Never use that name here!'

Mr Smith paled at the reprimand.

'Forgive me, sir,' Smith paused but his client said nothing. 'Since our meeting last week, Mr Black has sent details on how he might carry out your new direction.'

'And?'

'They're just what you asked for. His plans start small and gradually get bolder. All of them use his men, but the more ambitious involve our fighters too.'

Smith handed over several sheets of paper containing maps and diagrams that outlined the various options. His client flicked through them briefly.

'I want Black to plan a full-scale attack on the base the British are setting up at Harris Field. He can use all our men if he needs to, but I want his guarantee that when I give the order it will mean total defeat for the British.'

'Of course, sir,' Mr Smith kept his surprise at this new direction to himself. 'There is one other thing.'

'What?'

'Mr Black wants details of our army's operations. He says if he knows what they're doing in advance, he can work out what the British are doing too.' The client thought for a while.

'That makes sense. Tell Black he'll get what he wants.'

With that, Smith took back the papers, bowed deferentially and departed. Left alone, his client nodded to himself in quiet satisfaction. He had waited a long time for this.

11.

Less than twenty-four hours after arriving in New Devon, the personnel from 1JLR were boarding coaches once again. This time they were headed away from the capital to the forward base that everyone was all now calling *Hotel Fox*. The theatre reception briefings lasted all the previous afternoon, and most of the morning had been spent on the hundred metre range re-zeroing personal weapons.

Rob sat patiently in the passenger seat of his land rover, waiting for Mr Jones to finish the last-minute convoy checks. From the map in front of him, the route looked straightforward. Although the country appeared to be criss-crossed with dozens of roads, Rob knew from yesterday's briefing there were only three metalled routes into the hinterland that could accommodate heavy vehicles. All could be used to get to the forward base but the one to the south was most direct. Rob looked up as Mr Jones jumped into the driver's seat and fired up the engine.

'We're all set.'

The convoy slowly pulled out of the barracks. Mr Jones eased his land rover in behind the last coach, and they settled in for the long drive east. Although the weather was hot and the dust got everywhere, the journey was uneventful. The convoy reached its destination just as the sun was setting.

Sunrise was at 0645 hours, but Rob was up and about well before that. The field kitchen was still being built, so breakfast was individual rations packs. Rob didn't mind. They'd improved hugely during operations in Iraq and Afghanistan, and the food now was almost edible. Better still, it was all boil-in-a-bag. Rob simply dropped his selection into the large pot the field caterers had going and five minutes later he was eating something that tasted remarkably like sausage and baked beans. Mr Jones caught up with him just as he was finishing.

'Morning sir,' he called. 'Welcome to day one in the big brother house.'

'How did you sleep, RSM?' he inquired.

'Like a baby, as always. Plan for today, sir?' Rob had already thought through what needed to be done.

'First, we need to confirm the site layout. Ask Major Grey to join us for that. We'll also need a force protection input. At the same time, the 2IC can get the ops staff together and square away the battle rhythm. Getting comms up and running is also a priority.' Mr Jones nodded.

'Got it. Kick off at 0730?'

'Excellent,' confirmed Rob.

Harris Field had been built when West Africa Free State was still a British colony. Located in the middle of a large swath of savanna deep in the country's hinterland, it supported diamond mining operations until all the local mines had been bled dry. After that, the border force used it on and off for a few years as a forward operating base for its helicopters. Since the turn of the century, it had been largely abandoned. Covering almost twenty acres, much of the site was completely overgrown, although the hard dirt airstrip had escaped the worst of nature's advances. Running east to west, it was approximately twelve hundred metres long and sixty metres wide, comfortably large enough for C-130 Hercules aircraft to operate. Unsurprisingly, it had no lighting or navigation aids. There wasn't even a control tower. At the western end of the strip was a large hardstanding area that had once been used for aircraft parking. The savanna's ecosystem had been at work here too, and around the edges much of the concrete was cracked and crumbling.

Alongside the hardstanding were the site's only buildings. Perpendicular to the airstrip was an old aircraft hangar. Its large doors were badly bowed and obviously hadn't been opened in years, but the rest of the building was structurally sound. Beyond the hangar were two Nissen huts that looked like they had been lifted straight from a World War II film set. Even though most of the glass was missing from the windows and both corrugated steel roofs were covered in a heavy film of green moss, they were useable. There was a small parking area in front of the huts and a winding hard-packed track led away towards the perimeter fence.

Fifteen minutes after Rob had given his direction, he was in his land rover parked up next to the site entrance with Sarah, Dan, and Mr Jones. The RSM was behind the wheel as usual. The track onto the site was in good condition and Rob was confident it could comfortably take the regiment's fuel bowsers. The chain linked perimeter fence that marked the site's southern boundary ran parallel to an external metalled road. It was rusty and in extremely poor repair. Looking both up and down the fence line, Rob shook his head at the complete lack of security it offered. Seeing Rob's concern, Dan shrugged.

'I'm afraid it's worse than it looks, sir. The fence is down in a number of places. What's more, it doesn't cover anything like the entire perimeter. In fact, it only runs alongside the main road. The rest of the site has no physical barrier at all.' Rob considered what he had just been told.

'Okay, we've clearly not got the resources to fence in the entire airstrip. How do we square that?' Dan was expecting the question.

'Can I answer after we've done a complete tour?'

They drove slowly back up the track. To the right of the Nissen huts, a domestic site was busy taking shape. Sleeping accommodation was ten-man tents, most of which the advance party had already put up. Within each tent, there was room for individual sleeping pods made from mosquito netting. It wasn't much, but it did provide a little personal space. At the far end was a long row of portaloos that Sarah's team had hired, as well as space for shower cabins that were en route from the UK.

Between the Nissen huts and the accommodation tents, the caterers were hard at work building the field kitchen.

'These huts look somewhat run-down but they're useable,' said Mr Jones. 'The quick reaction force will work out of this one, and we're setting up a combined ops room in the other.'

Looping round behind the hangar, they drove on to the concrete hardstanding. 'The engineers are working on getting these doors open,' Mr Jones continued. 'Once that's done, we'll be able to store all the backup fuels kit in there, and there's plenty of room for vehicles too.'

'What about the bowsers?' asked Rob.

'Plan's still to use this hardstanding,' replied Mr Jones. 'We'll get decent-enough dispersal, but I'd be happier if we had some proper protection for them.'

Rob nodded thoughtfully. In a non-benign environment, the fuel trucks should be protected in revetments. They normally used HESCO barriers, which were wire mesh containers with heavy-duty fabric liners filled with earth or aggregate.

'Have we spoken with the Royal Engineers about that?' he asked.

'I have,' said Sarah. 'It's a possibility, but they've only got a limited amount of the stuff and we don't know what the demand is going to be up in New Devon yet.'

'And down here, constructing an explosive storage area for the ammunition will be a higher priority,' pointed out Dan.

'That's true,' agreed Sarah. 'I can't see you getting any blast protection on site, unless there's good intelligence to suggest this place is a target.'

'Okay,' said Rob. 'We'll just have to go for maximum dispersal instead. What's next?'

Mr Jones manoeuvred off the hardstanding and onto the dirt strip. He drove east for two hundred metres before slowing to a halt next to a large bund that had been dug approximately fifty metres from the southern edge of the airstrip. It was big enough for two large fuel tanks. Mr Jones consulted his notebook.

'We'll be laying the tanks and pipework later today. Still expecting the bowsers to pick up fuel before they make the journey down here. And now the ship is docking a day earlier than expected, we should see them on Monday.'

He slipped the land rover back into gear and headed off further down the dirt strip. The bunds had been dug one hundred metres apart. Three were finished, and a filthy yellow JCB was hard at work on the fourth. Mr Jones drove to the far end of the airstrip and turned around. The furthest bund was almost halfway down the runway, just over five hundred metres away from the Nissen huts. Looking back down the runway, Rob couldn't help commenting

'That's a hell of a lot of real estate to protect.'

'I agree sir,' said Dan. 'We've got a stack of barbed wire rolls on the ship, but nowhere near what we'd need for the entire perimeter.'

'So, what do you suggest?' asked Rob.

'First off, we need to tighten up security at the main entrance. Top priority is a chicane to control vehicles coming onto site. That's the best way to guard against suicide vehicle bombers. After that, we should fence off the domestic site. There's enough barbed wire and stakes for that. We'll build sangars at each corner and a control of entry from the hardstanding onto the runway.'

'What about the fuel bunds?' asked Sarah.

'That's definitely the problem area,' Dan conceded. 'They should be okay during the day. The refuelling points will be in use, so your guys can self-protect. It's overnight that worries me. We'll probably have enough wire to throw a barrier around them and we've got some motion sensors we can deploy. What I don't have is sufficient manpower to guard all four bunds when you're not using them. The best I can do is maintain roving patrols during the silent hours. I know it's not perfect but with the resources we have, it's the best we can do.' Rob considered all he had heard.

'Okay, let's go with that for now, but we have to be ready to test and adjust if the security situation worsens. I want a contingency plan for the permanent overnight guarding of the bunds, which can be rolled out immediately if required.

'Got it sir,' confirmed Dan. 'I'll work on that with Pete and the RSM. We're already planning to use 1JLR personnel for static guarding duties, at the main entrance and in the sangars. My gunners will be mobile and mainly off site. We need to be dominating ground four or five klicks around the airstrip to ensure safe lanes in and out for the Chinooks.'

'Okay,' said Rob. 'Time to get back, I think.' Mr Jones took the hint and they set off back down the runway.

That evening, the field kitchen served its first meal.

'How good was that?' said Rob pushing his plate away. 'I'm going to have to run at least five miles a day, or I'll leave here the size of a house.'

Sarah laughed.

'You'll be fine.'

'I told the RSM I'd check round the perimeter guards. Do you fancy coming along.'

'Sure,' said Sarah. 'Just let me get my kit.'

'Great, I need to grab a radio. See you outside the ops room in five.'

The sun had set but the night was still warm. A combination of clear sky and a full moon made it almost seem like daytime and Rob had no trouble picking out the sangars. Somewhere in the distance, they heard the chattering laugh of a hyena, distinctive above the rest of the savanna's background noise. If it wasn't for the body armour and helmet, thought Rob wryly, they could have been on an expensive African safari.

There was no intelligence to suggest the forward base was a target, but that didn't stop Rob from taking force protection very seriously. The ops room was manned twenty-four hours and he'd insisted on a full guard shift for the silent hours. Rob and Sarah kept their voices low as they made their way between the sangars.

'You're so lucky this op's come up during your command,' said Sarah. 'I know army COs who'd kill for this opportunity.'

'Yeah, that's what my brigade commander said.'

Sarah was a bit surprised at Rob's understated response.

'Don't be too enthusiastic,' she chided jokingly.

'No, it's not that,' said Rob. 'It's just ...'.

'Sorry,' said Sarah, sensing Rob's discomfort.

The savanna seemed to go quiet just at the wrong time. Sarah wasn't sure what else to say.

'Look,' Rob began again. 'Just after I commissioned, I was in a holding post at a training centre in Wales. There was an escape and evasion exercise for trainee pilots in the Brecon Beacons and I was leading one of the pursuit teams. Halfway through, the weather turned nasty. We came across a couple of civilians. One had fallen. He was hurt pretty bad. I wanted to get him off the mountain straight away, but my sergeant disagreed. When we called up exercise control, they ordered us to stay put. The weather was so bad even the search and rescue helicopter couldn't fly. The next morning, the guy was dead. We were so busy worrying about his broken ankle, we completely missed his fractured skull. I knew we should have got him to safety, but I didn't have the confidence to convince my sergeant or overrule exercise control.'

Sarah was shocked.

'But surely there was an investigation? A board of inquiry or something?'

'Sure,' said Rob. 'It was investigated to death.' He paused briefly at his own gallows humour.

'And?'

'And both the military board of inquiry and the civilian coroner said I did nothing wrong. But that doesn't mean a thing. If we'd got him straight to hospital that bloke would still be alive. I've had to live with that. Since then, tough calls have never been my strong suit.'

They arrived back at the domestic site.

'Look, sorry to have unloaded like that,' said Rob. 'Not something I share often.'

'No problem,' said Sarah. 'It must be a real burden. But you shouldn't beat yourself up over it. From what I've seen, you're more than capable of commanding Hotel Fox.'

'Thanks,' replied Rob, forcing a shaky smile. He didn't say anything, but Sarah's vote of confidence meant a lot.

12.

July 2022

It was Friday afternoon in Whitehall, exactly three weeks after Hotel Fox had been declared operational. And Admiral Bellis wasn't happy. He was guest of honour at a Royal Naval College dinner that evening and had been planning on leaving London early. Instead, he'd just learned the prime minister's private secretary had cancelled the next Operation *Weybourn* update. What's more, he had made it clear that there were no plans to rearrange it.

'Off to see the secretary of state,' he barked at his military assistant. This close to the weekend, the building was as empty as the Marie Celeste and the admiral passed no-one on his short walk to Tom Fletcher's office.

'Need a quick word with the minister,' he called to Fletcher's gatekeeper without stopping. The door was half open.

'Good afternoon minister. I wonder if I might have a quick word?' Tom Fletcher looked up irritably. He was halfway through reading about the indiscrete activities of a colleague on a backbenchers' WhatsApp group.

'Of course, admiral. What can I do for you?'

'My MA's just been told that Monday's *Weybourn* briefing with the prime minister has been cancelled. Not re-arranged, cancelled completely.'

'Ah,' said Fletcher cagily. He knew that the briefing had been removed from the prime minister's calendar days ago. 'Can I be blunt?'

'Please do, minister.' Bellis's response was terse.

'Well,' began Fletcher. 'To be honest, this whole *Weybourn* thing is no longer part of the news cycle, so the prime minister isn't really interested in it anymore. Don't get me wrong, he'll re-engage if he needs to, but right now the media's focus is somewhere else, and so is his.'

Bellis was exasperated.

'But these are our people out there. In harm's way. And it was the prime minister's decision to put them there.'

Fletcher shook his head. The military really do not understand politics.

'Not really in harm's way though, are they admiral? I mean, most of them are a hundred miles offshore. And if I remember, the Free State army hasn't had a single contact since we started supporting them almost a month ago.'

'That's not the point,' responded Bellis, growing steadily angrier.

'With respect, admiral, it's exactly the point. Nothing is happening over there, so no-one is interested over here. I'm sure that'll change if there's a bit of action, but until then the PM is confident you're on top of everything. He is right to be confident you're on top of everything, isn't he?' Fletcher smiled to himself. Outmanoeuvring Bellis was too easy.

'Of course, minister. Thank you for your time.' Bellis could see he wasn't going to get any more out of Fletcher, who was already back looking at his phone.

As he retreated to his office, Bellis motioned for his military assistant to join him.

'The minister said Op *Weybourn* is no longer in the news cycle. We've got to change that. Get on to the comms team. I want a big push on promoting the operation starting Monday. We need to get the media out to Free State and show them what we're doing. I want maximum publicity and I want it now. Maybe then the prime minister will start to take a bit more of an interest.'

'I'm on it,' said the military assistant. She returned to her desk and reached for the phone.

No early finish for me then, she thought to herself.

The following day Rob was up before the sun, as usual. Even though it was Saturday, the Chinooks were flying in support of the Free State army. Rob was impressed. They certainly were making every effort to track down the insurgents.

'Morning sir, welcome to day thirty in the big brother house,' called Mr Jones as he passed by on his way back from his morning ablutions. Rob smiled at the joke that kept on giving.

'Morning RSM. Looks like rain.' Mr Jones grunted in response and ducked into his tent as the first raindrops fell. Zipping up his jacket, Rob headed for the field kitchen and breakfast. He grabbed a bowl of cereal and headed for the nearest table where Pete Thurlow was busy demolishing a full English.

'Met man got it wrong then,' said Pete seeing Rob's damp jacket. 'I'm sure he forecast rain this afternoon.'

'Well, it's early,' replied Rob. 'But the cloud base looks quite high, so it shouldn't affect flying.'

'No chance of postponing the general's visit then?' said Pete.

'I guess not. But that's a good thing. I'm a bit surprised it's taken him this long to get down here. I mean, we've been operational for almost a month now.'

During his video conference the previous evening, General Wilkinson had announced his intention to visit Hotel Fox. He also expressed his dissatisfaction with the total lack of progress that had been made tracking down the insurgents. The collective conclusion was the Free State army needed more help.

'Are we still expecting the Free State army chief as well?' asked Pete. 'What's his name?'

'Karrick. General Karrick,' confirmed Rob. 'Yes, the plan is for both generals to fly in early this afternoon, have a quick tour of the site, meet the troops, and discuss options for further UK support. We can talk more at this morning's ops update but expect visit prep to be main effort for you and the RSM this morning.'

'Roger,' accepted Pete. As Rob's deputy, he knew that shitty little jobs came with the territory.

Rob and Mr Jones were waiting with two land rovers at the westernmost refuelling point. The morning's heavy showers had given way to bright sunshine. Most of the rainfall had already drained away into the savanna's porous soil, but two small Hamerkops were happily splashing away in a large puddle that remained inside the closest fuel bund. The local wildlife had proved remarkably tolerant of their new neighbours, except when big helicopters appeared, noisy and unannounced.

At 1400, exactly on schedule, a Chinook clattered overhead, prompting a hasty exit from the Hamerkops. It completed a low pass over the site before wheeling round and landing on the airstrip close to the vehicles. A loadmaster appeared, closely followed by four men, all in uniform. Rob recognised General Wilkinson and Major Phillips. Alongside them was a large, aggressive looking officer that had to be General Karrick. He was accompanied by a thin Free State army colonel. As they approached, Rob stepped forward and saluted smartly.

'General Karrick, General Wilkinson. Welcome to Forward Operating Base Hotel Fox. May I introduce my RSM, Sergeant Major Jones.'

'Good afternoon Rob. RSM,' replied General Wilkinson. 'This is General Karrick and his headquarters chief of staff Colonel Ele.' Jamie Phillips didn't get a mention. 'We're very much looking forward to our visit. Where do we start?'

'Windscreen tour,' said Rob indicating his vehicle. 'If you and General Karrick are okay to ride with me, we'll get going.'

Two hours later, it was clear that the visit had gone well. The visitors had been extremely interested to see around the forward base and had engaged enthusiastically with the troops manning the refuelling points. Even General Karrick had softened a little.

The two generals were sat in the field kitchen, discussing how the Free State army's campaign against the insurgents could be reinvigorated. The meeting was beginning to wind down when Mr Jones' radio squawked loudly. He listened for a second then quickly got up and left. Pete looked over to Rob, who held up his hand. Mr Jones was more than capable of dealing with whatever crisis might be developing.

As the two generals stood to shake hands, they heard a loud commotion outside. In strode Simon Nkaba, followed hurriedly by Dan Scrivener and Mr Jones.

'What the fuck's going on here?' snarled Simon.

'Minister Nkaba, how thoroughly pleasant to see you,' said General Wilkinson, full of charm. 'I promised General Karrick a tour of our forward base and we've just been swapping war stories. Actually, it's about time to leave. Can I offer you a flight back to New Devon?'

The pleasantness took much of the wind from Simon's sails, but he wasn't backing down.

'I know you want to get British troops out on the ground with your men Karrick,' he accused. 'But I won't let you. The president is on my side over this.'

General Karrick waded into the argument. In the background Colonel Ele leaned over to Rob and whispered softly.

'Nkaba's nephew is the border force liaison officer in our HQ. Everything we do gets back to him.'

General Wilkinson eventually managed to de-escalate the confrontation between the Free State ministers. Reluctantly Simon calmed down enough to accept the offer of a helicopter ride back to the capital.

'You,' he said, pointing dismissively to Mr Jones. 'Go and tell my driver I don't need him anymore.'

The RSM flashed an angry look in response, but tactfully did as he was bid. Rob was relieved the potential crisis had been averted and hustled his guests out towards the waiting transport.

'Stop!' shouted Simon. 'Where are they going?' He pointed to two vehicles that were just exiting the site. The stripped-down land rovers were all business. Doors and windscreens removed, camouflage netting lashed to the bonnet and extra jerry cans of fuel hanging from the side panels. Each had a general-purpose machine gun attached to an outrigger directly in front of the passenger seat and a larger, fifty-calibre gun secured to a ring-mount behind the vehicles' protective roll bar. The three-man crew looked menacing in helmets, goggles, and heavy body armour.

Squadron Leader Scrivener cut in.

'Those are just two of my WMIKs.'

'What?' thundered Simon.

'Weapon mounted installation kit. WMIK', replied Dan. 'They're basically customised land rover patrol vehicles.'

'I can see that,' replied Simon aggressively. 'Where are they going?'

'Operating procedures call for a patrol pattern approximately five klicks out from the airfield. We can't secure safe lanes for the Chinooks from inside the wire.'

Simon turned angrily to General Wilkinson.

'This is completely unacceptable. The agreement President Kirrundi reached with your prime minister was that no British soldiers would operate on Free State soil. Your men must stay on the base.'

Wilkinson was in a difficult position. As a soldier, he knew the significance of the patrols. As a general, he knew the importance of diplomacy. Diplomacy won.

'Rob, you will do as Mr Nkaba requests. Recall the patrol. From now on, you are to conduct all force protection operations from within the site perimeter.'

'But that's tactical madness,' blurted Dan.

'No, got it sir.' said Rob, talking over his force protection specialist. He knew Dan was right, but recognised General Wilkinson had no choice. 'Squadron Leader Scrivener, get the ops team to draw up a new force protection plan. Effective immediately.'

Simon smiled triumphantly. It was good to put the British general in his place.

13.

Sarah's heart was pumping like crazy, and her lungs were ready to burst. Her lightweight running vest was soaked as her body did what it could to avoid melting down completely. It was still early morning, but the African sun was merciless.

She approached the main entrance to the barracks and waved to the Free State soldiers standing guard. They all braced up rigidly to attention and saluted. Then they waved and cheered as she raced by. Sarah had been UK liaison officer to the Free State Army Headquarters for a little over three weeks, and she was very popular. The senior officers appreciated her professionalism and candour. Her fellow staff officers were pleased she just wanted to be part of the team. And the junior soldiers loved that she always took the time to speak to them. Few others did.

The fitness app on Sarah's watch measured the barrack's perimeter at exactly four kilometres. Her daily routine was two laps before breakfast and today she was on course for a personal best. Head down, she sprinted away from the main entrance. She glanced down at her watch, thirty-eight minutes dead. Just the final run for home to go.

Keep pushing hard! she screamed at herself as the officers' mess came into view.

Last two hundred metres!

Last one hundred!

Last fifty!

Maximum effort!

She hurtled past the main entrance and slowed up quickly, gasping for breath. That was tough. Thirty-nine minutes and seventeen seconds. Her best time by just five seconds.

But a personal best is a personal best. She congratulated herself and headed off for a well-earned shower.

Half an hour later, Sarah was stood in her regular place next to Lieutenant Colonel Koffi at the head of the map table. The morning briefing was just about to start. Until yesterday, she had been the only British officer in the headquarters. But since General Wilkinson's weekend meeting with General Karrick, another six staff officers from the Joint Force Headquarters had arrived to help the Free State army with its planning. In just twenty-four hours, some significant changes had been made to the way the campaign was being run and there was now a real buzz around the headquarters.

But hunting insurgents was not the main effort for the day. A large contingent of print-media defence correspondents had just arrived on the latest C-17 resupply aircraft from the UK. There was also a camera crew from the BBC and another from Sky. The party was accompanied by half a dozen minders from the Ministry of Defence's strategic communications team. As the most experienced media trained officer in country, General Wilkinson had tasked Sarah to travel with the group for the duration of their stay. She listened as Dai Evans outlined the timings for the day. He ended his briefing with the obligatory "any questions?" question.

'Not a question, just a change to your plan.' Jelani Achebe had been stood in the background but stepped forward as he spoke. 'As the border force liaison officer, I will also be accompanying the British media today.'

Evans started to protest, but Sarah silenced him with a quick shake of the head. Achebe had been the one bad thing about her liaison role in the Free State Army headquarters. Since their unpleasant exchange outside Colonel Ede's office, they had worked hard to avoid each other. It was clear that Achebe hated Sarah and she had little time for him either.

'Just make sure the ops staff add him to the manifest,' she said to Evans. 'I'll manage things at this end.' Evans accepted the direction without question. If it was okay with Sarah, it was okay with him. Jelani, on the other hand, did not even acknowledge the intervention Sarah had made on his behalf. He simply turned on his heel and strode from the room.

Sarah laughed to herself. Looking after the media was like herding cats. They never did what they were asked. In fact, you could usually rely on them to do completely the opposite. She was amazed when the coach from the high commission arrived at the main gate exactly on time. The passenger door opened with a hiss and Sarah jumped quickly up the steps.

'Keep everyone on the bus,' she said to the senior minder. Inquisitive heads were already looking around like a mob of meerkats, seeking out the next story. The media party had started their day with a presentation by the UK high commissioner. Next on their itinerary was a flight out to HMS Prince of Wales for a brief from the general, followed by lunch in the wardroom. In truth, Sarah was looking forward to that part too. Working in the Free State army headquarters was all well and good, but the abilities of the chefs left a lot to be desired. She followed Squadron Leader Evans onto the bus where he gave a quick safety brief. Most of the journalists had flown in a Chinook before, but it never hurt to hear the briefing again. Just as the coach was about to leave, Evans looked over to Sarah.

'Where's this border force wanker then? Is he so special that timings don't apply to him?' he asked angrily.

Sarah was just about to respond when she spotted Jelani ambling towards them. Head down and clearly in no hurry, he was absent-mindedly working the bolt of his assault rifle backwards and forwards.

'Anytime today,' hissed Evans, only half under his breath. 'This bloke thinks he's Lord God Almighty.'

'Calm down Dai,' said Sarah. 'He's not worth it.' Jelani reached the coach and slowly climbed the steps with complete indifference.

'Were you waiting for me?' he asked as he sat down in the first available seat. Sarah ignored him and nodded to the driver. They headed off to meet the Chinook.

With a cruising speed of one hundred and seventy knots, the Chinook ate up the miles to the aircraft carrier in little over half an hour. Shortly after landing, everyone was drinking coffee in the ship's main briefing room listening to General Wilkinson explain how the operation was progressing. Like most senior officers, he was well used to dealing with the media, and his charm and relaxed humour held their interest throughout. The buffet lunch was excellent, and a mix of the ship's officers and headquarters staff had an easy task keeping the conversation flowing. Two hours after arriving, the party was ready to get back on the Chinook and continue with their programme. As the minders worked to round up the stragglers, General Wilkinson took Sarah to one side.

'You know that CDS himself is behind this visit, don't you?' he asked.

Sarah nodded.

'It's vital that the rest of the day goes well. The political support for this op is not what we thought it was. Because it's not on the front pages anymore, the prime minister's lost interest. Our job is to get these journos really fired up and enthusiastic about what we're doing out here, so they get us back into the news cycle. Understood?'

'Absolutely sir,' replied Sarah. 'I'll make sure that message gets to the guys at Hotel Fox, but I know that Wing Commander Salmon is all over it. Squadron Leader Evans has arranged for us to join up with a couple of other Chinooks later. They're on a training sortie, getting the last Free State troops familiarised with heli-ops. The journos can see us working together, and the TV crews will be able to get some good footage. We can also square away some interviews if they want.'

'Excellent,' said the General, looking reassured. 'Just make sure it stays on the rails.'

Rob was at the first refuelling point, stood next to his land rover. He had binoculars to his eyes and was searching the horizon for the media-carrying Chinook. It was due anytime now. Behind him Mr Jones' professional eye ensured everything was ready for its arrival.

'Got it,' exclaimed Rob. 'Two o'clock, low over the trees.'

Mr Jones looked but the helicopter was still too far away to see with the naked eye.

'Right, you chaps, stand by,' he called to the team manning the refuelling point. 'That Chinook's flown all the way from the carrier. It'll need some more gas before its next sortie.'

The three-person team donned ear-defenders and set to work with a practised ease. First the pump was fired up and then the hose was dragged out from beside the pillow tanks to a spot close to the helicopter landing point. The third member of the team pulled on a pair of oversized orange gloves. She then sprinted away to a position approximately twenty metres upwind of the landing point. As the Chinook appeared, she raised both hands high above her head, making a V-shape with her arms. Seeing this, the pilot flared out and slowly manoeuvred towards her. With exaggerated motions, the marshaller directed the Chinook over the landing zone. Then she extended both arms out sideways parallel to the ground. The pilot responded by bringing his helicopter into the hover. The downward movement of her outstretched arms brought the Chinook towards the ground, and she confirmed it was clear to land by crossing her arms together in front of her.

'That was SAC Styles' first unsupervised helicopter marshal,' shouted Mr Jones over the noise of the shutting-down engines. Rob responded with a thumbs up.

'Looked spot on to me,' he called.

Once the Chinook had fully shut down, the loadmaster led everyone off via the rear ramp. Rob stepped forward to greet them.

'Welcome to Forward Operating Base Hotel Fox,' he said. 'I'm Wing Commander Rob Salmon and this is Mr Jones, my regimental sergeant major. As you've been cooped up in the back of that thing for the last hour or so, I thought we'd walk over to the main site.' He pointed the way. 'It'll only take five minutes and there's tea and coffee waiting.'

As the group began to move away from the refuelling point, Rob fell in step alongside Sarah.

'Hey there,' he said. 'How's it going?'

'Oh, hi sir.' Sarah replied with a smile. 'All good. Today's gone really well so far. We got out to the carrier on time and the general was just great. They were eating out of the palm of his hand.'

'I'm not surprised,' said Rob. 'He wasn't selected for this job because he's an idiot.'

'True,' agreed Sarah. 'And the Navy did us proud with lunch. All we need now is some sharp-end stuff from your team and some action shots of Free State soldiers with British helicopters. Shouldn't be too hard, don't you think?'

14.

'Just one final question,' the defence correspondent from Sky gave the slightest of smiles, like a lioness who has cornered her prey and is about to move in for the kill. Rob rubbed his jaw subconsciously in response. It wasn't a live interview, but he had never felt comfortable in front of a television camera. So far, he had coped all right with the questions that had been put to him, or at least he thought he had.

'Back in the UK, what you're doing is getting no media coverage and even the government seems far more focused on domestic issues. You've barely been out here a month but already no-one at home cares. How does that make you feel?'

Wow! thought Rob. *Thanks for that – leave the real zinger until last why don't you?* He cleared his throat to give him a couple more seconds thinking time before answering.

'Well, we are all extremely busy out here, focused on providing the assistance necessary for the Free State army to deal with the insurgency they are facing. To be honest, that doesn't leave much time to check the news from back home, so I can't really comment on that.' Rob hesitated for the shortest time. 'But what I can say is that all of the men and women under my command are dedicated to the task in hand and are doing an excellent job. What's more, they will continue to do so for as long as our government and the Free State president require us to.'

He folded his arms across his chest and looked straight into the camera. The next two seconds seemed like twenty.

'And we're good,' said the reporter eventually. 'Thanks for that.' Rob started to reply, but she had already turned away and was busy checking something with her cameraman.

'Well done,' said Sarah encouragingly. She had been stood to one side watching. 'Some good answers in there. Especially the last one. Textbook ABC.'

'Thanks,' said Rob, feeling a bit more reassured. 'It's one thing knowing "acknowledge, bridge, communicate." It's something else altogether putting it into practice in front of a camera.'

'You did great,' said Sarah. 'Come on, we need to start rounding everybody up if we're to make the RV with the other helicopters.' Rob nodded in agreement. His part of the media day was coming to an end, but the television crews and reporters still had the heli-ops training to look forward to.

Jim Farmer was the media team's pilot and before they left Hotel Fox he gave them a short explanation on how the final event would be run.

'Immediately after this briefing, we'll fly out to the rendezvous point and land on. It's no more than fifty miles from here, so our flight time should only be about fifteen minutes. The Free State soldiers will arrive in two Chinooks at 1600 hours and carry out a series of deplaning and emplaning drills. That will be the perfect time to get some good action shots – your MoD minders have maps of the exercise area and can help you pick the best spots for that. Once the drills have been completed, the Chinooks will shut down and you'll have time to talk to the crews and some of the Free State soldiers as well. Our departure time is 1645; we'll be back at Joseph Khalli barracks by 1730.'

Jim turned to the senior member of the media handling team.

'I'm assuming you have plans to get everyone back to their hotel from the barracks?' After receiving a nod in confirmation, he wound up the briefing. 'Right, if everyone's good with that, let's get back onboard.'

Rob followed Jim and Sarah as they headed for the Chinook.

'Has anyone considered force protection for this next event?' he asked.

'Shouldn't really be an issue,' said Jim. 'They'll be sixty odd Free State soldiers involved and this is the same ground we've used for all of the other familiarisation training. It's miles away from any reported insurgent activity.'

Rob stopped and looked at them both.

'That's what I'm concerned about. We've set a pattern that anyone who's smart will recognise. And all the time the drills are being run, the Free State soldiers won't be in any position to protect anyone. What's more, I'm not sure we should be relying on them for the safety of the UK press in the first place.'

'Well then, I guess it'll be down to me and Mr Grumpy then,' said Sarah, pointing to Lieutenant Achebe who was walking sullenly behind the journalists.

'Yes, I've been meaning to ask all afternoon. Who is that?' said Rob.

'That's Jelani Achebe,' said Sarah dourly. 'He's the border force liaison officer at the Free State Army HQ. He's also Simon Nkaba's nephew.'

'So that's who Colonel Ele was talking about last week,' said Rob, suddenly becoming more interested. 'And he's Nkaba's nephew?'

'Absolutely,' Sarah confirmed. 'Do you know him?'

'He gate-crashed the commander's meeting with General Karrick down here last Saturday. Got really pissed when he saw Dan's gunners heading off base in their WMIKs. Made General Wilkinson order us to stop all activity outside the wire. He's a real cock!'

'Well, it clearly runs in the family then,' said Sarah with a laugh.

'That's as may be,' replied Rob. 'But be careful around Achebe. If he really is like his uncle, I wouldn't trust him as far as I can throw him.'

'Don't worry about me,' said Sarah, still smiling. 'I'll be fine. And thanks for looking after us so well this afternoon, you've got a great team out here.' She turned and ran to catch up with the journalists as they started to board the Chinook.

But I do worry about you, thought Rob. *And a lot more than you know!*

Sarah was sat in the left-hand seat of the Chinook cockpit. They had been at the training area for about ten minutes and the journalists were busy scouting out the best vantage points to view the forthcoming drills. The co-pilot was in the main cabin checking on a hydraulic pipe that one of the loadmasters had noticed was leaking. Jim was still in the right-hand seat, explaining all about the Chinook's new avionics fit. But Sarah wasn't listening. Instead, she was thinking about Rob. It was clear from when they first met back in Northwood that he liked her, even if he had been a bit clumsy showing it. Sarah didn't mind that. He was smart and funny, and seemed genuinely interested in her. Sarah's tour with the Joint Force Headquarters had been full-on for the last two years and she'd had little time for dating. But perhaps with the forthcoming posting to Whitehall, that could change.

When this op is over, maybe we should explore things a bit further, she thought to herself. In the distance, she saw the two Chinooks, flying in formation towards the training area. She tuned back in to Jim.

'... it's the processing power on the new mission computer that's the real game changer. What the fuck was that?'

From the treeline approximately one hundred metres to their left a flash of light exploded, followed immediately by a smoke trail heading directly towards the approaching Chinooks.

'RPG!' screamed Sarah. They watched in horror as the rocket propelled grenade flashed between the helicopters, narrowly missing them both.

'Get this thing fired up, now!' Sarah shouted. At the same time, she leapt from the co-pilot's seat and dashed back into the main cabin. 'I'll get the journos rounded up.'

She unclipped the helmet from her webbing vest and jammed it on her head. A moment later, she was running towards the rear door, passing the co-pilot who was frantically heading in the other direction. As she jumped off the ramp, she was aware of the whine of the Chinook's auxiliary power unit starting up above her head. She was also aware of the zip of small arms fire around her, like a very unwelcome swarm of wasps. It was coming from the same direction as the RPG.

'Get on the helicopter. Now!' she screamed at the gaggle of journalists who were milling around looking dumbfounded. Glancing back, Sarah noticed Jelani Achebe still languidly sprawled on the nylon seating than ran down the length of the helicopter's fuselage. He appeared completely indifferent to the commotion all around him. In an instant she was in front of him, hauling him to his feet.

'On your feet, lieutenant. We've got work to do.'

Jelani reluctantly got up. It was obvious he would have been far happier staying exactly where he was.

'You're supposed to be an officer,' Sarah shouted. 'Time to prove it.' With a look of pure hatred, Jelani pushed past her down the ramp. Pausing only to pick up the assault rifle that he had left on the seat, Sarah followed him off the helicopter.

'Here,' she said, shoving it in his chest. 'You're going to need that!'

Sarah took a second to look round and assess the situation. Most of the journalists hadn't strayed too far from the helicopter and were already back on board. But both television crews were still some distance away on a small grassy knoll off to her right. With an exaggerated wave, she urged them to return to the helicopter. They needed no second bidding.

A second later, she felt something flick off her helmet. Whoever was firing at them was getting more accurate. Or luckier. Either way, it was time to do something about it. Reaching into an ammunition pouch, Sarah pulled out a magazine and slapped it onto her rifle.

'Come on lieutenant,' she called. 'We're up.'

Twenty metres away was a small copse of low-grown trees, which offered some cover from the incoming fire. She ran to it at a sprint and dived behind the nearest bush. A heavy thud followed by a loud grunt confirmed that Jelani had followed her.

'Get some covering fire down on that treeline,' she shouted at him. Without waiting for an answer, Sarah started firing. Single, aimed shots, just like the instructor at Sandhurst had taught her all those years ago. Suddenly to her right came the resounding clatter of Jelani's assault rifle on fully automatic. Within a few seconds his magazine was empty. The regular crack of Sarah's rifle continued before it was drowned out as Jelani reloaded and let loose again. At least it was disrupting the rate of fire from the treeline. Sarah looked back over her shoulder. The TV crews were hurrying towards to the Chinook as quickly as possible, not helped by the bulky equipment they were carrying. As she turned back to the fight, something away to her left caught Sarah's eye. It was a blue ball cap being frantically waved by someone pressed as close to the ground as was humanly possible. She recognised the cap. One of the broadsheet defence correspondents had been wearing it.

Jelani had emptied his second magazine and was in the process of loading another.

'Keep their heads down,' Sarah instructed. 'I'm off to get our friend.' Keeping as low as possible, Sarah dashed across the open ground. Behind her, Jelani was busy emptying his third magazine.

I wonder how many he's got? she thought as she slid down next to the terrified journalist.

'Thank you, thank you, thank you,' he gabbled. 'I only came over here because I needed a pee.'

'Not to worry, sir. You're safe now,' replied Sarah. She was tempted to try humour but thought better of it. 'Right, I'm going to get their heads down and then we're going to run like hell for the helicopter. Are you ready?' The journalist nodded nervously. Sarah knelt next to him and checked her magazine. It was half full.

Oh, what the heck! she thought and turned the selector to automatic. Aiming low, she gently squeezed the trigger. The weapon bucked as the remaining rounds flew away one after the other towards the treeline. In a second, it was empty. She stood up, replacing the magazine as she did so.

'Come on,' she yelled. 'Time to go.'

The journalist was old and overweight and his running like hell was no more than Sarah's fast jog. They were halfway to the Chinook when Sarah heard movement behind her. She turned to see Jelani retreating from the copse towards them. At least he'd had the sense to disengage when he saw them make their move. As he caught up with them, Sarah noticed he was no longer carrying his rifle.

'Where's your weapon?' she asked.

'Out of ammo.'

'What? You don't leave a weapon behind just because you're out of ammo. Go back and get it.'

'You go back and get it,' shouted Jelani. 'I'm off.'

Sarah turned to the journalist.

'Keep running for the chopper, I'll be with you in a minute.' Without even looking at Jelani, she turned and headed back to the copse of trees.

It took Sarah just a few seconds to locate Jelani's rifle, abandoned next to his firing point. As she bent down to pick it up, she suddenly realised she wasn't alone. She looked up and saw Jelani standing over her. A pistol in his hand.

'What are you playing at?' she demanded.

As she went to stand, Jelani fired. His single shot struck her high on the left thigh. Her leg gave way immediately in an explosion of pain. She rolled away, desperately trying to haul herself upwards. Jelani stepped forward and unleashed a massive kick. It caught Sarah on the side of the helmet. She fell back, unconscious.

'Useless bitch.' spat Jelani venomously. He turned and jogged back to the helicopter.

15.

Jim Farmer raced through the Chinook's pre-start up checks like a man possessed. His co-pilot threw himself into the left-hand seat and frantically joined in. The intercom was alive with updates from the two loadmasters as they hurried to get everyone back on board. Jim was head-down, stepping through the checklist to start the second T55-L-712 turboshaft engine.

'Fuck. Fuck. Fuck.' the co-pilot's scream was almost hysterical. Jim looked up. Out of the left-hand windscreen pane, he saw a man step out from the cover of the treeline. Even though he was almost a hundred metres away, Jim could see he was huge. But it wasn't the man's physique that caused the co-pilot to swear so violently. It was the grenade launcher he was bringing to his shoulder. Jim watched helplessly as the giant carefully took aim. He tensed up involuntarily. This was it. He was going to die.

It was impossible to tell the exact moment when the grenade was fired. In the blink of an eye, the fireball was upon them. And then it was gone, flashing high over the cockpit. The Chinook's engines all but drowning out the roar of the grenade as it flew passed.

'He missed. He fucking missed!'

The co-pilot's relief was short lived. As the smoke cleared, it quickly became obvious that their troubles were far from over. The man-mountain had tossed away the grenade launcher and picked up a heavy machine gun. He was advancing slowly towards them, carrying it one-handed, Rambo-style.

'Loadmaster, sitrep.' yelled Jim into his microphone. 'We need to go. Now!'

In the main cabin, chaos reigned. They were still taking incoming small arms fire. A cameraman was hit in the arm and collapsed onto the ramp. The senior loadmaster dragged him to safety. The second loadmaster was screaming at the nearest minder, trying to confirm if everyone was accounted for. Just then, they saw a figure labouring towards them waving a blue ball cap above his head.

'That's the last one,' yelled the minder. The loadmaster reached out a hand and pulled the journalist on board. A second later Jelani appeared and dived onto the ramp.

'Time to go,' he yelled.

'Go, go, go!'

Jim heard the loadmaster's cry over the intercom. That was all he needed. He wrenched the throttle to maximum and yanked up on the collective. The fifteen-ton helicopter rocketed skyward, like some startled prehistoric beast. As soon as he felt the cyclic become responsive, Jim threw the Chinook into the tightest bank possible, ignoring the high-pitched warning siren that screamed out from the engine control system. As they lurched stomach-churningly away from danger, Jim watched the machine gun carrying mountain disappear from view below him. He could have sworn the man was laughing.

Rob was hunched over a laptop in the corner of the Nissen hut, slightly removed from the main ops room set up. Even in another continent, the email monster had to be fed. He heard the call come in on the high frequency radio net.

'Hotel Fox ops, this is Checker zero-one, urgent message over.' Rob looked up from his screen. Checker zero-one was Jim's callsign, but he should have been on his way to Joseph Khalli barracks.

The ops controller reached quickly for his radio mike.

'Checker zero-one, this is Hotel Fox ops. Send, over.'

There was a long burst of static before Jim's voice came over the radio again.

'Hotel Fox ops. Be advised we are inbound your location. Arrival in zero-eight minutes. Ground contact encountered at the training area. We have one casualty and aircraft damage, severity unknown. Request medical support on arrival, over.'

'Checker zero-one, roger.' The ops controller's response was automatic, but he immediately looked over to Rob for further direction. Rob's response was automatic too.

'Get the crash team out to refuelling point one. Right now.' He turned to the force protection watchkeeper. 'Sound the stand-to.'

Rob raised his voice to the whole ops room.

'Listen up everyone. Until we know exactly what's going on, we must assume we're a target too. Treat this as a SIGACT. You know the drill. Stay calm and work the problem.'

He paused briefly letting his call to arms sink in.

'Okay, let's get to work.'

In a second, the ops team were back at it. There were standard operating procedures for a significant activity, or "SIGACT", which they had practised repeatedly during the regiment's work-up period. Straight away, that training came into its own as everyone focused on his or her initial response duties. The only person in the room not fixed by an immediate requirement to do something was Rob. Although he forced himself to appear unflustered, a thousand thoughts were crashing round his head.

What the hell had happened out there? And what about Sarah?

Jim had clearly said only one casualty, so the odds were against it being her. But Rob knew Sarah would have run towards the danger, and he couldn't get rid of the nagging fear that something had happened to her.

Rob's thoughts were interrupted by the sound of the Nissen hut door crashing open as Mr Jones entered at a run.

'Fire truck and crash ambulance are on their way. The doc is with them. Suggest we bring everyone back to the field kitchen. The caterers are knocking up some hot food, and there's plenty of tea and coffee available as well.'

'Thanks, Mr Jones. Good call.' Rob suspected that the journalists would need something a lot stronger than tea or coffee, but Hotel Fox was a dry site so that would have to wait until they got back to New Devon.

The door crashed open again and a breathless Dan Scrivener appeared.

'The site is fully stood to,' he said. 'Sangars are all manned. Nothing to report as yet. QRF is on standby. Do you want them at the refuelling point?'

'No, I don't think so,' decided Rob. 'There's a big enough welcome committee as it is. Pete's on top of things up there. He'll shout if he needs anything.'

Rob paused, ticking off the actions in his mind.

'What about the SINCREP?'

'I'm on it.' They all looked over to the young ops officer who was busy typing on her laptop.

'Well done,' said Rob. 'Hold fire until the chopper's down and we've got more of an idea what's happened. Send an immediate message to JFHQ to say we have a SIGACT running, and a full serious incident report will follow.'

'Already done, sir.' replied the ops officer. Rob looked across at Mr Jones who nodded approvingly.

We've trained them well.

'Okay, even better,' said Rob. 'Now, anything else?'

'That sounds like the Chinook coming in,' said Dan. The unmistakable sound of a large helicopter could clearly be heard over the background noise of the ops room. Rob turned to Mr Jones.

'Let's head to the field kitchen. Dan, you keep on top of things here. It won't be long before the general gets interested. Then it'll get really busy.'

As Rob and Mr Jones hurried over to the field kitchen, they could see the Chinook approaching the nearest refuelling point. From a distance, there was no obvious damage.

The field kitchen was made up of several large, interconnected tents. Half of them housed the mobile catering equipment; the other half were filled with trestle tables and canvas chairs. Apart from the old hangar, it was the biggest covered space on the site, and seldom empty. Everyone visited at least three times a day for meals, but it was also a focal point where the junior ranks congregated when off duty. Access to the site's only Wi-Fi hotspot for personal devices also guaranteed its popularity. But right now the dining area was completely empty. All non-essential site personnel were still stood to, guarding the site.

At that moment, Pete appeared, followed by a group of journalists. They looked dazed and dishevelled.

'What the hell happened?' Rob asked.

'Still not clear sir,' said Pete. 'This lot are all in shock. From what I can make out, they landed on okay but then came under small arms fire. No idea where from. One of the cameramen reckons he saw an RPG fired at the other Chinooks but can't confirm that yet.'

'What about the casualty? And where's Jim?' pressed Rob.

'It was the other cameraman. He took a round in his arm. Not serious. The doc's with him now.' Rob gave an audible sigh of relief. Sarah was okay!

'Everybody else?'

'The crew's still at the aircraft. They're checking out the damage. The rest of the pax should be down here any minute.'

'Thanks Pete,' said Rob. 'Mr Jones, I'm off up to the refuelling point. We need to get some accurate gen on what happened. Pete, stay with the journos. Get them whatever they need. I've a feeling CDS's plan for good publicity is just about to backfire, and badly.'

Rob's land rover was parked outside the ops room. He jumped in and headed off towards the nearest refuelling point. As he drove around the field kitchen, he saw another truck pulling up by the entrance. He slowed down, tempted to drive back and check on Sarah, but he knew he needed to speak with the Chinook crew first. The general would have lots of questions and he needed the answers. Reluctantly, he accelerated away towards the waiting helicopter.

Rob parked his vehicle next to the pillow tanks and jogged over to the Chinook. Jim was checking the undercarriage with one of the loadmasters but broke off when he saw Rob approaching.

'Hey sir,' he called.

'Jim, how are you?'

'I've had better days,' Jim replied. 'Everyone's a bit shaken, but we're all in one piece.'

'So, what happened?'

'We got to the training area as planned and landed on. The minders were sorting out the best place for the TV crews to set up and the rest of the journos were just kicking about. As the other Chinooks approached, we saw an RPG launched at them from a treeline to our left. It missed, but only just. They both bugged out immediately. I prepped for take-off while Major Grey went out and rounded everyone up. That took a bit longer than I expected. Then we came under fire ourselves – another RPG. I've no idea how, but it missed. As soon as Sergeant Halley confirmed we had everyone on board, I got the hell out of there. We knew the airframe had taken some small-arms hits so when I heard we also had a casualty on board, I decided to divert here rather than head all the way back to New Devon.'

'Sound like you made the right call,' said Rob. 'Now you've had a look at the damage, what do you think? Can you get airborne again?'

'Not a chance,' replied Jim. 'This frame's going nowhere until we get an experienced engineering team to check it out. They'll decide if it's safe to fly.'

'Okay, you're the expert. In that case, I need to get back to the ops room and start working on a plan to extract our guests. Can I give you guys a lift down to the field kitchen? There's hot food on.'

'Thanks for the offer sir, but no.' answered Jim. 'It'll be a while before we've finished up here.'

Rob hurried back to the land rover. He needed to update the ops team, but first he had to see Sarah. Just for a minute. He pulled up behind the truck and headed into the field kitchen. The journalists were all huddled together in small groups, slowly coming to terms with their near-death experience. A couple of medical orderlies were fussing around them but there was little response. Pete saw him come in and walked over.

'Did you get any gen from Jim?' he asked.

'A bit,' confirmed Rob. 'Enough for the SINCREP at least.' He looked around.

'Where's Major Grey?'

'No idea,' said Pete. 'I wanted to speak to her too, but she's not here. She didn't come down on either of the four tonners, I've checked. I assumed she was still at the refuelling point.'

'She's definitely not up there,' Rob said. 'If she's not up there and she's not down here, where the hell is she?'

'Oh shit,' swore Pete. 'Don't tell me she got left behind?'

Rob felt like he'd been kicked hard in the stomach. There was only one possible explanation. Somehow Sarah had never got back onto the helicopter.

'Sir, sir.'

Rob looked round to see the duty ops clerk running over.

'Squadron Leader Scrivener needs you back in the ops room right away. General Wilkinson wants to speak to you.'

16.

Rob followed the clerk back into the ops room, with Pete close on his heels. He took the handset that Dan was holding out for him. Before speaking into it, he turned to his deputy.

'Pete, get back to the field kitchen and find out anything you can about what happened to Major Grey. Make sure you speak with Jim and his crew too. And let's pray there's a simple explanation for all this.'

'What are you going to tell the general?' asked Pete.

'Everything we know.' replied Rob. *Which is not very much.*

He squeezed the pressel switch on the secure phone.

'General. Rob Salmon speaking.'

Unsurprisingly General Wilkinson did not engage in any small talk. Instead, he demanded an immediate update. Rob quickly passed on everything he'd just learnt from Jim.

'So, one civilian casualty and a Chinook with damage unknown at your location,' the General played back.

Rob gulped.

'Yes sir, but there's one other issue. Major Grey didn't make it onto the helicopter before it left the training area. We've only just found this out and are investigating further.'

'What? You're telling me she's still out there?'

'It would appear so sir. That's all I can confirm right now, but I recommend despatching an RAF Regiment section from here to check out the site. If they leave now, they can get there before nightfall.' There was silence on the other end of the phone for a few seconds.

'Negative. We're checking her personal locator beacon right now.'

Another pause.

'I've just been told it's not been activated. Either way, I don't want your people operating outside the wire. Not after that show with Nkaba on Saturday.'

'But what about Major Grey?' protested Rob.

'We have other resources Rob,' reassured the general. 'We also need to get the media party back to New Devon. The backup helicopter is still at the barracks, and so is Captain Willis's team. They're far better qualified to check out the training area and also have free rein to move about in country. I'll have the backup Chinook deploy them and then swing by your location to pick up the media. Is the injured cameraman fit to fly?'

'I'll have to check with the doc,' said Rob. 'But I'd be surprised if he isn't.'

'Good,' said the general. 'Sounds like you're well on top of things down there. Keep it up and come back directly to me if you need to.'

'Roger sir,' replied Rob, with more than a little relief.

As soon as the call was over, Rob checked with the ops team. 'What's the current threat situation?'

As usual, Dan was on top of things. 'Nothing to report from any of the sangars. If this was a co-ordinated attack, we'd be in contact by now. I recommend we stand the troops down.'

'Agreed,' said Rob. 'Good work everyone.'

Rob headed back to the field kitchen where he found Pete and Mr Jones.

'What more do we know?' he demanded.

'It's not at all clear,' said Pete. 'I've spoken to almost everyone but most of them are far too disoriented to remember anything clearly. As soon as the bullets started flying, they just rushed back on board the chopper without a second thought for anyone else.'

'That figures,' said Rob. 'What about Achebe? Did he see anything?'

'Well, he's not saying if he did. He reckons that he put down covering fire with Major Grey on the treeline where the shooting was coming from. Major Grey then ran off to help one of the other journalists and he was left on his own. By his account, he fought off the entire attack single handed until he ran out of ammunition. He claims he only just made it back before Jim took off.'

'Quite the hero,' said Rob, his voice thick with sarcasm. That didn't exactly fit with Sarah's view of Achebe. 'What about the journalist Sarah went to help. Have you spoken to him?'

'No, because I can't find him. No-one says they needed help. Maybe the Chinook crew will know more.' At that moment, Jim walked into the field kitchen with the rest of his crew. They made straight for Rob and Pete.

'I hear from Mr Jones that the backup Chinook is on its way. There's no need for us to stay here with the unserviceable frame, so we'll head back with the media group.'

But Rob wasn't interested in Jim's travel plans.

'Forget about that, Jim. What about Major Grey? How could you leave the training area without her?'

'Hang on a minute sir,' said Jim, getting defensive very quickly. 'All F-H was breaking loose. We'd just had a very near miss with an RPG and were seconds away from heavy machine gun incoming. If that had hit the cockpit, none of us would be here now.'

'But you left her behind!'

'We didn't know!' Jim shot back.

'Sir.' It was Sergeant Halley, one of the two loadmasters. 'I made the call. There was no way the boss could tell from up front if we had everyone on board, and Flight Sergeant Gill was busy with the casualty. It was my call. The strat comms lady confirmed everyone was on board, so I radioed that we were good to go. Then the Free State lieutenant ran up. He dived onto the ramp just as we were taking off. There was so much commotion nobody noticed the major was missing.'

'All right,' acknowledged Rob, calming down a little. 'Thank you, sergeant. I'm not suggesting you deliberately left Major Grey behind, but she is still out there and the more we know about what happened, the more likely we are to get her back.'

He thought for a second.

'Who was the last journalist to arrive? If we believe Lieutenant Achebe, he must be the person that Major Grey went to help.'

Sergeant Halley scratched his head.

'He was a fairly big chap. Wearing a black North Face jacket I think. And he had a blue ball cap. He was waving it as he ran up to the aircraft.'

Rob looked around the field kitchen but couldn't see anyone who fitting that description.

'Pete, track this bloke down quick as you can. We need to speak to him before the second Chinook gets here. Once the media party have gone, we've no chance of getting any more information out of them.'

It was past seven o'clock when the second Chinook arrived at Hotel Fox. At any other time, its breath-taking appearance out of the shimmering setting sun would have had the journalists reaching for their camera phones. But right now they were still struggling with the trauma of the attack, and it hardly even registered. All they wanted was to get back to New Devon, to a stiff drink and a safe bed.

'I managed to track down mister blue-cap,' said Pete. 'But he wasn't that helpful. He got separated from the main group of journalists and Major Grey went back to get him. After that it's all a bit confused. He reckons she left him to give more covering fire and he made it to the Chinook on his own. When he got on board, he ran to the front to get away from the incoming fire. He didn't take any notice of what happened after that and just assumed Major Grey had got on board as well.'

'So why didn't he come forward earlier when you were trying to track him down?'

'No idea. He's clearly embarrassed that he needed rescuing, but it's not obvious he's hiding anything.'

'I don't know,' said Rob. 'Something's missing. Or somebody's taking the piss. There are just too many holes in all this. Did you speak to Achebe again?'

'I did,' Pete confirmed. 'But he was even less helpful than before. I get the distinct impression he doesn't like Major Grey. Or any of us for that matter. I don't trust him, but I can't find anything to prove he's lying.'

'Okay, Pete, thanks. Once the second Chinook gets away, you need to get all this down on paper. Tonight's SITREP is going to take a while to put together.'

It has been an extremely long day. The second Chinook left without incident and Rob was back in his corner of the operations room doing a very bad job of clearing down the day's emails. The daily situation report had been sent and the night shift was now on duty. All was quiet.

Rob needed to talk to someone, and at times like this there was only one candidate. He reached for the secure phone and punched in a number from memory. It took an age but eventually the connection was made.

'Rebecca Salmon, Head Africa Department.' Rob had no doubt his sister would still be at her desk, even after ten o'clock.

'Hi Becca, it's me,' Rob said wearily.

'Rob. It's great to hear your voice. Sounds like you've had a really lousy day.'

Rebecca had already seen the reports on the day's activities, so was fully aware what her brother had been dealing with.

'You're not wrong,' confirmed Rob. 'If you don't mind, I just need to unload for a bit.'

'Of course,' said Rebecca. She listened as Rob replayed the day's events. Normally she just acted as an independent sounding board, but tonight she had skin in the game.

'Rob, there's a couple of things you've gone over that just don't make sense. First off, who misses a stationery Chinook with an RPG from point blank range? I mean, it's not exactly a small target. And then they didn't open fire straight away with the heavy machine gun? Why? It's almost as if they didn't actually want to take it out.'

'But that makes absolutely no sense,' said Rob. He was tired. And seldom kept up with his sister at the best of times.

'Then the pilot reported that the shooter was laughing when they made their escape. What's that all about?'

'I've no idea,' confessed Rob.

'But that's not the really big thing,' said Rebecca. Not waiting for Rob to respond, she continued. 'Weybourn is supposed to be a counter insurgency operation, right? The Free State army fighting an insurgency with your support. An insurgency presumably started by disaffected Free Statians, from deep in the country's hinterland.'

'You know it is,' retorted Rob. 'So what?'

'So how come the first time anyone actually sees an insurgent, it's a white man?'

17.

The following morning, Rob brought Pete, Dan, and Mr Jones together to discuss the fallout from the previous day. Although Rob had been pleased with the way things had gone, he knew there was always room for improvement.

'During the stand-to, there was confusion over the actions of some duty personnel,' Dan reported. 'A number continued with their primary task, while others manned their allocated defensive position. We need to be clearer on exactly which duty personnel should stay at their posts, and which are needed to defend the site.'

'Right,' agreed Rob. 'But I don't see any major issues here. You and Pete should be able to work out those sections that must always be manned. The ops room and the medical post for example. If we're supporting flying, I'd also expect the refuelling points to remain open. Not sure there's much beyond that though. Anything else Dan?'

'Yes sir. We need to push back on the general's direction not to patrol outside the wire. It goes against all our procedures and is leaving us dangerously exposed.'

'I don't disagree,' replied Rob. 'But I can't see him changing his mind. Even yesterday when I suggested deploying gunners to the training area, he pushed back. That run-in with Nkaba last weekend really had an impact.'

But Dan wasn't ready to back down.

'How about the fuel convoys then? After what happened yesterday, it's clear someone sees us as a target now. We're sending convoys out almost every day and there's only so many routes they can take. It's impossible not to set patterns. After all, their destination is always the same.'

'Fair point,' conceded Rob. 'What are you suggesting?'

'We send a WMIK with them. Just one land rover and a three-man fire-team. It's relatively discrete. They could even peel off when the tankers reach the outskirts of New Devon and join up again for the return journey. The chances of anyone targeting the convoy in the final few miles through the city is pretty slim.'

Rob was impressed. Dan had clearly thought this through.

'Thoughts?' he asked, looking at Pete and Mr Jones.

'I think it's a good idea,' said Pete.

'Me too,' agreed Mr Jones. 'And if we cop any flak from the general, it's always easier to ask for forgiveness after the event.' Rob smiled. Mr Jones had been around long enough to know how the game was played.

'Okay, it's decided,' said Rob. 'Next convoy's Saturday?

Mr Jones nodded.

'As soon as we're ready, we send a WMIK out with every convoy. Dan, Pete. The convoy commanders will need to work with the RAF Regiment training section to confirm actions on. They'll also need some practise drills, so everyone's up to speed. Providing you're both happy they know what they're doing, we'll start running escorts straight away. Any questions?'

Before anyone could answer, the sound of the tent flap being pulled open distracted them. Stooping low, the ops controller entered. He paused to let his eyes adjust from the bright sunshine outside.

'Sorry to bother you sir,' he said looking at Rob. 'We have visitors.'

The visitors were Terry Willis and his team. The backup Chinook had dropped them off at the training area the previous afternoon and they had spent most of the night searching for Sarah. While the two SAS troopers refuelled their vehicle and chased down a much-needed brew, Terry and his staff sergeant updated Rob on what they had learned.

'We searched the whole training area and as much of the land surrounding it as we could. No sign of Major Grey. Or her weapon or any of her kit. We got the exact GPS coordinates where the Chinook landed from Squadron Leader Farmer, so we know we were looking in the right place. The obvious location for the enemy forces' attack was the nearest treeline and when we checked it out, we found stacks of empty cartridges littered around. Probably about half a dozen shooters. We backtracked to the landing site and came by a small copse of trees that would have made ideal defensive cover. Sure enough, we found plenty of brass there too. Both five point five-six and seven point six-two.'

'The five-five-six cases would have come from Major Grey's weapon, wouldn't they?' interjected Rob.

'That's what we think,' said Staff Sergeant Hayes. 'And the border force use Hungarian AMP-69s. That takes seven-six-two millimetre. Wasn't there a border force officer on the manifest?'

'Yes, Lieutenant Achebe,' confirmed Rob. 'We spoke to him yesterday and he reckoned he'd covered the return of the journalists to the helicopter with Major Grey.'

'Well there must have been almost a hundred seven-six-two cartridges there,' continued Terry. 'It looked like they'd all been fired from the same position. Far fewer five-five-sixes. No more than a dozen or so.'

'Anything else?' asked Rob.

'Yes,' replied Terry. 'But it's not good. There was also a lot of dried blood, close to the seven-six-two firing point.'

'But we know Achebe wasn't injured. Where did it come from?'

'We don't know for sure, but we did find this.' Terry held up a small plastic bag with a single cartridge case in it. 'It's a nine millimetre, almost certainly from a handgun. We scoured the whole area but there weren't any more.'

'That doesn't make much sense,' said Rob. 'Is that all you found?'

'No. This morning Corporal Farrell sent me yesterday's SITREPs. When we read about Major Grey helping the journalist, we widened our search and found half a magazine's worth of five-five-six cases about fifty metres beyond the copse of trees. That suggests the Major put down covering fire before sending the journalist back to the helicopter.'

'But the timeline doesn't make sense,' said Rob. 'If the blood's not Achebe's, it got to be Sarah's. And if she was injured during the initial engagement, how come she managed to get to the journalist and help him? And why wasn't there any blood beyond the copse of trees.'

'And why didn't the journalist say that the major had been injured?' added Hayes. 'He can't have missed that, surely?'

'Of course not. And where does the nine-millimetre round fit in?' Rob was getting really concerned now. 'I said yesterday someone was taking the piss. It's got to be either Achebe or the journalist.'

'But the journalist didn't have a handgun and there's no evidence to suggest he was anywhere near the copse of trees,' said Terry. 'Major Grey was carrying a Glock, I guess he could have got hold of that.'

'No chance,' replied Rob. 'How many journalists know how to use a Glock, and can you see Major Grey allowing him to take it off her? No, this is all about Achebe. We need to question him again. He knows exactly what happened yesterday.'

Rob paused for a few seconds, thinking through options.

'Terry, I suggest you write up your report now. You can send it to the JFHQ from here. I'll call the general and explain what we know. Given who Achebe is, General Wilkinson is the only person who's got any chance of getting him handed over.'

Jelani Achebe was feeling extremely upbeat. The previous day had turned out much better than he could have hoped. When he left the relative safety of the Chinook, he'd been really concerned. But the buzz he'd felt during the engagement, and the feeling of invincibility he got once it was over, was the best feeling he'd ever had. To cap it all, he'd successfully got away with shooting the British major and leaving her for dead. And the dumb journalist had helped him by only telling half the story of his rescue. Jelani had no idea why he'd done that, but he didn't care. Even the dull ache from his bruised foot was welcome.

Jelani's staff car pulled up outside New Devon International Airport. Limping slightly, he got out and looked on as his driver removed two bags and an expensive-looking rifle case from the boot. The driver was very careful, knowing that even the slightest of knocks would mean a volley of abuse and probably a punch from his passenger. He clicked his fingers and a wizened old porter shuffled over.

'You be bloody careful with that,' demanded Jelani angrily, as the porter heaved his rifle case onto a trolley. 'It's worth far more than you.'

Not waiting for the porter, and without a word of thanks to his driver, Jelani marched into the terminal and headed for the business class check-in. The terminal was quiet and the few passengers around were quick to get out of his way. Like rats on a sinking ship, they instinctively knew it was better to be somewhere else. Jelani was disappointed not to be flying first class, but the National Shooting Association could only afford business and his uncle had refused to pay for an upgrade. There was no queue, and he handed his passport over to the check-in agent.

'Do you have any luggage?' she asked pleasantly.

'Of course I do,' snapped Jelani. He had no time for mere staff. 'Get up here,' he shouted at the porter who was still making his way carefully across the terminal with Jelani's bags. 'I haven't got all day.'

The porter reached the check-in desk and began lifting the bags onto the scales.

'Is that a gun case?' inquired the check-in agent politely. She was determined to remain courteous even though her customer clearly was not.

'What does it look like?' Jelani shot back. 'Of course it's a gun case.'

'Do you have the necessary paperwork, sir?' Still polite.

'Of course I've got the bloody paperwork,' Jelani had got one of the functionaries at the interior ministry to complete all the necessary documentation before he left that morning. He reached into his pocket and shoved a crumpled form at her.

'Here.' The agent checked the form and returned it with Jelani's passport and his boarding card.

'The flight leaves at two o'clock from Gate One. The executive lounge is just down the …'

'I know where it is,' interrupted Jelani rudely. He snatched his passport and boarding card and walked away without another word.

The check-in agent looked at the porter and rolled her eyes.

'*Aja!*' The porter almost spat the word.

The check in agent was shocked. Even though Jelani was no longer in earshot, she hadn't expected the porter to call him a dog.

'He no *Afirika,*' continued the porter in a mix of Yoruba and broken English. He pinched his own pitted black cheek hard. 'This *Afirika.*'

18.

Admiral Bellis knew it was going to be a very difficult meeting. The prime minister was furious, and he wanted everyone in the cabinet room to know it. The other five occupants could hardly miss his anger but displayed markedly different reactions to it. Sat next to the prime minister was his chief advisor. Cedric Ratley was well used to seeing his boss like this and knew the best response was to keep his mouth shut and let everyone else cop the flack. Tom Fletcher was his usual sycophantic self, trying to avoid the worst of the prime minister's castigations, while at the same time making sure everyone knew the current crisis was not of his making. Further down the table, deliberately distancing himself from the defence minister, was the new foreign secretary, George Grierson. As an elder statesman of his party, he considered himself to be above the prime minister's haranguing, but nevertheless couldn't completely ignore it. That was because the final member of the quintet in the prime minister's sights worked for him. And Hilary Blythe had still not been able to come up with any concrete information about the assassination of Grierson's predecessor.

'So just remind me again, why did we send the journalists to West Africa Free State?' Brownlow looked pointedly at Tom Fletcher, who said nothing but turned his head very deliberately in the direction of Admiral Bellis.

'CDS, perhaps you'd care to explain.'

Recognising there was no chance of any top cover from his minister, Bellis cleared his throat. He felt like a convicted wrongdoer facing the gallows.

'Well prime minister, it was clear to me that Operation Weybourn had fallen from the public's view, and I felt it necessary to make sure the excellent work our servicemen and women are doing out in Free State was being fully recognised.'

Even as he said it, Bellis knew his response sounded lame.

'You felt it necessary?' said the prime minister, not hiding his astonishment. 'You felt it necessary? You don't decide what's necessary. Your job is to do what I tell you. You don't dictate what this government feeds to the media – I've got a bloody communications team for that.'

Brown could sense the admiral wilting before his verbal assault.

'What you should be doing is not letting members of the press get shot. But you can't even manage that can you? And a BBC cameraman, for God's sake.' The prime minister paused but Bellis had no reply.

'Do you have any idea of the damage you've caused? Read the damn headlines. You've made us look like a bunch of idiots chasing around Africa without a clue. How difficult can it be to hunt down a rag-tag bunch of mis-fit losers in such a piss-ridden, third world country?'

Bellis winced at Brownlow's vulgarity but knew he only had himself to blame for the onslaught. With no other option, he fell back on the obvious.

'Prime minister, I must remind you that we are supporting the Free State army in its operation against the insurgents. We are not making the decisions. That was the clear direction from the National Security Council. I should also stress that our eight, medium-lift helicopters are operating across a country one and a half times the size of Wales. Finding an insurgent force of less than one thousand hidden in an area that size is like looking for a needle in a haystack.'

Anthony Brownlow looked ready to explode. No-one talked to him like that. But before he could respond, Cedric Ratley intervened.

'Perhaps we should move on, prime minister,' he suggested. 'I'm sure the number ten media team can pull together something to deal with the fallout from this. And I've no doubt the news cycle will quickly move onto something else. Might our time be better spent considering the plight of the officer who is missing?'

He searched for a name.

'Major Grey,' offered Hilary.

'Yes, Major Grey,' agreed Ratley. 'What are we doing about that situation?'

Anthony Brownlow nodded grudgingly but still glared at Admiral Bellis. He wasn't going to forget that show of disrespect anytime soon.

Hilary did not always see eye to eye with George Bellis, but she did know he was an ally who, right now, needed some protection.

'Maybe, I can help there,' she offered. 'You will recall, prime minister, that you gave SIS the lead in investigating Mr Harknell's assassination. As such, we've taken on the coordinating role for all intelligence out of West Africa Free State. Yesterday, a special forces team searched the training area where Major Grey went missing but found no trace of her. They did, however, find evidence that she may have been wounded during the attack on the Chinook. Our assessment is she's likely to be in the hands of the insurgents.'

'That's just bloody brilliant,' exclaimed Brownlow. 'So now we can expect a video of her beheading to be all over the internet.'

'No sir,' said Hilary firmly. 'We cannot expect that. There is no evidence whatsoever that the insurgency is driven by Islamist extremism. I agree that Major Grey remains in danger. But if they'd wanted her dead, they'd most likely have killed her straight away and left her on the training area for us to find.'

'And why would they have done that?' asked the prime minister.

'Because it sends a message. It says, we're in control and we can kill your soldiers whenever and wherever we choose.'

Brownlow hated it when someone thought through the situation quicker than he did.

'So, what are you doing about it?' he shot back angrily.

'We're continuing to work the intelligence,' said Hilary. 'It's only a matter of time before we get a break.'

'And General Wilkinson has provided additional planning support to the Free State Army HQ from his staff on the Prince of Wales,' added Admiral Bellis. 'From now on, we'll be pulling the strings in the pursuit of the insurgents.'

'Well, something had better make a difference. And soon,' Brownlow's look could have killed. 'Otherwise, you'll both be out of a job.'

Sarah slowly regained consciousness. She was in the back of an off-road vehicle travelling way too fast on a heavily rutted and pothole filled road. Her hands were tightly bound behind her, and she could do nothing to stop being tossed around the cargo space, like a small boat at the mercy of a violent storm. She was being assaulted by pain. The ache in her thigh was intense but that didn't come close to the waves of agony exploding in her head. She could sense the swelling to the side of her face, and her left eye was almost completely closed. What's more, every bump in the road seemed to pitch Sarah against a sharp edge from the row of metal crates stacked on the floor beside her. She couldn't even scream out in pain, because of the gag that was knotted tightly over her mouth.

Just when it seemed as if her suffering would never end, the vehicle slowed down and swung off the uneven road. It didn't stop, but the new track was more challenging for the driver, and he was forced to slow down. That was a godsend for Sarah. The pitching stopped and she managed to drag herself away from the crates and onto some large half-filled sandbags.

Sarah's eyes gradually became accustomed to the darkness, and she recognised the trappings of a military vehicle. The sides and the roof of the cargo space were hard-skinned, and the floor was interspersed with heavy, tie-down hooks. The metalwork was painted black rather than green. Not a land rover, maybe a Mercedes G-Wagon or Russian equivalent. Her webbing vest was thrown in the far corner, and she could see her personal location beacon clipped to a side pouch. If she could somehow get over there and activate it. But there was no way she could scramble over the crates with her hands bound behind her and trying to work them free only made the nylon cable tie cut into her wrists more fiercely.

For a second, Sarah felt the despair wash over her.

Get a grip!

She dug deep, forcing her training to take over.

First, evaluate the situation. That wasn't hard. She'd been shot in the leg and kicked unconscious by someone who was supposed to be on her side. Now she was a captive of person or persons unknown. She looked down at her thigh. Her camouflage trousers had been cut open along the seam and someone had applied a field dressing to her wound. It was a professional piece of work and had stopped the bleeding. The persistent ache suggested that the anonymous consideration hadn't stretched to pain relief, but at least she was no longer in danger of bleeding to death.

Take the positives. If they wanted me dead, they wouldn't have bothered with first aid.

Next, identify the best course of action to facilitate her escape. Again, not difficult. She wasn't going anywhere other than where the driver of the vehicle decided. And until she was able to get up, she had no idea if she could even walk. Cracking on regardless after taking a bullet to the leg was fine in Hollywood, but Sarah knew the real world was somewhat different. She pushed herself against the sandbags and discovered all the pockets in her combat shirt had been emptied. Then, more in hope than expectation, she glanced at the holster strapped to her good thigh. It was empty.

Come on, you weren't really expecting them to miss that, were you?

Exhausted from both the physical and mental effort, she rolled back into the most comfortable position she could and waited for her journey to end.

Amazingly Sarah managed to fall asleep and was only wakened by the judder of the vehicle as the driver switched off the engine. Outside, she could hear footsteps and people talking, but too quietly to catch what was being said. Then the rear cargo door was opened. Sarah tensed up. It was dark outside, and she couldn't make out anything other than the vague outline of a couple of bodies stood close together.

'Hey, lady. Get out,' the voice was deep and the accent unmistakably South African.

Sarah stayed where she was.

'I said, get out.'

Realising that there was little to be gained in disobeying further, Sarah struggled to move towards the cargo door, but was unable to make it over the metal crates. Her protestations were muffled by the gag, but the message got through.

'Get her out of there.'

Sarah was aware of someone climbing into the vehicle and then two strong hands took hold of her shirt and dragged her roughly over the tailgate. The pain in her thigh was like fire as it scraped over the hard metal surface, and she collapsed in a heap. The same hands reached down and heaved her to her feet.

Strongly favouring her good leg, Sarah was just about able to stand. She looked up defiantly at the man in front of her. He was huge, dwarfing the rest of the growing crowd that was quickly gathering around her. He was wearing dark camouflage trousers and a black vest. On his head was a grey, badge-less beret.

'And who have we got here?' he asked.

Sarah eyes burned. *How the fuck do you expect me to answer like this?*

He reached down and ripped the gag away.

'Let's try again,' he said. 'Who are you?'

'Major Grey, British army,' Sarah replied, offering nothing more.

'How come you're so unpopular?'

Sarah was confused.

'My men saw some skinny little black kid pop you one in the leg with a Glock and then kick your head in. Don't think that makes him your friend.'

'That's none of your business,' said Sarah defiantly.

'It is my business,' said the South African. He leaned in close to Sarah, their faces only inches apart. The mix of beer and cigarettes on his breath was disgusting.

'And I'll tell you why. I'm in charge round here. That makes everything my business. That means everything I say goes. So, don't piss me off. Most of the locals have never seen a white girl in their lives. Especially not a pretty one like you. They'd jump at the chance to get to know you better and the only thing that's stopping them is me and my buddies here.' He jerked his thumb at the three similarly dressed men behind him. 'So, you just sit tight and behave, and you'll come to no harm. Mess me about and I can't guarantee what might happen.'

Sarah nodded resignedly. Her courses of action had just narrowed considerably.

19.

Corporal Marsden was on top of the world. Not only was his promotion confirmed the day before deploying, but today he was also going to command his first vehicle convoy. It may only be two fuel tankers on the now routine run to New Devon International Airport, but it was a big step up. There was also talk within the regiment that Operation *Weybourn* was being added to the qualifying list for the general service medal. If that happened, he'd be getting his first gong too. Marsden had completed the convoy commander's course earlier in the year. It was unusual to do the course before being promoted, but his flight commander had confidence in him. Now Marsden was determined to prove it was well placed.

His team had spent the previous afternoon working through practise drills under the professional eye of the RAF Regiment training section. From now on, all the fuel convoys would be accompanied by a WMIK patrol vehicle. Marsden had been relieved to find out that the three-person fire team would be led by a lance corporal, which meant Marsden would still be in overall command of the convoy. That said, the training instructor had made it very clear that when it came to tactical decision making, Marsden would be expected to listen to his RAF Regiment colleague.

Marsden checked his watch. Three minutes to seven. Time to mount up. His driver, Private Bryony Leigh, was already in the cab. Senior Aircraftsman Ben Smith and Private "Dolly" Parton made up the rest of his small team. Marsden looked across at the RAF Regiment gunners, already in their patrol vehicle. Lance Corporal Jamie James gave him a thumbs up. Marsden returned it with a grin. As he walked round to the passenger door, he saw the regimental sergeant major striding purposefully towards him.

'Everything good to go, corporal?' asked Mr Jones.

'Absolutely sir,' replied Marsden, the grin still on his face. 'Can't wait to get out there.'

'Good,' said Mr Jones. 'But don't forget, you're in command now. That's a big step up. After what happened at the training area on Wednesday, Major Thurlow was seriously considering replacing your crew with a more experienced team. But your flight commander argued that we should stick with you, and I agreed with him. Don't let me down.'

Marsden nodded, replacing his grin with a determined look.

'I won't sir,' he confirmed in the most serious voice he could muster. 'You can count on me.'

The journey to the airport was uneventful. There were three different convoy routes between Hotel Fox and New Devon. Route *Murrayfield* took the northern-most road and Route *Twickenham* the southern-most. The route that they were using today – Route *Lansowne* ran directly though the centre of the country. For most of the journey, the roads were empty. Just a few beaten-up old SUVs and the odd rust-covered tractor. As they got closer to the capital, the traffic picked up, but nothing to stop the drivers keeping to the mandated convoy speed of forty kilometres per hour. In fact, the biggest problem Corporal Marsden had was making sure his drivers stayed alert. The monotony of the drive was enough to send anyone to sleep.

As the convoy reached the outskirts of the city, they pulled over into a layby where a Royal Engineer section was hard at work rebuilding a dilapidated Free State army guard post. Marsden jumped down from his cab and jogged over to the patrol vehicle. 'You guys hold here. We should be back in a couple of hours, but if there's any delay, I'll give you a shout.'

'Roger that,' replied James. His men were looking forward to getting a brew on and spending the hottest part of the day lounging in the shade.

The remainder of the journey was slow going as the heavy vehicles negotiated New Devon's narrow, crumbling roads and crazy drivers. Only on the final few kilometres along the country's single stretch of dual carriageway did the drivers manage to get back up to their convoy speed.

By now, the bowsers were a familiar sight at the airport, and they were waved through the security barrier without a second glance. They headed over to the aviation fuel farm and Private Leigh manoeuvred her vehicle expertly up the short ramp to the offtake point, stopping as the cab drew exactly level with the control point. The local supervisor appeared from his tiny hut wearing a floppy sunhat and filthy overalls. He ambled over and started dragging out hoses, refusing Leigh's offer of help. Forty minutes later, both bowsers were full, and the paperwork completed. They were ready to head for home. Corporal Marsden made a note of the departure time in his convoy commander's log, 1240 hours. Everything was going like clockwork, he thought.

As the two bowsers roared past the security post and back onto the dual carriageway, one of the guards reached for a mobile phone. He dialled a number, waited for it to be answered and said simply.

'Two trucks leaving the airport now.'

Half an hour later, the convoy arrived back at the guard post and the gunners reluctantly left the shade they had been enjoying. Pausing only for a quick comms check, the bowsers pulled back onto the road and disappeared down Route *Lansdowne*, with the patrol vehicle falling in behind them.

The man-mountain took the brief call and followed it up with one of his own. Less than ten miles from Harris Field, one of his compatriots acknowledged the updated information gruffly and hung up. Leaving the comfort of his air-conditioned G-Wagon, he rounded up the dozen insurgent fighters lounging nearby with a shout.

'Right, you lot. Time to go to work.'

The small team didn't look much, but they were the pick of the fighters the mercenaries had been training. Dressed in an assortment of camouflage gear, most carried AK-47 automatic rifles that were older than they were. The remainder made do with the slightly more modern, but less favoured copy, the Chinese Type 56. None were trusted with anything more substantial. The mercenary was stood on the brow of a low hill. Looking westward, he could see the weather-beaten asphalt of the country's main highway as it snaked along the valley floor towards them. The incline that brought the road to where they were standing was not overly steep, but it was enough to force a heavy truck to drop down through the gears to tackle it. The South African frowned. Looking back into the setting sun was a problem he should have foreseen. But it was too late to worry about that now. Leaving one of the men as a lookout, he led the rest to the position he had chosen just over one hundred metres further down the road. Parking the G-Wagon out of sight behind some low scrub, he shouted to get them ready.

Corporal Marsden was hot and tired. There was no air conditioning in the bowser's cab and the draught from the open window did little to reduce the temperature. At least they were almost home. As the convoy entered the valley, he knew they were no more than fifteen kilometres from Hotel Fox. He looked across at Private Leigh who was concentrating on the broad winding bends that were a feature of Route *Lansdowne.*

'Anything good planned for when we get back?' he asked.

'What, when we get back tonight, or when we get back to Stafford?' replied Leigh, with a brief glance across at him.

'When we get back tonight.'

'Oh, the usual,' confirmed Leigh without enthusiasm. 'Catching up on Facebook if the Wi-Fi's working. And I should face time my kid sister. It's her birthday tomorrow.' She gunned the engine and changed down through the gears in preparation for the climb out of the valley. 'Won't be sorry to get out this cab neither. I really need a shower.'

Neither Marsden nor Leigh saw the camouflage coated figure as he turned and made an exaggerated wave towards his colleagues.

On seeing the signal, the mercenary began his final checks. His men had stolen a low trailer from a farmstead earlier in the day and towed it to the ambush site using an ancient three-ton Bedford truck that used to belong to the Free State army. That truck was now parked down a nearby track, ready for a quick getaway if needed. The trailer had been dragged across the road and tipped onto its side blocking both lanes. The fighters had taken cover behind it with their weapons pointed towards the brow of the hill. Satisfied all was in order, the mercenary walked back across the front of the trailer and took up a position close by the scrub where his vehicle was hidden. Regardless of how his charges performed, he was not planning on hanging around for too long.

Private Leigh's bowser was one of the oldest in the regiment and its engine was tired. It had been designed for use in northwest Europe, not Africa, and was struggling with the heat and the dust.

'You'll never get up the hill in this gear,' Marsden told her. 'You need to change down again.' Leigh tutted crossly. She got on okay with Marsden but didn't need him to tell her how to drive. Revving the engine hard, she sought a lower gear, but the gearbox was as old as the engine and refused to respond. The synchromesh crashed wildly and the tanker slowed to a crawl. Behind her, Senior Aircraftman Smith cursed as he was forced to reduce his speed to keep a safe distance between the two tankers.

'Get in you git!' she shouted, hammering the accelerator, and crashing the gearbox again. This time it worked. The engine engaged and the tanker responded with a heavy lurch. It battled up the last few yards of the hill and Leigh swung the wheel to take the final bend.

As the roof of the tanker's cab came into view, the mercenary saw the fighters near him tense up, fingers tight on the trigger.

'Wait for my command,' he yelled.

The bowser traversed the brow of the hill reluctantly, as if it knew what was coming. Leigh was still fully engrossed in battling the engine, and it took a second or two for her to refocus and take in the scene in front of her.

At that point, the mercenary gave the order to fire.

As one, a dozen assault rifles opened up. The fire was wild and inaccurate, but it was still the most unnerving second both Marsden and Leigh had experienced in their short lives. With a screeching shudder, the cab pitched forward as Leigh stomped down on the brake with all her might. The bowser crashed to a stop in an instant. Even though they had been travelling at such a slow speed, the deceleration was enough to hurl Marsden forward towards the windscreen. He recovered quickly and snatched the radio mike from the hook above his head.

'Hotel Fox ops, this is Trucker six-one. Contact, wait, out!'

20.

As soon as the last word was out of his mouth, Marsden released the transmit button and whipped the radio's frequency switch over to the convoy's tactical channel. Abandoning formal radio procedure and call signs, he screamed into the mike.

'Ben, back up. Back the fuck up!' At that moment, an AK-47 round fizzed through the windscreen, quickly followed by two more. The toughened glass fractured into a thousand tiny crystals but didn't shatter. Marsden felt no pain and when he looked over at Private Leigh, he couldn't see any blood. Taking that as a good sign, he keyed the mike again.

'Jamie. Get up here. We need help. Now!' Not waiting for a response, he grabbed his rifle and shouted to Leigh. 'Get the wagon back below the ridge line and then call in the contact update.'

'Where are you going?'

'To be a hero,' Marsden responded with a bravado he certainly wasn't feeling. He wrenched the passenger door open and jumped out of the cab.

Leigh's hands were shaking so much that she could barely keep hold of the steering wheel. She could hear the incoming rounds as they pinged off the engine cowling in front of her. The sound was just like the X-Box games they played during downtime at Hotel Fox, but this was very much for real. Glancing in her wing mirror, she could see Ben reversing back down the hill. Gritting her teeth, she reached for the gear stick and prepared to do the same.

The RAF Regiment WMIK had been following a safe fifty metres behind the second tanker as the convoy started climbing out of the valley. The first thing they knew of the trouble up ahead was when Marsden's screamed order came over the radio.

'Go, go, go.' shouted James. The WMIK raced towards the top of the hill. It careered round the offside of Leigh's tanker and skidded to a halt in front of it. In the second it took for James to work out where the danger was coming from, Private Leigh already had her bowser moving backwards. James leapt up and ripped out the restraining clip from the outrigger mounted in front of him. Kneeling on the passenger seat, he swivelled the machine gun in the direction of the trailer and opened fire. As Marsden ran up, the third gunner jumped out of the land rover, weapon at the ready.

James briefly held his fire.

'Mark, get out there and outflank them,' he shouted, pointing away to his right. He didn't wait for a reply before putting down more fire on the trailer. At that moment, Private Parton arrived on the scene, raising the number in Marsden's private army to three. Gesturing for them to follow, Marsden charged off into the undergrowth.

Private Leigh's heart rate was still through the roof, even though she had successfully reversed back round the bend and out of the kill zone. Behind her, Smith had his vehicle even further down the slope. Leaving the engine running, she reached across for the radio mike that was swinging freely above the dashboard. Remembering to switch frequencies, she took a couple of deep breaths and hit the transmit button.

'Hotel Fox ops, this is Trucker six-two, stand by for contact update, over.' It had been less than three minutes since Marsden's initial message and the ops room had only just begun its own immediate response drills.

'Trucker six-two, this is Hotel Fox ops, send, over.'

As succinctly as possible, Leigh explained what had happened. The ops controller came back with a single follow-up question to confirm the convoy's exact location. Leigh punched a button on the side of the commercial sat-nav that had been fitted to all the tankers before they left Stafford and read off the GPS co-ordinates.

'Roger, Trucker six-two, stand by. Hotel Fox ops out.'

Rob was breathing hard as he looked across at the ops controller. He'd just sprinted all the way from the medical post where he'd been deep in conversation with the doc.

'What do we know?' he demanded.

'Still very sketchy sir,' replied the ops controller. 'It looks like the convoy has come under attack on Route *Lansdowne* approximately fifteen kilometres northwest of our location. They're still in contact, although both tankers have withdrawn from the kill zone and are currently out of danger. Casualties unknown. Enemy strength unknown. Current actions of the RAF Regiment fire team unknown.'

'Are there any Free State army units in the vicinity?'

'Negative,' answered Dan Scrivener, who had been in the ops room when the contact report came in. 'The last tasking completed at 1600 local. The Free State troops will be back in barracks by now and the Chinooks heading back to the carrier.'

'That's not helpful,' grumbled Rob. 'What do you suggest Dan?'

'First off, we need to stand-to here,' said Dan. 'Same as the training area attack, we don't know if this is part of something bigger, something co-ordinated. Hotel Fox may be a target too. But we can't ignore the convoy. We should send the QRF. Immediately. I know we're short of information, but we can update them on route. If the fire team is outgunned, they'll hunker down and wait for the cavalry.'

Rob deliberated for the briefest of moments. 'Okay, do it.'

Corporal Marsden led his three-man army at a run for approximately fifty metres, before stopping in a crouch. They had entered the undergrowth at right angles to the road, and looking back, he could just make out the muzzle flashes from James' machine gun. Keeping parallel to the road, Marsden led his men cautiously towards the enemy. He didn't want to rush and give away his position, but he knew he couldn't hang about either. The patrol vehicle was completely in the open and even its overwhelming firepower could be undone by a single lucky shot. When he judged himself to be roughly level with the trailer, Marsden whispered to his men to take up firing positions. He quietly pulled back the working parts of his rifle and let them slide forward, loading a round into the breech. Then he carefully thumbed the safety catch to "off".

Lance Corporal James fed a fresh belt of ammunition into his machine gun. Next to him, the driver was breaking open another ammo box. Still plenty, but it wouldn't do to run out. It had only been a few minutes since the ambush had begun, but already the firefight had reached something of a stalemate. With his superior weight of fire, James could keep the enemy's heads down, but on his own he couldn't dislodge them from their position. On the other hand, the attackers were never going to rush the patrol vehicle and none of them could shoot accurately enough to hit either crew member.

Come on Mark, where are you?

Crouched low by the side of the trailer, the South African mercenary was far from happy. This was supposed to be the simple shooting-up of a couple of fuel tankers. Nothing fancy, but a good opportunity to blood a few of their newly trained fighters.

The RAF Regiment fire team was not part of the plan. Its appearance over the brow of the hill had changed everything. Now his men were going to have to learn how to conduct a withdrawal under fire, on the job. And he wasn't planning on hanging around to help them. He'd seen the British soldiers dash off into the undergrowth as the machine gun had opened up and knew it was only a matter of time before his men would be outflanked.

The machine gun fell silent. Looking up, the mercenary saw its operator stepping through the reload drill, calmly and efficiently like the well-trained soldier he obviously was. Sensing his opportunity, the mercenary crawled away from the trailer and headed towards the G-Wagon. The fighter nearest to him was lying on the ground, motionless. Half his head blown away. The next man was on his knees, nursing a shattered elbow. No-one noticed they were about to be abandoned. As the mercenary slid behind the wheel, the machine gun began firing again.

Every man for himself, he thought as he swung the vehicle around and accelerated away.

Corporal Marsden heard the machine gun go quiet and realised that James must be reloading. As soon as James started up again, he'd give the order to fire. He racked his brains to remember the sequence of the fire control order he'd been taught during the pre-deployment ground defence lectures.

Bollocks to that, he said to himself. *This isn't a bloody test.*

'Stand by,' he whispered hoarsely. His mouth was dry as sandpaper and his right hand shook as he gripped his rifle. Then he heard the familiar chatter of James' machine gun.

'Open Fire!'

It turned out his men didn't need a fire control order after all. They knew exactly what to do. The flanking attack was too much for the enemy fighters. With no-one to lead them, they quickly decided they'd had enough. As one, they turned and ran for the three-tonner, slowing only to drag away their dead and wounded. As soon as he saw them withdraw, James ceased firing. He knew the rules of engagement and they did not allow him to engage enemy combatants who were running away.

Marsden ordered his men to cease fire too. He was less sure of the rules, but he couldn't see any more targets. Cautiously, he advanced towards the road. When he saw the patrol vehicle moving slowly in the same direction, he realised the fight was over.

The enemy position was deserted. In the distance, a billowing dust trail betrayed the fighters' speedy withdrawal. James jumped down from the patrol vehicle.

'Are you all okay?' he asked, a little unsure of what to do next.

'Not a scratch on anyone,' replied Marsden. 'Shitty-death, how did we get away with that?'

'No idea,' said James. 'But I'm not complaining. We need to check the rest of the guys are okay and report back to Hotel Fox.' They all piled into the land rover and headed back up the road to where the bowsers were safely parked.

Private Leigh heard the land rover before she saw it. She had moved her bowser to the side of the road and shut off the engine. The radiator must have taken a round because the temperature gauge had gone through the roof. As the WMIK came into view, she was stood warily by the side of her cab, grim faced, rifle at the ready. When she realised the danger was over, she slowly lowered her weapon and cracked the broadest smile of the day.

21.

The quick reaction force covered the fifteen kilometres from Hotel Fox to the ambush site in as many minutes. When they got there, the two bowsers still hidden away below the brow of the hill. Covering them was the WMIK with one gunner behind the wheel and another manning the fifty-calibre machine gun. The lead bowser's engine cover was open, and the rest of the team were staring earnestly at the engine. Although none were technically qualified to assess the damage, they all agreed that the four bullet holes in the radiator were probably enough to stop the vehicle from being driven again anytime soon. The sergeant commanding the quick reaction force finished his brief appraisal and radioed back to the ops room.

At Hotel Fox, Dan Scrivener found Rob in the field kitchen.

'The QRF's reached the ambush site, sir. No sign of any enemy forces and the home team's safe and unharmed. One of the bowsers has been shot up quite badly and the convoy commander is fairly sure it's undriveable. The recovery vehicle's on standby, but it's getting a bit late in the day.'

'Timings?' asked Rob.

'It'll take the recovery team around half an hour to get to the ambush site. Another half an hour to rig the bowser and then the journey back.'

'We can't leave the bowser out there unguarded overnight,' said Rob.

'No,' agreed Dan. 'So, either everyone who's out there stays there, or we spin up a separate team to deploy and secure the site until morning.'

'That sounds like a lot of effort. Plus, I'm not happy about the force protection implications. There could be hundreds of enemy fighters in the area.'

'I agree,' Dan said. 'We can spare another WMIK to accompany the recovery team and they can be on the road in a few minutes. That definitely sounds like the best option to me.'

'Okay, let's do it,' commanded Rob. 'And make sure the ops team keeps the JFHQ up to speed on everything we're doing. You know how hot the general is on knowing the after-action activity has been properly squared away.'

The recovery vehicle was easily the slowest vehicle in the British army's inventory and Dan's estimated journey time for it to reach the ambush site was optimistic. But the team was good at its job, and it took no more than twenty minutes to hook up the damaged bowser. Under the watchful eye of the QRF, the convoy safely negotiated the remainder of the route to Hotel Fox and arrived no more than a couple of hours later than originally planned.

It was well into the evening and Rob was reading through the draft situation report when the call came though from General Wilkinson.

'Now everything has calmed down a bit, how's it going?' the general asked.

'It's been another hectic day sir, but I think we've done okay,' responded Rob honestly. 'The convoy commander is new in rank, in fact this was his first run out in command. He held his team together well. His driver, Private Leigh, was impressive too. Getting her vehicle out of the kill zone as swiftly as she did was excellent work.'

'And what's the situation now?' followed up the general.

'All the vehicles have been recovered back here. One of the bowsers is badly damaged and will probably need an engine change. We'll run the after-action review first thing in the morning. As you know, general, there's only three routes out of the hinterland that can accommodate our fuel bowsers. The insurgents must have had dickers out and probably someone with eyes on the airport as well.'

Before he could continue, the general came back.

'I saw from the SINCREP that you had WMIK in the convoy. How long has that been going on?'

Bugger, thought Rob. In the words of Mr Jones, it was time to ask for forgiveness.

'Actually general, today was the first time. We carried out a review after the training area incident. I judged the threat to our convoys was now high enough to warrant dedicated force protection.'

'And how does that fit with my instruction to carry out all FP activity from within the perimeter of the forward base?' the general asked pointedly.

Rob already had his answer prepared.

'I suppose we saw that as being relevant to the specific defence of Hotel Fox, rather than force protection in general,' he offered.

The general paused deliberately, just to let Rob squirm for a second or two. Then he responded.

'Just as well that you did then. Because if I'm reading the SINCREP correctly, it was the WMIK that saved the convoy.'

'That's true sir,' agreed Rob.

'Good work, Rob,' General Wilkinson recognised proactive decision making when he saw it, even if it hadn't exactly been to the letter of his orders. 'But don't make a habit of going against your commander's direction, even though in this case it was the right thing to do.'

'Thanks sir,' said Rob, extremely relieved. 'Got it.' He was just about to hang up when he suddenly remembered.

'General, before you go. Have you had any success tracking down Lieutenant Achebe?'

'Ah, well remembered,' said the general. 'No, we haven't. He's not been seen at the Free State Army HQ since Wednesday. Our team at JK barracks are looking out for him, so if he shows, we'll know.'

'But he won't show, will he sir?' pushed Rob. 'If he's got something to hide, he'll keep as far away from us as he can.'

'So, what do you suggest?' asked the general, his exasperation showing.

'Isn't there any way you can up the ante sir?' responded Rob. 'It's been five days now. Can't the high commissioner do anything?'

'We've got to be a bit careful. I can't just go throwing accusations around, given who Achebe is. Don't forget, we're still the visitors here.'

Rob's complete lack of empathy with his commander's concerns shot down the phone like a guided missile.

'Okay Rob, I get it,' said the general. 'I want to get Major Grey back safely just as much as you do. I'm flying into New Devon first thing Monday. I'll take it up with the high commissioner then.'

'Thanks, sir.' Rob knew he'd pushed the general harder than he should. But if it helped to find Sarah, he didn't care.

The following morning was bright and sunny. Rob was up early checking the refuelling teams on station to support the first wave of heli-ops. As he walked back through the domestic site to the ops room, he saw Mr Jones emerge from the field kitchen.

'Morning RSM,' he called.

'Morning sir,' replied Mr Jones in his normal upbeat fashion. 'Welcome to day thirty-seven in the big brother house.'

Rob waved in response. He wondered if Mr Jones would keep his standard greeting up for the duration of the operation.

Probably.

As Rob pushed open the door to the ops room, the secure phone on his desk began to ring. Recognising the number, he picked it up.

'Good morning, Becca. This is a pleasant surprise. How come you're working on a Sunday?'

'Right now, every day's a workday. How is the search for Major Grey going?' she asked. Although her brother hadn't said as much, Rebecca could tell that his concern for Sarah's wellbeing extended beyond the professional.

'Still no news,' said Rob. 'But General Wilkinson has re-tasked Terry Willis and his team to help in the search. They joined a Free State army op yesterday. It was acting on some new intelligence about an insurgent training camp. When they got there the site was empty, but it had clearly been in use until very recently. Terry's team is still out on the ground and are feeding back regular intelligence to the JFHQ. I'm sure we'll get a lead soon.'

'That's pretty positive,' said Rebecca. 'And what about you? I read your SINCREP. It looks like your convoy team did well.'

'Yes, it could have been a lot worse,' admitted Rob. 'We added a WMIK to the fuel convoy, even though technically it was counter to the commander's direction on FP activity outside the wire. Without it, I don't think they'd have survived the contact.'

'I wanted to talk to you about that,' replied Rebecca. 'Have you done your after-action review yet?'

'No, we're doing it this morning,' confirmed Rob. 'Why, something on your mind?'

'Yes, but I don't want you to take it the wrong way,' said Rebecca cautiously.

'Can't guarantee that,' joked Rob.

But his sister was deadly serious.

'I'm wondering why the ambush was so poorly prepared and executed,' she blurted out.

'What? I'm not sure I follow,' said Rob, not joking any more.

'Bear with me,' she continued. 'The location for the ambush was well chosen, knowing the tankers would have to slow down to get up the hill. Although facing west wasn't smart, there probably wasn't any other option. But the position of the lead-blocking element was rubbish. Your report said it was over one hundred metres from the brow of the hill. That's a long way for poorly trained fighters to be firing from. I bet for every shot that hit your tanker, dozens missed. Why not have them fifty metres closer, or seventy-five even? It was almost as if they let the bowsers withdraw safely back down the hill.'

'I'm not sure I agree with that,' said Rob. 'Have you ever tried reversing a thirty-ton articulated fuel truck round a bend and down off the crest of a hill while under fire?'

'No, and I'm sure I couldn't. But I'd expect your drivers to be able to, and so would the insurgents, don't you think?'

Rob thought about it. Perhaps his sister had a point.

'And what about the rear-blocking element?' Rebecca asked next.

'What about it?' replied Rob. 'There wasn't one.'

'Exactly,' said Rebecca. 'Even I know an ambush should always have troops deployed to cut off the enemy's retreat. So why didn't they?'

'No idea,' confessed Rob. 'Maybe they only had a limited number of fighters on hand. But what about the WMIK? Yesterday was the first day we'd sent one out with a fuel convoy, so there's no way they could have planned for that. And without it, we'd probably have lost both bowsers.'

'Okay, I'll grant you they wouldn't have known about that. But intelligence analysis is an art not a science, you know that. The fact remains whoever set up that ambush kept his lead-blocking element far enough away to allow your vehicles to manoeuvre out of the kill zone, and then gave them the opportunity to escape completely by not deploying troops to their rear.'

'But why would anyone do that?' questioned Rob.

Rebecca didn't have an answer.

'I don't know. The same reason why they didn't take Jim Farmer's Chinook out on the training site I guess.' She thought for a moment. 'We're definitely not seeing the big picture here. There's too much tactical detail and it's taking our attention away from what's really important.'

'And what's that?' asked her brother.

'Damned if I know,' Rebecca admitted. 'But I'm going to find out!'

Almost a hundred miles east of Hotel Fox, in a camp only just inside the West African Free State border, Sarah was beginning a fifth day of captivity. In that time, her world had been reduced to a dusty patch of ground between two ancient canvas tents that looked like they first saw use in the nineteenth century.

Sarah pulled on the rusty chain shackled to her ankle. It gave her no more than a few metres freedom from an equally rusty post hammered deep into the ground. Next to the post was a dull yellow bucket that served as her latrine. There was no shelter and her every move could be viewed by anyone in the camp who wanted. For the first twenty-four hours, that had been extremely unpleasant, but she quickly learned to ignore the gawking looks. Night-time brought a little relief, as power in the camp was a limited commodity so there were no external lights.

Sarah hadn't seen soap and water since her run around JK barracks and the odour coming off her uniform was worse than the men's locker room in Northwood. But that didn't bother her. Although it smelt terrible, her body was healing. The dull ache in her thigh persisted, but it had reduced to a manageable level. Better still, she no longer had the exploding pain in her head and her left eye was almost fully open.

Sarah had been a model prisoner. She made no complaints, gratefully took the little food that had been offered, and showed no sign of wanting to escape. The reward for her subservience was the cleaning and redressing of her wound by one of the mercenaries. After a few days, she realised she had become an accepted feature in the camp. Most of the fighters still verbally abused her at every opportunity, but they were careful to keep their distance. The man-mountain had made it clear she was not to be touched and his word was law.

But Sarah's submissive approach was a front. From day one, she had been listening and observing. Turning the humiliation of having every move watched to her advantage, she built up a comprehensive picture of the pattern of life in the camp. Like a permanently on-station reconnaissance drone, she knew where every guard was posted and how long they spent there. She also learned which fighters were diligent and which ones were lazy. Every waking hour was spent plotting her escape. Sarah knew an opportunity would come her way sometime, and she was determined to be ready for it.

22.

The Final Week – Monday

Rebecca was sat in the ante room outside the chief's office. The clock on the wall clicked round to half past seven. It was too early for the chief's PA. After speaking with Rob on Sunday morning, Rebecca had spent the rest of the day at her desk.

Not for the first time, she thought ruefully. And probably not the last either James had just begun a rotational duty as bronze commander liaison officer, which meant he was at thirty minutes notice to respond to a terrorist incident anywhere within the UK. Because of that, he was confined to the SAS depot at Hereford for the next two weeks. And Rebecca didn't begrudge working the weekend. Without her boyfriend around, Saturdays and Sundays were somewhat dull anyway.

The chief's PA arrived at quarter to eight, ten minutes before her boss walked in.

'Good morning, Rebecca,' Hilary called as she disappeared into her office. 'Give me a minute to get the coffee machine going and you can come through.' Five minutes later, Hilary reappeared, coffee in each hand, and motioned for Rebecca to join her.

'I'm not sure when we're going to get to update the foreign secretary this week. The Indian prime minister flies in with a massive trade delegation on Wednesday and all the major departments are fixed on the visit.'

'I know,' said Rebecca. 'James is on duty this week and the Met police are lining up stacks of major incident scenarios to rehearse over the next few days. There's a state banquet on

Thursday and the trade fair starts Friday. I'm pretty sure both prime ministers will be there on Sunday.'

'You're right,' confirmed Hilary. 'But that's not what we're here to talk about. What's the latest on West Africa Free State?'

Rebecca handed Hilary a slim briefing folder.

'I've kept the paperwork to a minimum. The report is a précis of my analysis, and the flags contain the relevant intelligence summaries. Everything's on the Africa Department team site, which your PA has access to.'

Hilary nodded.

Rebecca took a deep breath and launched in.

'There's still a lot we don't know about what's happening in Free State now, but I'm convinced this isn't an insurgency aimed at overthrowing the government.'

Hilary looked surprised but kept quiet.

'From the outset, the insurgent activity has been sporadic and inconsistent,' continued Rebecca. 'Some of the local people have been brutally terrorised to make them fall into line. But there are also cases where villages have been given food and medical support. I can't find any obvious ethnic or geographical reasons for the different approaches. It just doesn't follow any of the classic insurgency case studies I've read up on. Then there's the input from Colonel Ele. I dug out his dissertation from the Royal College of Defence Studies. It's a really good piece of work, well researched and very well written. He's adamant what they're experiencing is not traditional insurgency.'

'Okay,' conceded Hilary. 'But just because it isn't in our playbook, doesn't mean it's not for real,'

'No, I accept that,' said Rebecca. 'But you've also got to factor in how the UK's been drawn in. The foreign secretary's assassination was bound to provoke a response and who would knowingly make an insurgency task harder by adding British soldiers to their enemy forces list? And then there's the direct attacks on the training area and the fuel convoy. I'm convinced the insurgents held back. In both cases. They could have inflicted far more damage but chose not to.'

'Why on earth would they do that?' asked Hilary astonished. 'It makes no sense.'

Rebecca paused for a few seconds before responding.

'To be honest, ma'am, this is where the analysis gets a bit flaky. But I think whoever is behind this is not targeting the Free State government at all. They're targeting us. Starting an insurgency is excellent cover for building a private army and the reason the violence's been sporadic and inconsistent could be because there's never been the intention of it ever getting the momentum to challenge President Kirrundi. It could just be a ruse to get UK troops into Free State, where they are vulnerable. The fact they've been holding back in their attacks is probably a mixture of not wanting to commit too many fighters but also not wanting to overplay their hand.

'So, what are you suggesting is going to happen next?'

'I think they're building up to some sort of spectacular event. Something truly devastating. I don't know what that could be yet, but I strongly believe finding it out must be our highest priority.'

Hilary thought for a moment. This was not the conclusion she had expected Rebecca to reach, but she trusted her subordinate.

'I agree there's a lot of ifs and buts in there. And some of your deductions are a little tenuous. But what you're suggesting is plausible. The obvious question is, who's behind it all? Free State as a country has nothing to gain from attacking the UK in this way. And there's no intelligence to suggest Islamic extremism or in fact any major non-state actor being involved. I made that very clear to the prime minister only last week. So, what's the motive?'

'That's the hole in my analysis,' admitted Rebecca. 'No matter how hard I search, I can't see who would gain from all this. But I'm convinced I'm right.'

Hilary started. A thought had suddenly struck her.

'Something doesn't add up,' she said. 'Go back to what you said about UK troops being vulnerable. What if we'd sent the spearhead battalion? After all, that was the prime minister's preferred option. There's no way they'd have been in any danger from a bunch of poorly trained insurgent fighters. Your theory only works because we haven't deployed combat troops, but no-one could have planned for that in advance.'

Rebecca had to stop and think.

'Whose decision was it to only send support troops?' she asked.

'As far as I recall, it came directly from President Kirrundi,' replied Hilary. 'Someone in the Ministry of Defence would know, I can ask Admiral Bellis. But you're surely not suggesting that the Free State president is behind this, are you?'

'No, definitely not,' said Rebecca with conviction. 'He's one of the most honest and effective leaders in the whole of Africa. But he doesn't govern in isolation. Something of this importance is bound to have been discussed by his cabinet, and they have advisors in much the same way as our ministers do. There's tons of people who could have influenced that decision.'

'I agree,' said Hilary. 'But you're still suggesting whoever is behind this is near the top of the Free State government. We need to tread carefully. Because if we're wrong, it could be very embarrassing for the UK and career ending for us.' The prime minister's parting shot from last week's meeting was still very much uppermost in Hilary's mind.

'I understand,' said Rebecca, but she was already thinking ahead. 'I know just who might be able to shed some light on this for us. Leave it with me ma'am, I have a favour to call in.'

'Okay,' said Hilary. 'But don't take too long. If your analysis is right, we may not have much time.'

No more than a couple of miles away from Vauxhall Cross, Jelani Achebe was checking out of his hotel. His long weekend in London had been excellent, at least what he could remember of it. On the downside, his credit card had taken a real hammering, leaving him a little worried where the money to cover next month's bill was going to come from. But then he glanced down at the rifle case on the floor next to him and remembered why he was in London in the first place. If he was successful in his endeavour, surely his uncle would be happy to cover it.

The valet service brought his hire car to the front door of the hotel and the concierge had his bags put in the boot. The satnav told him it was less than forty miles to Bisley, but the estimated journey time was almost two hours. Jelani grumbled to himself.

Just another shitty thing about this shitty country.

He punched in the post code to the Royal Berkshire, the only five-star hotel he'd managed to find anywhere near Bisley and swung the SUV out into the heavy London traffic.

Rob had been quiet and reserved all day. He knew he should snap out of it. The troops very quickly picked up on the mood of their commanding officer and if he appeared downbeat, they soon would too. Almost a week had passed since Sarah had disappeared and they were no nearer finding out what had happened to her or where she was. He'd heard nothing from the general's meeting with the high commissioner and Achebe still hadn't shown at the Free State Army Headquarters. Rob had tried to be positive in his call with Rebecca yesterday, but he certainly wasn't feeling that now. In fact, without talking to Achebe, he couldn't see how they were ever going to track Sarah down.

The other concern he couldn't shake was his sister's theory about last week's SIGACTs. Rob had long since accepted that he was the twin with fewer brain cells. In his military mind, if it looked like a duck and sounded like a duck, it probably was a duck. Trying to get his head around the idea that the attack on the training area and then the convoy ambush may not be entirely what they appeared to be, was making it hurt.

Pull yourself together, he chided himself.

His duty was to lead and that was best served by putting his concerns to one side. Let those with access to the bigger picture worry about the bigger picture. He resolved to snap out of it straight away.

'Boss,' it was Pete. 'Commander's VTC in five minutes.'

Rob looked up and nodded.

'I'll be there.'

General Wilkinson had switched his regular commander's conference from daily to weekly after the deployed force had reached full operating capability. But as a result of the previous week's attacks, he had reverted to a daily update. The conference format was standard. Following the usual briefing from the staff leads in the headquarters, each of the unit commanders gave a short report and then the general summed up at the end.

'As you all know,' he began. 'A week ago, we augmented the Free State army staff with additional plans and intelligence personnel from this HQ. That investment is now starting to pay off. You've just heard from the operations brief that the Free State army had its first significant contact with insurgent fighters earlier today. Following intel from Captain Willis, we dropped two Free State companies near the village of Siguiri, close to where the abandoned training camp was discovered over the weekend. They got into a prolonged firefight. Several insurgent fighters were killed and over a dozen captured. We've already begun questioning the detainees and I'm confident we'll get more information from that. It's taken a while, but today's action could be the start of a domino-effect that rolls up the bulk of insurgent fighters very quickly.

'So, the message to everyone is, stand by for a busy few days, but also be prepared for retaliatory action. We still don't know how capable the opposing force is, but last week's events show that we shouldn't underestimate them. Any questions?'

Rob raised his hand and pressed the unmute button on his remote control.

'General, given what you've just said, will you now consider rescinding the order regarding force protection at Hotel Fox? We'd be far better placed to meet the increased threat by dominating the ground outside the wire again.'

General Wilkinson leaned back in his chair grim faced. He had been expecting Rob's request.

'Thank you, Rob. That's a fair point and I get exactly where you're coming from. But until we get actionable intelligence about an attack on your location, I'm not prepared to relax the current restrictions.'

'But sir, that may be too late,' Rob responded forcefully.

'It may be,' accepted the general. 'But that's a risk I'm willing to take.'

Rob realised there was no point pushing it any further. The general had heard him out and stuck to his guns. Rob knew that his job was now to get behind his commander's direction, even if he did completely disagree with it.

23.

The Final Week – Tuesday

Rob watched the sun rise slowly over the hills to the east of Hotel Fox. It appeared almost shyly, a deep orange glow spreading light and warmth in equal measure. To Rob it was one of those breath-taking sights that made Africa so special. Reluctantly, he turned away and headed to the field kitchen and breakfast. He caught up with Mr Jones on the way.

'Morning sir,' said Mr Jones. As always, he had a smile on his face. 'Welcome to day forty in the big brother house.' Rob was pretty sure he hadn't missed a day.

'Morning RSM,' replied Rob, determined to be equally cheerful. 'Have timings for the first wave been confirmed?'

'Yes sir. Just checked with the ops controller. A six-ship left the carrier at zero six thirty as planned. They'll deploy the first two companies and loop back through us before picking up the next two. Should be here around zero nine hundred.'

Today's operation was the largest and most ambitious to date. All eight Chinooks were tasked solidly throughout the day. That including a dedicated, CASEVAC frame at JK barracks to cater for the wounded. Almost one thousand Free State troops were allocated to a major search and destroy mission that the planners had swiftly put together, based on intelligence collected from the captured insurgent fighters. The plan included allocated refuelling windows, but Rob knew from experience they could be called upon at any time throughout the day. No plan survives first contact with the enemy.

'We need to make sure everyone stays focused,' he continued. 'Refuelling and force protection. There's a lot can go wrong today.'

As Rob expected, the carefully calculated timings in the operations order were overtaken by events almost straight away. Before long, Chinooks were turning up unannounced as their tasking was changed by the planning staff. All four refuelling points were constantly in use, like a well-placed motorway service station at the start of a bank holiday weekend.

The first wave of Free State soldiers located the enemy much sooner than anticipated and the fighting quickly spread. A second Chinook was pressed into service to ferry the wounded back to hospital in New Devon.

At the furthest refuelling point Lance Corporal Marsden was hard at work with his team. He'd lost count of the number of helicopters to come through that morning. As he waited for the latest Chinook to finish sucking gas, he wandered round to the ramp. Marsden always marvelled at the sheer size and power of the helicopters. The huge rotors whirring above him, and the roaring engines reminded him of the mega-cool robots from the Transformer films he'd seen as a child. Massive and invincible.

He stared up into the Chinook and his jaw dropped. It was packed with dead and dying soldiers, like a super-sized ambulance. Some were laid out on canvas stretchers, others sat numbly on the airframe's red nylon seats. Here and there, medics were flitting about, fighting to keep the critically injured alive with little more than a few blood-stained bandages and words of encouragement.

Just a couple of metres away, a soldier was curled in a ball on the aircraft floor staring silently up at him. Pain etched across his face. Marsden tore his eyes away from the soldier's accusing stare, only for them to be drawn to the bloodied stump where his right foot should have been. A crude torniquet was only half doing its job and blood still seeped from the shattered ankle, forming a macabre, boot-shaped pool next to it. The carnage was like nothing Marsden had ever seen, and he recoiled in horror.

Suddenly he felt a hand on his shoulder. The refuelling was finished, and the loadmaster was urging him back from the helicopter as it prepared for take-off. Dazed, Marsden stumbled away from the sickening sight.

The refuelling team were not the only ones to see the CASEVAC helicopter ferrying through the forward base. Less than half a mile from the eastern end of Harris Field, the savanna gave way to a gentle roll of hills, covered with low scrubland punctuated by large clumps of acacia trees. Parked beneath the trees halfway up the nearest hill was a G-Wagon and a three-ton Bedford truck. Both hidden under a large, low-slung camouflage net. The man-mountain thought it unlikely they'd be seen by the helicopter crews overhead, but he wasn't taking any chances. The elevation gave an excellent view of Harris Field, spread out below like a child's jigsaw on a deep-pile carpet. Looking down the length of the dirt airstrip through powerful binoculars, he could easily make out the four refuelling points stretching away from his position. In the distance, he could also see a tented accommodation site and large wooden hangar. Beyond that, he counted six green and black fuel tankers parked up on concrete hardstanding.

Behind him, four insurgent fighters were hard at work under the watchful eye of another mercenary. They were digging pits for the two M2 mortars they had just unloaded from the back of the Bedford. Two more fighters were busy fetching and carrying ammunition. With a range of less than two kilometres, the mortars would not reach much beyond the nearest refuelling point. But that was okay. It was plenty close enough.

Back at Hotel Fox, Rob was slowly working his way along the refuelling points. He could have driven but he was in no hurry. The sun was hot on his back, but the late-afternoon breeze kept the temperature tolerable. He stopped at each point to talk with the junior non-commissioned officer in charge and their refuelling crew. Although it was getting late, there was no indication that the day's mission was nearing completion. The sergeant overseeing refuelling operations had been swapping out his crews at regular intervals throughout the day to make sure everyone remained sharp.

As Rob left the third refuelling point, he saw Mark Marsden. Rob hadn't had the opportunity to talk to his newest corporal since the attack on his convoy.

'Corporal Marsden, hold up,' he called. Marsden paused long enough for Rob to fall in step alongside him. 'How are you after last week?'

'I'm good sir, thanks,' replied Marsden. 'It was a bit scary at the time, but we've all been kept really busy since we got back. To be honest I've not had much chance to think about it.'

'Busy is good,' agreed Rob. 'But you will need to talk about it at some point. When that time comes, don't fight it. Facing up to the experience is important. The worst thing you can do is hide it all away. That's not being macho, it's foolish.'

'No, I get it sir,' said Marsden. 'And thanks for the advice.' They walked along in silence for a minute, then Rob asked.

'What brings you all the way down here anyway?'

'Oh, my brother Tony's working refuelling point four,' replied Marsden.

The rest of his explanation was drowned out by the noise of an incoming Chinook. It landed at the final refuelling point, one hundred metres beyond the pillow tanks. With its rotors still turning, a loadmaster jumped down from the ramp and unclipped the protective cowling over the fuel intake point. Twenty metres back, the hose operator stood waiting. He waved her forward.

Crouched against the howling downdraught, Rob and Corporal Marsden jammed their ear-defenders on their heads and watched as the hose operator advanced slowly towards the helicopter, dragging the heavy hose behind her. With the loadmaster's help, she connected the Avery-Hardoll coupling to the helicopter's fuel intake point. It locked into place with a hefty twist. After a nod from the loadmaster, the hose operator motioned to her colleague at the pump. The pumpman gave a thumbs up, cranked the motor to maximum and opened the valve.

Rob and Corporal Marsden retreated a few metres to get away from the worst effects of the downdraft. In the cockpit, Rob could see the pilots busy doing whatever pilots did during a rotors-turning refuel. He wondered if one was Jim, but they both had black visors pulled firmly down so it was impossible to tell.

Then, without warning, the ground in front of the helicopter erupted into a huge spew of dirt that crashed down over them. Before his brain had time to process anything, Rob was blown off his feet by a violent shock wave. He rolled over, covered head to foot in grit and dust from the explosion.

Before he could get up, a second blast shook the ground. This time much closer to the pillow tanks. The insurgency had announced itself to Hotel Fox, literally with a bang.

24.

Rob scrambled onto his hands and knees and peered through the billowing dust. Two explosions one after the other. No obvious threat within visual range. Almost certainly mortars.

They'd be re-aiming now, having seen the first fall of shot. There wasn't much time. In front of him, the Chinook was still sat there, rotors turning. Rob couldn't see any significant damage. The refuelling hose remained attached but unattended. The loadmaster and the hose operator were both lying on the ground unmoving. Looking towards the pillow tanks, Rob couldn't see the pump operator either.

'Tony!'

Even above the noise of the Chinook's engine, Rob heard Corporal Marsden, who was also staring back towards the pillow tanks. Marsden took off towards his brother, but Rob grabbed him.

'Get to the pump first,' he yelled. 'We need to get that Chinook airborne.'

Marsden looked at him, eyes wide with shock. Rob tried again.

'Go-and-turn-off-the-pump!'

The confusion lasted another second. Then a glimmer of comprehension flickered across Marsden's face.

He nodded.

Rob let him go and headed for the Chinook. As he got there, the second loadmaster jumped off the ramp and ran over to his fallen comrade. Rob ducked down to examine the hose operator, just as the third round hit.

It exploded on the port side of the helicopter. A good fifty metres away. Rob braced himself. Seconds later a fourth round struck. Another geyser of dirt erupted skywards, but it fell well clear.

The bastard's over-compensated. Rob knew their luck couldn't hold. They were bracketed. And a direct hit on the Chinook would be carnage.

He flung a glance towards Marsden who was now crouched over the pump. Marsden looked up and made an exaggerated cut-throat motion in Rob's direction.

The valve was closed.

Rob jumped up and grasped the coupling. He wrenched it hard anticlockwise.

Nothing.

His hands were streaked with dust and sweat. He struggled to get a grip. The seconds ticked past, each one taking them closer to disaster.

He twisted again, as hard as he could. More seconds gone. This time he felt movement. A third attempt was rewarded with a dull clunk as the coupling disconnected and the hose fell free.

Rob let go immediately and raced to help the loadmaster. As they dragged his unconscious colleague onto to the ramp, the engine noise was louder than ever. There was no way they would hear the incoming whistling of the next rounds before they landed.

Peering inside the cargo bay, Rob saw a full load of Free State soldiers all still strapped in. Their eyes were wide and fear sparked around them like an electric storm. The sense of terror was so great, he could smell it.

He jumped back and gave the loadmaster an urgent thumbs-up.

'Get going, right now!' he screamed.

The loadmaster didn't hear a word, but he knew what to do. Within seconds, the message reached the pilot, and the giant mortar magnet was clawing its way upwards towards safety.

Rob just managed to stay on his feet as the huge helicopter roared away. The dust and grime whipped up by its downdraft stung his eyes and choked him. He gasped for breath, coughing and spluttering. The stench of aviation fuel was everywhere.

As he watched the Chinook go, Rob knew the greatest disaster had been averted. But his relief was short-lived. The refuelling team was still right in middle of the kill zone, and they were fast running out of time.

The hose operator still hadn't moved. Rob dropped to his knees and rolled her over. It was Senior Aircraftwoman Styles. Her goggles had been ripped off and a torrent of blood was running down her face. Rob quickly checked for signs of life.

None.

Before he could do anything, Rob heard the whistle of more incoming rounds. Without thinking, he crouched protectively over Style's body. The blast rocked him backwards and he felt a sharp crack on the side of his head.

A second later, another round landed right next to the pillow tanks, blasting packed earth from the bund wall everywhere and ripping open the nearest tank. Gallons of aviation fuel began to gush out, adding to the chaos.

The mortar team now had the range bang on. Rob knew that even an average crew could put a round down every ten seconds or so. They had to get out of there, and fast.

Rob dragged SAC Styles up into a sitting position and, with a huge groan, hauled her over his shoulder. He shuffled for a second to get his balance and set off as fast as he could.

Looking over to the pillow tanks, Rob saw Corporal Marsden hunched over the body of his younger brother. Not far away lay the third member of the refuelling team, still wearing his bright orange marshalling gloves. His helmet was missing and one of his legs was bent back at an impossible angle.

More whistles and the next two rounds exploded directly on the landing zone where the Chinook had been. The blast wave hit Rob a second later. He staggered but kept moving.

'We've got to get out of here,' yelled Rob.

'He's not breathing,' Marsden shouted back at him.

'If we don't get out of here right now, none of us will be.'

Marsden looked down at his brother but the instinct to obey his commanding officer was stronger. He stood up and hefted his brother onto his shoulder like he was no more than a child. Rob looked around.

'The marshaller,' he shouted. Together they grabbed the shoulder straps of his webbing vest and started pulling. It took an age to get away from the refuelling point. Rob's thighs were burning and the pain in his back was excruciating. Catching his breath, he looked over his shoulder. They must be clear by now. At that moment, they heard the whistling sound again. More incoming. The noise seemed to be coming from directly above them.

Two rounds impacted within a millisecond of each other. Right on top of the pillow tanks. They ignited immediately, sending a mighty fireball spiralling high into the sky. The explosion was deafening, and the blast wave crashed violently across the airstrip.

Rob was hurled into the air. Styles' body ripped from his grasp. Time seemed to stand still as he flailed about uncontrollably. Then he crashed down with rib-cracking force, driving the air from his lungs. Heavily winded, he wallowed on the ground for a second, like a beached whale. An eardrum had surely burst, strangely muting the sound of falling debris all around him.

On the hillside, the man-mountain looked down on the devastation he had caused. He'd wanted to get the Chinook but was caught out by how quickly the pilot had managed to escape from the kill zone. Still, seeing the fuel tanks ignite had been almost as good. All in all, a job well done.

'Right, get these mortars broken down and back on the truck. Quickly. I want to be well away from here when the Brits show up.'

Slowly Rob gained control over his heaving lungs and clambered back to his feet. Aviation fuel was still burning uncontrollably within what was left of the bund. Small fires flickered all around him caused by the burning rubber fabric from the exploded tanks. The force of the blast had wrenched the heavy fuel pump from its connecting hoses and hurled it a hundred metres across the airstrip. The filter was nowhere to be seen.

Subconsciously Rob was counting the seconds. He reached twenty without hearing the whistle of incoming rounds. The attack was over.

He immediately turned his attention to SAC Styles. He checked her breathing again. Still nothing. Tipping her head back, he could see her airway was clear and started CPR.

Thirty compressions followed by two rescue breaths.

And repeat.

And repeat again.

It was exhausting work, but Rob wasn't giving up. Nothing else mattered. The muscles in his arms and shoulders screamed in pain and his own heart ached in desperation at the lack of response from Styles. Eventually a hand touched his shoulder. It was the doc.

'I've got it now,' he said quietly.

Rob fell back, shattered.

When he looked up, he saw Pete and Mr Jones standing over him.

'You all right sir?' asked Pete.

'Yeah, yeah, I'm fine,' he heard himself answer.

'Clearly, you're not though are you sir.' said Mr Jones in the matter-of-fact voice he reserved for the rare occasions when he had to tell his boss he was wrong. 'Else what's all that blood pouring down your face?'

Rob put his hand to the side of his head. It came back wet. Then the pain started. A medic appeared with a field dressing. He slapped it on with the maximum of efficiency and the minimum of compassion.

'You need to let the doc see that sir,' he said, stating the obvious.

'Yes, thanks,' said Rob with much more gratitude than he felt. 'I will.'

Mr Jones helped him up. The whole world was spinning wildly, and it took a moment for Rob to get his balance.

Right then Corporal Marsden shouted wildly.

'Fucking yes!'

The medic who had taken over resuscitating his brother pulled away suddenly as Tony heaved air into his lungs and started coughing. The older sibling pumped his fist softly.

'Knew you'd be okay,' he whispered.

Rob looked at Styles and then at the doctor, who shook his head.

'I'm sorry sir. There was nothing you could have done. The trauma from the explosion was fatal.'

No! Rob screamed silently to himself.

He turned away biting his lip hard. In all the operations he'd been on, he'd never lost a serviceman or woman under his command. The enormity of Styles' death suddenly felt like a huge weight crushing down, threatening to overwhelm him. For a second, he almost gave in. Then he forced the pain and guilt to the back of his mind. There was still work to be done.

'Thanks doc,' he said in a faltering voice. Then he straightened up, embracing the responsibility of command. When he next spoke, his voice was firm and clear.

'Mr Jones, stay here and see the crash team gets this fire under control. Pete, we need to get back to the ops room. This mortar attack could be the start of something much bigger. Until we know what we're up against, Hotel Fox is shut down. Get the word back to the JFHQ and make sure the Chinooks stay well clear.'

The rest of the afternoon passed without incident. Squadron Leader Scrivener led a heavily armed patrol out to the firing point. As expected, their assailants were long gone. All that remained were the two mortar pits and some fresh tyre tracks. Ignoring General Wilkinson's direction, the patrol spent the next two hours checking out other potential firing locations outside the wire. On hearing all were clear, Rob ordered the re-opening of his remaining three refuelling points. Only then did he allow himself to go to the medical post where the doc cleaned and stitched his head wound. He returned to the ops room just as a call came in from General Wilkinson.

'Rob, how's it going down there now?'

'All under control sir,' said Rob. 'The fire is out and we're recovering the destroyed refuelling kit. We've got spare pillow tanks, but we'll need to get some engineer plant back down here to rebuild the bund before we can get them into use.'

'What about casualties?'

'Well sir, as you know, we had one fatality. SAC Styles. We've already passed details to your admin team, and I know they've forwarded them on to Northwood. Styles was twenty-two years old. She wasn't married and lived in single living accommodation at Stafford. Our rear party will co-ordinate all the necessary liaison with her next of kin.

'The other two members of the refuelling team, Lance Corporal Marsden and Private Langley were both injured. Marsden was knocked unconscious but is recovering well and can probably stay in theatre. Langley is in a serious condition and the doc's discussing AEROMED options with your medical staff.

'And what about you?' asked Wilkinson. 'The SINCREP said you were injured too.'

'I guess so,' confessed Rob. 'I took a bit of shrapnel in the head, but the doc has stitched me up and apart from a thumping headache, I'm fine.'

'If you say so,' said the general. 'But don't overdo it. You've got a good command team down there. Make sure you use them.'

'Of course, general.'

'What can you tell us about the attack?'

'The QRF's already been out to the firing point. We think they used M2 mortars. Anything bigger and the whole of the site would have been within range. We found two mortar pits, which tallies with how the rounds came in. Whoever set this up knew what they were doing. It's a good thing the Chinook got away when it did. It was a sitting duck. Talking of the Chinook sir, I assume it got back to JK barracks okay? And how's the loadmaster?'

'He's fine,' confirmed the general. 'But he won't be on flying duties for a while. And the frame made it back here without any problems.' The general paused before asking his final question. 'How's morale?'

It was Rob's turn to pause. He was mindful of not antagonising his commander, but he had an obligation to tell it how it was.

'To be honest sir, it's not great,' he started. 'This is the first time we've experienced a fatality on ops, and Styles was extremely popular. What's more, there is a feeling it could have been avoided. The gunners are especially hacked off. If they'd been patrolling outside the wire, they reckon they'd have stopped the attack in the first place.'

'I appreciate your honesty, Rob,' said the general. 'What do you think?'

'General, there's no way of knowing what might have happened. But that's irrelevant. You considered our input before you made your decision. We can't ask for anything more than that.'

25

Deep in the Free State hinterland, the sun was beginning to set. Before long, another day in captivity would be over. Her seventh. Sarah glanced down at the lines she'd scuffed out of the dirt with the heel of her boot. Each morning, she added another. Tomorrow would be Wednesday again. The psychological challenge was increasing by the day. Eventually, she knew, it would crush her.

Two mercenaries emerged from the nearest tent and walked by. They kept well away. The man-mountain's no-touch rule clearly applied to them too.

'Hey, lady,' one of them called. 'You're gonna get wet tonight.' He jerked a thumb up at the sky. 'There's a big thunderstorm coming.'

Sarah ignored their laughter. That was just what she had been waiting for.

The storm broke three hours later. It began with fat, heavy raindrops that fell unhurriedly, almost in slow motion. When they finally hit the ground, they seemed to bounce right back up again. Sarah had seen rain like that before. In the military, it was known as Forrest Gump rain, after the character's experiences in Vietnam. For Sarah, it conjured memories of never-ending training exercises as an officer cadet at Sandhurst.

A different world.

Before long, the rain changed, turning into a huge deluge that hammered down in long straight streaks. What Sarah's grandmother used to call stair rods of rain. Within seconds, Sarah was soaked to the skin. The ground around her quickly became waterlogged and small rivers began to form, snaking away towards the lower ground. Not a soul was in sight. The entire camp was hunkered down, trying to stay dry. One of the rivers flowed over a large stone buried next to Sarah's metal post. For the past couple of nights, she had worked hard to loosen it. Then, each morning, she had gently re-packed the loosened earth back around it, to hide her progress. Now she started kicking at it again. The waterlogged ground gave way far more easily and within a few minutes, it was completely free. She picked it up, her fingers just long enough to grasp it comfortably. It was slightly larger than a cricket ball. But much heavier. A jagged seam ran across the top, making it the perfect tool for the job in hand.

Stage one complete.

Sarah checked again for visible signs of life. Still none. The rain was coming down even harder now. No-one in their right mind would be out in this. Way in the distance, she saw the sky light up with the first flash of lightning. Slowly she counted. It took just over fifteen seconds before the corresponding rumble of thunder rolled in. Around five klicks away.

A minute later, more lightning sheeted across the sky. Maybe twelve seconds this time before the thundercrack reached her. It was moving closer.

Almost time for stage two.

Sarah sat down and grabbed the chain secured to her ankle. She pulled it taut. No way could she break it free from the post, but that wasn't the plan. The chain was old and caked in rust, and the links closest to the shackle round her ankle looked in really bad shape. A few good blows might be enough to split them apart. And now Sarah had a hammer. She waited impatiently as the thunderstorm drew closer. Finally, the gap between lightning and thunder was just a few seconds. Close enough to predict.

Sarah glanced round the camp yet again. The rain was still driving down, and no-one wanted to be out in it. Her pulse quickened and she started to shake in anticipation. It was now or never.

Keeping the chain taut, Sarah lifted the stone high above her head. A blinding flash of lightning momentarily turned night into day. A second later, a mighty thunderclap echoed across the sky. With perfect timing, Sarah brought the stone crashing down, the smash of rock on metal completely masked by the thunder's roar.

Almost immediately, another lightning flash lit up the sky. Thunder was instantaneous. The storm was directly overhead. Again, Sarah smashed the stone downwards. She caught the weak links full on causing blue sparks to spit back at her. Someone must surely have seen that. She scanned around quickly. Still no movement.

In the next minute, Sarah rained down half a dozen solid blows, but the chain refused to give way. The gap between lightning and thunder slowly started to creep up again. The storm was moving on.

Sarah was getting desperate. Only two or three more blows before the thunder would no longer disguise her actions. Concentrating hard, she lined up the jagged seam and let fly again. More sparks but the chain held firm. Once more. Same result.

The storm was a mile away now. More lightning. But weaker and less prolonged this time.

One, two three, four …

On five, Sarah brought the stone down with all her might. A perfect strike. A large shard of metal span crazily upwards and Sarah instinctively ducked away. When she looked back down, the chain was in two.

She had done it!

Sarah took a few deep breaths to compose herself.

Stage two complete.

The most difficult part might be over, but the most dangerous was still to come. Although the camp was quiet, the guards were still out there. And the rain was just starting to ease. Time was not on Sarah's side. She stood up, feeling a twinge in her thigh – a reminder that the next part of escape would need guile rather than strength.

Sarah thought through her plan. First off, head west. The camp was bound to be deep in the hinterland, far from prying eyes. The best chance of getting to safety would be to head towards the hinterland's more populated areas. That's where the Free State army patrols must be. Once the storm's cleared, it should be possible to navigate by the stars. Daylight was a threat, so Sarah's aim was to make maximum progress under cover of darkness and then hide up before the sun rose.

The first challenge was to get away without being seen. The direct route west went right through the middle of the camp. Not ideal, but better than taking the shortest route out and then skirting by all the guards. The rain was much lighter now. She needed to get moving. Sarah took one last look around. She'd miss this place like a hole in the head.

Sarah moved slowly away from the metal post. If anyone was watching, they'd know straight away she was no longer chained up. The thunder was still echoing in the distance. The only other noise was the background gurgle of flood water flowing through the camp. Sarah stepped quietly but purposefully. The edge of the camp getting nearer and nearer. There was no obvious boundary. No picket posts or barbed wire fence. The camp simply ended where the hard-trodden dirt stopped, and the undergrowth began.

Sarah reached that point undetected. Just a few more metres and she'd made it. Sarah stole a final glance backwards. She couldn't believe her luck. The camp was still deserted.

Then, as she started to quicken her stride, she tripped over something dark and shadowy in the long grass. She cursed silently stumbling forward and almost falling. Then the shadow moved. It was a guard, sleeping under an old poncho roll out of the rain.

But not asleep anymore.

Sarah watched as he sat up slowly, like a zombie. She was close enough to smell the odour from his unwashed body. It was foul. The poncho slid off his back, as the confused guard twisted round trying to work out what had disturbed him.

Instinctively, Sarah took a pace forward and swung her stone. It connected with the side of his head with a resounding crack.

The guard fell back, dazed. In an instant, Sarah was on his chest, pinning him down. The guard's eyes were wide open in fear as he struggled to get free. But Sarah was having none of that. She raised the stone and sent it crashing down again. The guard's head snapped to one side and his struggling ceased.

Sarah climbed off the guard's chest. He was unconscious but still breathing. Sarah checked his pockets. Empty. Not even a water bottle on his belt. She lifted the poncho roll and found the guard's weapon. An ancient, wooden-stocked AK-47. The exposed metal was covered with rust, but she knew it would still work just fine. She checked it was loaded with a round in the chamber and thumbed on the safety.

Sarah knew that the guards were relieved every two hours and estimated the last change-over had been no more than fifteen minutes before the storm started. That meant her handiwork would be discovered within the hour. Of course, someone might notice her absence any time before that. She needed to put as much distance between herself and the camp as she could. And quickly.

Taking a second to cover the guard's body with his poncho roll, Sarah looked up to the sky. The rain had all but stopped and the clouds were quickly clearing. It didn't take long to locate the long-handled pan of the Big Dipper, glistening brightly in the darkness. From there, the North Star was easy to find. Keeping it roughly in her thee o'clock, Sarah set off westwards at a brisk jog.

26.

The Final Week – Wednesday

Jelani checked the forecast again. The weather across the whole of England was hot and sunny until the end of the week when heavy rain was due in the south-east. He wasn't sure how that might affect his weekend plans but decided to worry about that closer to the time. Jelani had spent the last day and a half on one of the eight hundred metre ranges at Bisley. First, he re-zeroed his rifle and then he practised relentlessly to get used to the local conditions. In truth, the current hot weather made it much like shooting at home, but Jelani wasn't taking any chances. He hadn't come here just to make up the numbers.

The Imperial Meeting ran over four days. It involved a series of shoots to whittle down the competitors to a final group that would compete on Saturday for the Queen's Prize. Jelani was scheduled to compete in the very first shoot on Wednesday morning. He had already fired his allocation of practise ammunition and was warmed up and confident. The preliminary rounds shouldn't be a problem, providing he took them seriously. Back at High Rocks, he had gone over the likely scores he'd have to shoot to progress through each round with his instructor. Knowles knew exactly who had shot what to win the Queen's Prize every year going back to before Jelani was born. Jelani knew even his worst practise score should be good enough to see him through the first two days and then his average should get a place in Saturday's final. After that, it was as much about who could hold their nerve as who had the most talent. And Jelani was determined to hold his nerve.

Admiral Bellis' staff car swept through the gates and into Northwood Headquarters, closely followed by his personal protection team in their dark grey Range Rover. The chief of joint operations' military assistant was waiting to escort him to his boss' second floor office. Admiral Bellis was in very familiar surroundings. Not only had he been chief of joint operations himself a few years back, he could also remember when the site had been a Royal Naval shore establishment before the creation of the Permanent Joint Headquarters. Back then, it had been called HMS Warrior and was where British forces had been commanded during the Falkland War.

The current chief of joint operations was a Royal Marine, Lieutenant General Gordon Wallace. Wallace was the archetypal marine: wiry, taciturn, and hard as nails. The two senior officers had known each other for years and got on well. Most of their correspondence was electronic, but Bellis tried to visit Northwood every few months to get a feel for the atmospherics within the operational headquarters and gauge morale at the working level.

The military assistant led Admiral Bellis straight into his boss' office. General Wallace hurried around from behind his desk to meet him.

'Good afternoon admiral,' began Wallace. 'You know Jayne Reilley and Bill Davis.' Bellis nodded. 'I've asked them to join us in case you want to get into the detail of any of the ongoing operations.'

Of course,' replied Bellis. 'Always happy to hear from the experts. I know you've got many other operations on your plate, but it's Weybourn that's firmly back on the political agenda.'

'Understood,' said Wallace. 'Then that's where we'll start. Bill.'

Brigadier Bill Davis was responsible for the oversight of all UK operations worldwide.

'Sir, you'll have read our report on yesterday's attack at Hotel Fox. Latest information is SAC Styles' repatriation flight will be on Friday. Arriving at RAF Brize Norton 1530 hours local. All standard procedures are in place this end. The Oxford coroner is standing by to receive the body and the local police will escort the hearse as normal.'

The brigadier paused but Bellis nodded for him to continue.

'Of the other four casualties, Wing Commander Salmon is already back at work and Lance Corporal Marsden is expected to recover sufficiently to remain in theatre. Sergeant Manning, the air loadmaster, and Private Langley are currently in the sickbay on HMS Prince of Wales. Both serious but stable. We're waiting on an AEROMED decision from the Joint Force Headquarters later today.

'Hotel Fox is fully operational again, but after the intensity of yesterday's combat, General Wilkinson estimates it will be a few days before the Free State army is ready to conduct operations.'

Sensing the admiral wanted to come in, Davis paused again.

'Have we seen the after-action report from yesterday's mission yet?'

'Just received,' confirmed Davis. 'We'll have a full briefing note ready by close of play today, but I can give you the bare bones now sir, if you wish.'

Bellis nodded.

'The Free State army deployed six companies from their first and third infantry battalions, as well as one company from second battalion. That was the mission reserve. We had all eight Chinooks committed yesterday and between them they flew over fifty hours.

'The search phase of the mission went as planned. It resulted in several minor contacts and one major one, which lasted on and off for over six hours. That prompted the deployment of the mission reserve. Casualty data is still being processed, but early indications are that fifteen Free State soldiers were killed and between thirty and forty were medevacked to the Role Four hospital in New Devon.

'Enemy losses are harder to gauge. Initial indications suggest high. And with minimal access to medical facilities, that's likely to be a limiting factor on the enemy's ability to return to the field.'

'So, are we saying yesterday's engagement was a turning point?'

Air Commodore Jane Reilley answered.

'It's too early to say sir. Since General Wilkinson up gunned the Free State army's intelligence and planning capability, the campaign has taken a turn for the better. But our information is that the insurgency has hundreds of fighters. Until we know for sure how badly they were hit yesterday, it's impossible to determine how much of a threat they still pose.'

'Okay, thanks, I get all that,' said Bellis. 'What about the SIS view that this whole insurgency is not about the overthrow of President Korrundi? Do you have an opinion on that?'

Reilley thought hard before responding. She had a good working relationship with the SIS's Africa Department and didn't want to jeopardise it.

'Sir, we've seen all of the intelligence that they've collected and read their analysis as well. In our view, there are simply too many unknowns in their hypothesis. I mean, it could be accurate, but it's held together by a lot of assumptions and conjecture. So, it could also be way off the mark.'

Bellis nodded thoughtfully.

'Is there anything else on the intelligence front that I need to know about?'

'Sir, there is one other thing. JFHQ have now de-briefed all the fighters that were captured last weekend. They were only foot soldiers, so no surprise the intelligence is pretty thin. However, they all confirmed one thing. It appears that all enemy troops are being massed at a single location in the next few days. None of them knew where or why, but we got it from them separately, so I'm reasonably confident it's reliable.'

'Interesting,' said Bellis. 'What's your assessment?'

'That's a hard call,' responded Reilley. 'If they were planning an attack on New Devon, you wouldn't expect them to gather their forces that far away. They'd stay dispersed for OPSEC and to reduce their vulnerability.'

'Makes sense,' said Bellis. 'So why would they do it?'

'Because,' butted in Davis, 'If they're planning a local op, they'd need to concentrate their forces. There's no way they could carry out a co-ordinated attack without getting their troops together beforehand.'

'But what would the target be then?' asked Bellis, suspecting he already knew the answer.

General Wallace was first to answer.

'There is only one obvious target,' he stated bluntly. 'Hotel Fox.'

Rebecca looked out over the River Thames, shimmering in the heat of the late afternoon sun. Like most government buildings Vauxhall Cross did not have air conditioning and by this time of the day it was really noticeable. The clock on the wall passed five, and Rebecca looked down with envy on the masses of commuters making their way home. An early finish and a glass of wine in the garden of her local pub sounded wonderful.

But that was never going to happen.

She turned back to the pile of intelligence summaries waiting to be read. Although the situation in Free State was top priority, she was still responsible for intelligence analysis covering the whole of Africa. And, she reflected ruefully, it was a big place. From somewhere under a weighty report on the impact of ivory poaching in Botswana came the metallic ring of her secure phone. Shoving the papers aside, she grabbed the receiver.

'Rebecca Salmon, good afternoon.'

'Rebecca, hi, it's Ed Banks.' Colonel Banks was the UK Defence Attaché for Free State, as well as neighbouring Guinea and Sierra Leone.

'Ed hi, how are you?'

'Good thanks,' he replied. 'Look, I got your message about the Free State government's decision-making around Op Weybourn. Given the urgency, I thought I'd call you back rather than spend the next two hours tapping out an email.'

'Thanks,' said Rebecca. 'It is urgent, so I really appreciate it.'

'Okay. My source in the Free State government is a stenographer who works in the presidential palace. She normally only handles low-level stuff, but her supervisor's been long-term sick, so she's covering her work too. And that includes all of the president's meetings.'

What a stroke of luck, thought Rebecca.

'Anyway,' went on Banks. 'I met with her earlier today and she remembers the meeting where the deployment of UK forces was discussed. There were only three attendees. The president, the chief of the army and the interior minister. They spent some time arguing if they should invite UK forces into the country at all. Eventually they hit upon the compromise of just asking for support forces, which would avoid the fall-out from British combat troops potentially killing local nationals. They all decided that was the way to go.'

'That's really helpful,' said Rebecca. 'Did she tell you who suggested the compromise in the first place?'

Rebecca held her breath.

'She did,' confirmed Banks. 'It was the interior minister, Simon Nkaba.'

Sarah waited until the sun had completely set before emerging cautiously from her makeshift hide. There was no way the local fighters would have night-vision equipment, but she couldn't be sure about the South African mercenaries. The euphoria of the previous night's escape had long since passed. Although she had made good progress during the darkness and even managed a few hours exhausted sleep in the heat of the day, her situation wasn't great. What's more, it was only likely to get worse. She hadn't eaten for almost thirty-six hours and only managed a few mouthfuls of rainwater after last night's storm. Without food and, more importantly, water, inside her, Sarah knew her chances of getting out of the hinterland in one piece were slim.

And that was before she factored in the full-on search mission she knew the man-mountain had kicked off as soon as he'd realised she was missing. The headlights from the mercenaries'

G-Wagons cutting through the darkness were impossible to miss and she had wisely kept well away from the dirt tracks that criss-crossed the hinterland. Well before first light, Sarah had selected her lay-up position and taken the time to camouflage it as best she could. Burrowed deep into the undergrowth, she had been well hidden from the half-heated patrols mounted by the insurgent fighters. Instead, she had been eaten alive by the mosquitos, bugs and ticks that had happily welcomed her into their home.

Ignoring the growling in her stomach that sounded loud enough to be heard in New Devon, Sarah orientated herself west and began a second long night's march towards safety.

27.

The Final Week – Thursday

For the second time in four days, Rebecca was outside the chief's office first thing. Realising the importance, Hilary's PA had cleared her calendar and shortly after eight o'clock Rebecca was sat in one of the now-familiar easy chairs, coffee in hand. It took only a few minutes to pass on the intelligence from Colonel Banks.

'Where does that leave us?' asked Hilary, after considering the new information briefly.

'Well, it doesn't prove anything on its own, but it adds a useful piece to the jigsaw,' suggested Rebecca. 'I don't think we should drop everything just to focus on Nkaba, but I've got a couple of my best people tracking down as much information as we can about him. Unsurprisingly, there's nothing readily to hand, but we've already put the feelers out across the five-eyes community, and there's bound to be a stack of open-source material available as well. If he's linked to the insurgency, we'll find out.'

'Good,' nodded Hilary. 'But we need to move fast. If they are planning a spectacular, we haven't got much time.'

'Actually, that's the other thing I need to brief you on,' said Rebecca. 'General Wilkinson released details from the interrogation of the captured fighters. His report suggests that all the insurgents are being massed in one place, ready for a major operation.'

'A move on the capital?'

'No, that's unlikely. They'd stay dispersed until they got a lot closer. A force that size would be far too easy to locate and interdict. My view is their target is much closer to where they're currently operating.'

Rebecca paused to let her boss catch up. It didn't take long.

'The only obvious place is Hotel Fox.'

'Exactly!'

It was all quiet in the hide that the SAS team had been cooped up in for the last twenty-four hours. Located on the top of a gentle rise, it provided excellent concealment as well as the perfect view over the former insurgent training camp. Captain Willis and Staff Sergeant Hayes had disagreed on the plan to mount surveillance on the empty camp. Hayes considered it a waste of time, arguing that the bird they were after would have long since flown the nest. Terry thought differently. The bad guys knew the Free State army had turned the site over only a few days ago but found nothing. They may well believe it was now safe to return. If so, the surveillance plan was a smart move. A game of bluff and double bluff. But as dawn broke on their second morning in the hide, Terry was beginning to doubt that wisdom. Maybe the enemy were not as clever as he'd thought. After a quick discussion with Hayes, he decided to call it a day. Just then he heard the unmistakable rumble of a Bedford truck. As he reached for his binoculars, a convoy of three vehicles drove slowly into view below him. They parked up in the middle of the site and around thirty insurgent fighters climbed out stiffly. A few wandered over to the nearest treeline to relieve themselves. The rest headed towards the largest hut and quickly disappeared.

'What do you think?' Terry whispered.

'Looks like a simple pit-stop,' came Hayes' reply. 'They've not unloaded anything from the trucks, apart from a bit of scran. I reckon they're just stopping for breakfast.'

'You're probably right,' agreed Terry. 'Doesn't look like they're expecting any trouble though. They haven't even posted any sentries.' By now the entire group was in the hut. 'Wonder where they're headed?'

'Well, if the intelligence is accurate, they'll be joining up with all the rest of their mates,' said Hayes. 'It would be handy to find out where that jamboree is taking place.'

Terry looked at his staff sergeant. They were clearly thinking the same thing.

'Do you reckon you could get a tracker on one of those trucks?' he asked.

'No problem,' replied Hayes. He reached for his pack and, with a silent stretch, hauled himself up. 'Keep me covered boss. And if any of those bastards decide to take a stroll while I'm down there, give me a shout on channel two.'

He reached into a pouch on his web-belt and pulled out an earpiece, which he deftly hooked in place under his helmet as he clambered out of the hide. Within a few seconds, he was crawling away towards the training camp.

Hayes briefly moved out of sight as he worked his way stealthily down the slope. He reappeared as he reached the edge of the clearing. It looked empty, but he still paused to make sure.

'Boss, are we good?' he called softly into his radio.

'We're good, Jay,' confirmed Terry. 'All tangos still in the large hut in the centre of the compound.'

'Ack. I'm going in.'

Crouching low, Hayes sprinted across the open ground until he reached the closest outbuilding. He flattened himself against the wall and took a second to catch his breath. Slowly he peered around the corner. No movement from the big hut, which was now less than twenty metres to his right. The three trucks were parked just beyond the hut, facing him. This was the dangerous bit. If he got caught out in the open as he approached the trucks, his chances of survival were zero. Removing that thought from his mind, Hayes ducked low again and ran for the nearest truck. A second later he was crouching down by the off-side front wheel. Almost at once, he heard noise from the hut as the door was opened.

'Two tangos leaving the building, heading in your direction,'

Terry's update confirmed what he already suspected.

Shit!

Hayes slid quickly underneath the truck and pressed himself tight against the front axle. He could hear the voices of the two fighters as they sauntered over towards the trucks. They stopped directly in front of cab under which Hayes was hidden and lit a cigarette. Looking out, he could see their dust-caked boots, almost close enough to touch. Hayes considered his options. There was little chance of the two tangos discovering him, but he'd never get back to the hide without been seen. However, unless they thinned out pretty quick, he was definitely going to be trapped when their mates showed up. Taking them both out quietly would be tough and even if he managed it, they'd surely be missed. And that would defeat the object of the exercise. He made his choice. Quietly, he removed the tracker from his webbing pouch and turned it on. Reaching up, he attached it to the inside of the nearest wheel arch. The strong magnet on the underside of the device held it firmly in place. Then he reached for his combat knife and slowly slid it from its sheath. Silently, he slid away from the under the engine block. Getting to a point where he could roll out and quickly spring to his feet, he stopped and steadied himself.

'Jay, the tangos have finished their smokes. Looks like they're about to head back to the hut.' Terry's intervention was about as timely as it could get. Hayes remained motionless. Then, out of the corner of his eye, he saw a still-burning cigarette butt flicked into the dust. Seconds later, another followed.

'Stand by. Tangos are moving,' a short pause followed before Terry radioed again. 'Jay, it's all clear. Suggest you bug out now. Quick as you like!'

Hayes rolled out from under the truck, stood up and casually took a second to dust himself off. Then he calmly jogged back to the safety of the hide.

Barely a minute after Hayes arrived back in the hide, the fighters began spilling out from the hut. Terry shook his head at the shambolic way they ambled back to the trucks and the age it took them all to get back on board. Eventually, they were ready to move out and the small convoy left the training camp as unhurriedly as they had arrived.

As soon as the last vehicle was out of sight, the SAS team set to work. One of the troopers doubled off to retrieve their hidden land rover while the other gathered up their gear. Hayes had his mobile phone out and was busy synching it to the tracker.

'Got it,' he said. 'Good signal, heading west approximately one klick away.'

'What's the range of that thing?' asked Terry.

'Should be good for up to ten klicks,' confirmed Hayes.

'Okay, best we get cracking. Be a shame to lose them after all the effort you just put in.'

'Roger that,' replied Hayes.

The SAS team spent the rest of the day cautiously following the convoy. It stopped twice more before finally reaching its destination just as dusk was falling. Hayes pulled the land rover off the road and into cover when it became clear that the convoy had finally stopped. Terry checked his map. The trucks were in the middle of what appeared to be an old diamond mine. He was surprised to see they were less than twenty klicks from Harris Field. Deciding to wait until dark before moving in any closer, he instructed his men to break out the ration packs and get a brew on.

After a quick meal of cold chicken curry, Terry and Hayes returned to the map to identify a good observation point. Judging from the contours, it looked as if the mine had been built into the side of a steep escarpment that separated a large area of savanna lowland, from the densely forested highlands beyond it. The ground directly in front of the escarpment was shaped like a large, shallow bowl. The map indicated that the bowl contained several various-sized buildings. Probably storage sheds and the like, thought Terry. He had also seen enough of the country's geography to know the surrounding hills would be a mix of woodland and grassland, ideal for establishing an observation post. They chose the largest hill.

It took until midnight for the SAS team to move into position. The site they selected was perfect and they quickly set about building a hide. Its location gave them an excellent view of the mine and through his night vision goggles, Terry had no difficulty picking out eight separate buildings. Four were sizable storage sheds, the remainder looked like they'd been built for administrative use. He couldn't see if any were occupied, but judging by the amount of movement below, he suspected they all were. He counted over thirty trucks of various vintage scattered around, as well as a few more modern G-Wagons. If the insurgent fighters were being gathered together, this looked like a likely place. Terry decided to get an initial intelligence report off to the Joint Force Headquarters straight away, before concentrating on a more detailed assessment in the morning.

28.

For a second night, Sarah made good progress. Under a clear sky, she'd kept the North Star to her right and maintained a steady pace out of the hinterland towards safety. Only once did she see headlights searching for her, and they had been far enough away to ignore. As before, she found a good lay-up position while it was still dark and settled in for another day of being eaten alive. But even though Sarah was exhausted, sleep proved impossible. It was getting too difficult to ignore the screaming hunger pangs coming from her stomach and the splitting headache told her that dehydration was fast becoming an even bigger problem. By mid-morning, Sarah knew she had to change her plan. Food and water were now the priority.

Decision made, Sarah listened hard for a long time. The savanna vegetation around her was alive with noise. But it was all the background sounds of the hinterland she expected to hear. The reassuring chirp of crickets and croaking of frogs. Even the infuriating whine of the squadron of mosquitos zipping about above her head suggested all was as it should be.

Cautiously Sarah emerged from the hide. Staying low, she turned slowly though a full 360 degrees, like a wary submariner's periscope, checking for danger from every direction. The sun was bright, and she had to squint to see any distance. Not far away, a dirt track meandered east to west. Probably where last night's vehicles had been driving. Apart from the track, there was nothing man-made in sight. Encouraged by the lack of any obvious threats, Sarah slung the captured AK47 over one shoulder and set off.

When she reached the track, Sarah had a choice. Following it should eventually lead to a village, where there would be food and water. But her pursuers were vehicle-borne so keeping to the track was bound to increase the risk of being recaptured. Sarah was beginning to get desperate. Another day without sustenance and she would really be in trouble. Reluctantly, she turned to her left and begin following the track towards the west.

Without a watch, it was difficult for Sarah to know exactly how long she had been walking, but the sun had definitely moved beyond its highest point. She regularly checked up and down the track for the tell-tale dust cloud that would signal vehicles travelling towards her. But she didn't see a sole. It was as if Sarah was the only person left on the planet. The sun beat down relentlessly and her reserves of both energy and spirit were reaching a critical low. She feared the next time she stopped for rest, she might not have the strength to get back up again.

Sarah paused as the track crossed the crest of a low hill. Below her, through the haze of the afternoon sun, she could just make out another track running perpendicular to her own. Where they met, she saw a cluster of small buildings. There were no more than twenty or so, haphazardly dotted around the intersection. Probably not enough to be called a village. A hamlet perhaps? It didn't matter to Sarah. What mattered was the possibility of something to eat and drink.

It took Sarah five minutes to cover half the distance to the crossroads. She stopped again. The nearest building was no more than half a kilometre away. There were no obvious signs of life below her. More importantly, there was nothing that looked military anywhere in sight. No jeeps or trucks parked up. No sentry posts or barbed wire fencing. Nothing at all to suggest the place was being used by insurgent fighters. Then some movement caught Sarah's eye. Out of a long, narrow building burst several children, their laughter and shouting loud enough for Sarah to hear. At that distance, they were little more than dots of white and grey uniform, but the sense of normality that the end of a day's schooling conveyed was unmistakeable. With a positive stride, Sarah set back off down the track.

The schoolchildren had disappeared by the time Sarah reached the edge of the village and all was quiet again. She looked down at the assault rifle in her hands. Keep or toss? Sarah was loathe to get rid of her only form of protection, but she couldn't afford to look threatening to the people whose help she so desperately needed. She unclipped the magazine and hurled it as far away as she could. Then she dropped the weapon behind a large bush and kicked up the earth around it to hide it from view. Satisfied that it couldn't be seen from the track, she straightened up and headed for the nearest building.

It was eerily quiet as Sarah walked towards the crossroads, reminding her of a similar, tense scene from Ice Station Zebra. One of her favourite movies. Only here, it was fifty degrees hotter! She reached the crossroads and stopped. Looking around, it felt like there were dozens of eyes staring at her, but still she saw no-one. Then, behind her, she sensed movement. Sarah turned round quickly. From nowhere, a group of villagers had appeared. Maybe nine or ten. Mostly women but a few old men too. None of fighting age. One of the women had a baby perched solidly on her thigh. It was coughing uncomfortably, but that was the only sound.

More movement. Sarah turned again and was confronted with more villagers. In front and behind her now. Just staring, saying nothing. An uneasy standoff that Sarah knew she had to break, and quickly.

She slowly opened her arms out wide, as unthreateningly as she could.

'British,' she said. 'British soldier … friend?'

No reaction. None of the villagers moved. The baby's coughing still the only sound.

Sarah tried again.

'British soldier,' she said. 'I need your help …'

Then, one of the older men raised his arm and pointed at Sarah.

'*Kiniun*,' he called loudly. '*Funfun kiniun*.'

At once, everyone around started shouting.

'*Funfun kiniun. Funfun kiniun.*' Arms high, they moved towards Sarah, still shouting.

'No!' replied Sarah, as loudly as she could. 'I'm a British soldier. Not white lion. Not ... white ... lion.' Her protests were ignored. The crowd closed in on Sarah and swept her up. They jostled and pushed her away from the crossroads, towards a squat, ramshackle hut. She was thrown down violently outside it. Sarah looked up at the dirty grey curtain that served as a door. It was pulled aside, and a withered old man slowly shuffled out. Shielding his eyes from the sun, he looked first at the crowd in front of him. Then he looked down at Sarah.

At once the crowd started up again. Screaming and shouting over each other in an effort to be heard. The high-pitched screams of the women and the lower, almost gravelly tone of the old men. Sarah had no clue what they were saying but the frequent use of *kiniun* and the animated pointing towards her told a very clear story.

The old man listened and then held up a thin, bony hand. At once, the crowd stopped. In a quiet, halting voice, he spoke to Sarah in Yoruba.

'I'm sorry,' she responded with growing desperation. 'I don't understand what you're saying. I am a British soldier. I'm fighting with your army, and I need your help.'

Sarah lapsed into silence. The old man looked down at her, deep in thought. The crowd waited, quiet but on edge. Then, from the door of the schoolhouse, came a cry.

'*Baba agba. Baba agba!*'

The old man was jolted from his thinking. He looked up as the crowd parted and the young school mistress ran towards them. Her blouse was the same brilliant white as the shirts of her schoolchildren, but her kind, rounded face was set with a determined urgency. Breathless, she stopped next to Sarah and began speaking, rapidly in Yoruba.

Sarah could only look on incomprehensively as the argument grew. It was clear from the reaction of the crowd that the school mistress was disagreeing with them, and their displeasure got steadily louder. The old man listened impassively for a while, then he raised his hand again. Immediate silence. He pointed at Sarah and asked a question.

The crowd seemed to edge even closer, as the school mistress reached down and helped Sarah to her feet.

'I'm Monifa,' she said. 'This is my grandfather, Chibuike. He is the chief elder of our village. Who are you and why do you come here?'

Sarah struggled to contain her relief on hearing the question being asked in English.

'I'm Major Sarah Grey of the British army. I am fighting with the West African Free State army against the rebel soldiers, the *kiniun*, who are terrorising your people. I was captured by the *kiniun* a week ago, but I escaped. Now I need to get back to New Devon, but I'm desperately short of food and water, and I need your help.'

'How do we know your story is true?' said Monifa. 'How do we know you are not *funfun kiniun*?'

'Look at me,' said Sarah. Her blond hair was matted and full of knots. Her face was black with grime, and her clothing was filthy. The ripped seam in her trousers had torn even further and the exposed bandage on her thigh was unrecognizable. The shackle still hung at her ankle and the short length of chain attached to it dragged in the dirt behind her. She had no weapon.

'How many *funfun kiniun* have you seen looking like this?'

Monifa looked Sarah up and down and then broke into a smile.

'I believe you,' she said. 'Because you really do look like shit!'

The rest of the day was all a bit of a blur for Sarah. As soon as Chibuike had endorsed his granddaughter's acceptance of Sarah's story, the rest of the villagers couldn't do enough to help. Food and water were quickly provided, and an old man skilfully removed the shackle from Sarah's ankle with a hammer and chisel. As she kicked the chain off into the dirt, Sarah reflected on her good fortune. If Monifa had turned up just a few minutes later, it might have been a very different story.

As the sun set, Sarah relaxed in an old iron bathtub in the tiny, two-room shack behind the schoolhouse where Monifa lived. The water, drawn from a large outdoor tank, had been heated all day by the sun and was still luxuriously warm. Sarah spent at least half an hour scraping the muck and grime from her exhausted body and was finally beginning to feel human again.

'Hey, girl. Are you going to be in that bath for ever?' Monifa said jokingly as she stuck her head round the bathroom door. 'Get yourself out here and let me put a clean bandage on that leg of yours.'

Sarah stretched her leg out straight and examined her thigh. Considering what she'd been through in the last week, it was healing remarkably well. It was still painful, and the scar was going to be horrible, but Sarah knew it could have been so much worse. Even though the bullet was still inside her, the wound remained free from infection. When she finally made it back home, the medics would insist on cutting her open again and removing the bullet, and that was not going to be pleasant. But one thing at a time.

Sarah dragged herself reluctantly out of the bath and wrapped a towel around her. It was old and threadbare, but at that moment it was better than the softest, most sumptuous towel in any five-star hotel. She hopped into Monifa's living room, come kitchen, come bedroom, and collapsed into an ancient, worn-out settee.

Monifa took down an old round biscuit tin from the shelf above her sink and knelt in front of Sarah. The tin doubled as a first aid box, and she quickly cleaned and dried Sarah's wound before treating it with iodine and expertly bandaging it.

'That was impressive for a teacher,' complimented Sarah.

'Well, I haven't always been a teacher,' said Monifa.

'No?'

'No. I worked for five years as a nurse in the Joseph Khalli hospital in New Devon,' said Monifa with evident pride. 'Did all my nurse's training and finished up as a sister in the casualty department.'

'I guess that's where you learned English then,' said Sarah.

Monifa nodded.

'So, what brought you back here?'

'My older sister was the school mistress here until last summer. Then one day the kiniun came. It was the first time they had been to our village. They demanded the children go with them. Boys and girls. My sister refused, so they took her instead. We haven't seen her since. The children still needed a teacher, so here I am.'

Monifa blinked hard to keep the tears from her eyes.

'I'm so sorry,' said Sarah. She leaned forward, took Monifa in her arms and hugged her hard. 'I can't even begin to imagine how tough that must be.' Monifa pulled away, wiping at the tears that were now flowing freely down her face.

'Do the kiniun ever come back here?'

'Sometimes. But not so much. We have seen your helicopters flying overhead in the last few weeks. I think the *kiniun* are hiding from them.'

At that moment, the peacefulness of the village was shattered by the roar of vehicle engines. Screeching tyres and hard-revved engines echoed across the crossroads. The sound of automatic gunfire added to the chaos. Monifa leapt up and peered through a large crack in the door.

'There are three big black jeeps, all driving around fast. The men are firing guns up into the sky. It's the *funfun kiniun*.'

'Shit, shit, shit,' said Sarah. She jumped up from the settee and grabbed her clothes.

'You must go,' said Monifa. 'We cannot let you get captured again.' Sarah was not about to disagree.

'Go through the bathroom. The wood behind the tub is old and rotted. You can escape that way.'

'What about you?' said Sarah. 'What are you going to do?'

'I must go to my grandfather. The *funfun kiniun* don't speak good Yoruba.'

'Thank you for everything,' said Sarah.

'No, thank you,' replied Monifa. 'Get back to New Devon and help our army kill all the *kiniun*. That is the only way.'

They hugged briefly and then Monifa slipped out of the door and was gone. By the time Monifa reached the crossroads, the G-Wagons had stopped circling and the mercenaries were busy rounding up the villagers. Her grandfather was dragged from his hut and thrown to the floor in front of the nearest vehicle. The villagers looked on, helpless.

The man-mountain peered down scornfully at Chibuike. 'We are looking for a woman soldier,' he said. 'A British woman soldier. This tall, walking with a limp.' He indicated someone of Sarah's height. 'Has she been here?'

Chibuike shook his head, not understanding.

'My grandfather doesn't speak English,' said Monifa, stepping forward to face the man-mountain.

'Well best you translate for him, little lady,' said the man-mountain.

'I don't need to,' replied Monifa. 'We haven't seen anyone like you describe.'

'Don't lie to me,' said the man-mountain. 'We'll search every last shack in this shitty little place, and if we find anything, you'll wish you hadn't.'

'Do what you like,' said Monifa defiantly. 'We've nothing to hide.'

'Hey boss,' a voice from behind the vehicles caused them both to turn around. 'Look what I've found?'

Monifa's heart sank. One of the mercenaries was holding up the shackle and chain. The man-mountain recognised them immediately.

'Lying whore!' he stepped forward and slapped Monifa hard across the face. She fell with a cry. Her grandfather tried to clamber to his feet and help her, but the man-mountain felled him with a single, savage kick.

Monifa got to her knees and stared up at the man-mountain. A trickle of blood ran down from her split lip and dripped onto the dusty ground.

'I told you not to lie. Now where is she?' The man-mountain raised his hand again. Monifa shied away but remained quiet.

'All right,' said the man-mountain. 'We can do this the hard way.' He turned to one of the mercenaries and pointed at Chibuike. 'Break his neck. But do it slowly.' The mercenary grinned an evil grin.

'My pleasure, boss.'

'No!' screamed Monifa. 'Leave him alone.'

'Last chance,' said the man-mountain, fixing Monifa with a hard stare. 'Start talking.'

Monifa looked at her grandfather, still doubled over in pain.

Sorry grandpa, she mouthed silently.

'Right, that's it,' said the man-mountain angrily. 'Kill him.'

'Stop!' the cry rang out over the crossroads. Everyone looked up. Standing in front of the schoolhouse was Sarah.

'Leave them be,' she shouted. 'It's me you want.'

The man-mountain gave a triumphant shout.

'Take her,' he ordered. 'Quickly. We've wasted enough time out here. We need to get back to the mine. There's work to do.'

Sarah allowed herself to be dragged to the nearest G-Wagon. As she was pushed into the back, she looked over to Monifa and gave a silent nod. The man-mountain followed her gaze.

'Don't think you've got away with this, you fucking whore,' he raged at Monifa. 'We'll be back, and when we do, we'll raze your whole fucking village to the ground.'

29.

The Final Week – Friday

Admiral Bellis' walk down the fifth-floor corridor in the Ministry of Defence felt much like a condemned man's journey to the gallows. He knew today was going to be a particularly difficult day and it hadn't started well with an immediate summons to see the secretary of state. The smile that Fletcher's gatekeeper offered was more conspiratorial than welcoming as he ushered the admiral into his boss' office without delay.

Tom Fletcher got straight to the point.

'The PM and I are both extremely disappointed with the recent turn of events in Free State. Even though we've somehow managed to keep the convoy ambush out of the news, the disappearance of Major Grey and now the attack on the refuelling site are casting this government in an extremely poor light.' He gave Bellis a pompous look.

'Today's repatriation of the airwoman into RAF Brize Norton is hardly going to improve the situation. The PM wants to know what you're doing about it.'

It was pretty much the broadside that the admiral was expecting.

'Well minister, you'll have seen the latest update from Northwood and in particular the successful search and destroy mission on Tuesday. General Wilkinson believes that maintaining this tempo for the next few weeks will break the back of the insurgency.'

'But what about the casualties. The whole reason for not sending combat troops in the first place was you said there wouldn't be any,' Fletcher shot back.

'Minister, that is simply not true,' corrected Bellis, working hard to keep his contribution to the argument objective. 'The military advice was never that this operation could be undertaken without casualties. You can't make an omelette without breaking eggs.'

'Don't give me that bollocks.' Fletcher was only too happy to take his anger out on his subordinate. 'In the build-up to this operation, your reticence on the subject of casualties was deafening. And while we're about it, what progress have you made on finding and rescuing Major Grey?'

Bellis remained silent. Although he had seen the report detailing the massing of insurgent fighters at the diamond mine, there was no indication that Major Grey was being held there too. And even if she was, he knew the British forces in Free State did not have the resources to mount a rescue mission.

'I've a meeting with the PM to discuss where we stand on this operation later this morning. After that, he will want to give further direction to the defence and security organisations involved. See to it that a suitable video conference is organized for later in the day.' Fletcher ordered Bellis dismissively.

'Of course, minister,' replied the admiral, still keeping his anger in check. 'You are aware that I planned to travel to Brize Norton this afternoon for the repatriation of SAC Styles.'

Fletcher exploded.

'For Christ's sake, Bellis. The PM's an inch from firing you right now. Don't you understand? Send someone else to Brize Norton. I want you on that VTC.'

Bellis nodded his acknowledgement formally but didn't say a word. Grim faced, he turned and left the room.

Sarah had no way of knowing that she'd just been the subject of a heated conversation between the defence secretary and the chief of the defence staff. She also didn't know that last night's journey had ended at the diamond mine Terry Willis and his team had under surveillance. She had been hauled from the back of the G-Wagon and immediately thrown into a small stone-walled storeroom. In the two-second gap in between, she'd had no time to take in any of her surroundings.

Although she was hardly over the moon at being back in captivity, there was no doubt Sarah's new prison was an improvement over the previous set-up. For a start, she was no longer chained to a post. Even though the storeroom measured only a few metres square, it was huge compared to the tiny freedom of movement the chain had permitted. It had two windows set high on opposite walls, which offered a reasonable amount of light. Both were windowless but the heavy iron bars fixed over them took away any thought of escape. At least they offered some airflow that should help to bring down the sweltering afternoon temperatures and also lesson slightly the foetid smell already building up from the galvanised steel bucket that served as her toilet.

Sarah had another cause for optimism. The two fighters who brought her food that morning had displayed an extremely lackadaisical attitude towards the task, clearly thinking their captive posed no threat. The routine they adopted was a simple one. The first fighter was the guard. He unlocked the heavy wooden door and then moved aside to let his colleague amble in carrying the food and water. He hadn't even bothered to unsling his weapon. Then his mate let Sarah take the food and water directly from him. From that moment, Sarah was back plotting. First, she needed to encourage their sloppiness by appearing as grateful and subservient as she could. Then she needed to work out the best way to take them down and when to strike. She may have willingly given herself up yesterday to save Monifa's grandfather, but that wasn't going to stop her trying to escape again as soon as she possibly could.

It was mid-afternoon when the large white Lexus SUV nosed its way slowly down the cobbled road that ran along the New Devon waterfront. The driver carefully negotiated the worst of the potholes before halting in front of a large metal bollard onto which a couple of unkempt and barely seaworthy fishing boats were moored. A stiff breeze was blowing in off the sea, strong enough to make waves that caused the boats to bump continuously into each other. The front seat passenger got out and surveyed the area from behind a pair of large, mirrored sunglasses. Deciding that all was as it should be, he reached over and opened the rear door for his principal to alight.

Simon Nkaba climbed out of the vehicle and also looked around. He was wearing a khaki linen suit and open necked grey shirt. He too saw nothing out of the ordinary. Just then he felt his mobile phone vibrate. He reached into his pocket and checked the screen.

Just finished the last shoot off, made it into tomorrows final, all set for Sunday, will keep you posted. JA. Not bothering to reply, he returned the phone to his pocket. Then he nodded to his security detail and walked across the street towards an old and nondescript single-storey bar. Without pausing, he pushed open the dull green door.

It took a few seconds for Simon's eyes to adjust from the bright sunlight outside. He blinked a couple of times and then quickly identified the door to the backroom, exactly where Mr Smith had said it would be. Without looking left or right, he strode across the bar and thrust it open. As expected, there was just one occupant in the room. As Simon entered, he stood up.

'Mr Black, I presume,' said Simon.

Max Kruger nodded. 'And you must be the money.'

Corporal Farrell was bored. Now that the new training team was fully up and running, he wasn't needed to support any of the Free State army training serials. All he had left to do was monitor the comms net for Captain Willis's and his team out in the hinterland. He had been doing that twelve-on, twelve-off with Signaller Talbot for the last week. It was definitely the unglamorous part of special forces work they never told you about when you volunteered. He'd even got bored whacking the bad guys on the latest edition of Call of Duty.

He was idly surfing the internet, when the icon for the looker-listener app on his laptop began flashing. They only had one active device in place, so he knew exactly where it was transmitting from. In the few weeks since he'd installed it, it had tripped half a dozen times. Mostly, it had been old man Bacchi seeking some peace and quiet to do his paperwork. But on one occasion, a local call-girl had picked the lock to the backroom and bent over the desk to entertain a client. That had been worth watching back a couple of time. Farrell double-clicked the icon to start the application. A new window opened displaying the video feed from the camera. The door to the backroom was being closed by a tall man in a black polo shirt and grey cargo pants. As he sat down in the single chair, he turned towards the camera. In glorious HD, the moustachioed face was unmistakable.

Farrell immediately checked to make sure the app was recording properly and then racked up the volume to maximum. It was sensitive enough to register the impatient drumming of Kruger's fingers on the table. Farrell then paired the laptop to his mobile phone. He knew this recording could be crucial, so he made sure he had a backup running. No sooner had he confirmed both systems were working, the door on screen opened again and in walked a large, well dressed black man.

Kruger recognised Simon immediately but if he was surprised, he kept it to himself. In this clash of alpha males, he was certainly not going to be first to show any sign of weakness.

'I said it to Mr Smith, and I'll say it to you. Breaking OPSEC like this is a bad idea,' opened Kruger, determined to start on the front foot.

'You can say what you like,' countered Simon aggressively. 'This is my operation, and I'll decide what is and isn't a bad idea.'

'Of course,' conceded Kruger. 'But what's so important that you had to come out to this seedy little shit-hole and meet me face to face?'

'The end game,' said Simon simply. 'The next forty-eight hours is the end game and I need to know it's going to run exactly as planned.' That took Kruger by surprise. He'd always thought the attacks against the British forces were just a sideshow. Now it seemed they were the main event.

'Tell me about the spectacular attack I asked for,' pressed Simon.

'Everything's ready,' said Kruger. 'We have almost one thousand competent fighters assembled at an abandoned diamond mine approximately ten miles from the British base at Harris Field.'

Simon cut in immediately.

'Just one thousand? Back in May, you said you'd already trained more than that.'

'We have trained more than that,' Kruger replied. 'But in the last week, we've had two significant contacts with the Free State army. The British are assisting with their planning now, and that's making a big difference. We've lost over ten per cent of our manpower either killed or injured. Not that it matters, the British force at Harris Field is less than two hundred and most of them are just support troops. Hell, we estimate almost fifty are women. We'll outnumber them more than five to one. That's more than enough to guarantee your spectacular.'

'It'd better be,' said Simon.

'But I should warn you, it won't come cheap. They have significant firepower, especially in their vehicles. And once they work out there's no chance of surrender, they'll fight hard. Our fatalities could be in the hundreds with many more injured. After this, your insurgency will be finished.'

'You let me worry about that,' said Simon. 'How will you attack the British?' Kruger could see that Simon wasn't interested in the detail, so he kept it high level.

'We'll move out from the diamond mine after dark tomorrow. We've got enough transport to move the force in a couple of runs. A mile from Harris Field, we'll divide into two groups. One will engage the base head on, the other will attack from the flank. The first force will fix them, and the second will roll them up. We'll go in at first light.'

'No, you'll not attack until twelve o'clock,' instructed Simon.

'That's a bad idea,' replied Kruger. 'Resistance is always lowest at dawn and besides, waiting a further five hours means we'll have to deploy during daylight. That'll make us more vulnerable and there's every chance we'll lose the element of surprise.'

'You'll have to work round that,' insisted Simon. 'Because you will attack at midday.'

'Why?' asked Kruger. 'What's so important about midday?'

'That's my business,' said Simon.

'It's my business too,' retorted Kruger. 'You pay me for my military experience and I'm telling you waiting beyond first light will jeopardise the mission. And I'm not prepared to put the life of my employees in danger for no good reason.'

'All right,' said Simon. 'Your attack on Harris Field is not all I have planned. At the same time on Sunday in England, another spectacular attack will happen. And for maximum effect, I want them both to happen at exactly the same time.'

Jesus, what is this guy on? thought Kruger. But at the end of the day, he was only really concerned about the money.

'Okay,' he said. 'I can make that work. Twelve o'clock on Sunday it is.'

'Good,' replied Simon. 'Then we're done here. I have one final concern about your plan. With all the fighters massed in one place, how do you know you won't be attacked first?'

'What, by the Free State army?' asked Kruger with surprise. 'I don't think that's likely. For a start, they don't know where we are, and secondly, they're not capable of operating above company level. To take us on, they'd need almost their entire army.'

'But with the extra training the British have given them, it's a risk,' insisted Simon.

'Well, it's a bloody small one,' conceded Kruger grudgingly. 'But if you're worried, it wouldn't take much to fix the Free State army in their barracks.'

'How could you do that,' asked Simon.

'Oh, you needn't be concerned with the detail,' said Kruger. 'I'll make sure the Free State army has more than enough to worry about.'

The looker-listener clicked off thirty seconds after Kruger left the room. Corporal Farrell quickly checked that both the laptop and his phone had successfully captured the full recording. Then he reached for the secure comms and called his boss. From the hide overlooking the diamond mine, Terry listened intently to the update from his corporal. He knew that he personally didn't need to see the recording, but it needed to go up the chain of command fast.

'Email it out to the intelligence contact list soon as you can,' he commanded. 'And make sure a copy gets to Rebecca Salmon. She's head of the Africa department at SIS.'

'Roger that, boss,' acknowledged Farrell. The recording was a large file and even zipped it took a couple of attempts before he got a delivery receipt from across the network. Less than thirty seconds later, he received a read receipt from Vauxhall Cross.

30.

Half an hour before the prime minister's video conference was due to start, Rebecca was back in the chief's office. Hilary watched in silence as the recording from Corporal Farrell's looker-listener device played through in full on one of the large plasma screens built into the wall opposite her desk. Her first response was cautious.

'How do we know this actually is Nkaba?' she asked.

'We don't yet know for sure,' replied Rebecca. 'A copy of the recording is down with the tech boys right now. The video should be good enough for facial recognition. They're also tracking down an audio recording of Nkaba so we can check for a voice match too. I put it in as a flash request, so we'll have an answer by the end of the day.'

'But not in time for the prime minister's VTC.' Hilary was clearly frustrated. She thought for a second. 'What has your team managed to track down on Nkaba?'

It was Rebecca's turn to show disappointment.

'To be honest ma'am, not a lot. He's the son of one of the country's new political elite that emerged during Joseph Khalli's time. And he's been close to the current president for years. They met in prep school and practically grew up as brothers. In fact, they went up to Oxford together in 1987, Christ Church College.'

'So, we were there at the same time,' Hilary mused aloud. 'Yes, I remember. There were three of them. Korrundi, Nkaba and another boy. Can't remember his name. Think they were the first students to come to Oxford from West Africa Free State since independence.' She paused, still thinking quickly.

'In fact, wait. No, I'm sure I remember Nkaba was also involved in ...' Hilary clicked her fingers and pointed to a bookshelf. 'Rebecca pass me that book, will you? No, the next one, with the blue binding. That's it.' Rebecca heaved a large, heavy book from the shelf and handed it over. It was expensively bound in brown leather and the thick layer of dust suggested it hadn't been opened in ages.

'In my final year at Somerville, I was the president of the Oxford Union,' Hilary explained. 'Every few years or so, the Union publishes a record of debates. All mine are in here.' She held up the book so Rebecca could see the title *Debates of the Oxford Union 1985-1995*. 'I'm sure Nkaba was involved in one.' She opened it at the contents page and began searching.

'Of course.' her finger stopped halfway down the list for academic year 1988-89. 'There was a debate about British imperialistic policy in Africa. Around Easter time, I think. If memory serves, Nkaba was the lead student arguing against the motion. It was a really big deal at the time. Quite emotive if I recall.'

'Yes,' she said flicking to the page that recorded the debate in detail. 'Here we are. I persuaded Sir Hugh Anderson to come as a visiting speaker. He was permanent secretary at the Foreign & Commonwealth Office at the time. Anyway, it was a disaster for Nkaba. His speech was atrocious, and he got ripped to pieces in the Q&A too. There, the motion was carried by two hundred and ten votes to fourteen. One of the most one-sided results in the history of Oxford debating.'

'Okay,' said Rebecca slowly. 'I agree that must have made him pretty pissed off, but I'm struggling to find a link. I mean how …'

'I'm not,' interrupted Hilary. 'The lead student arguing for the motion was … Anthony Brownlow.' They looked at each other, momentarily speechless. Another piece of the jigsaw had just fallen into place.

'So what are we saying?' asked Rebecca, almost to herself. 'This whole thing is all about Nkaba getting back at Brownlow, because of a debate at Oxford over thirty years' ago?'

'It could be,' answered Hilary. 'You said yourself it was never about an insurgency in Free State. And back then, Brownlow was a real spoiled brat. He wouldn't have stopped gloating about winning that debate for months afterwards. It must have been really humiliating for Nkaba.'

'But thirty years ago?' repeated Rebecca. 'Really? Has Nkaba really spent his whole life plotting to get even?'

'Why not?' replied Hilary. 'Wasn't it Talleyrand who said, "revenge is a dish best served cold"?'

'Well yes,' said Rebecca. 'But it's still a big leap if you ask me.'

'Okay,' accepted Hilary. 'Maybe you're right. Maybe there's more to it than just the debate. But it's all stacking up against Nkaba. He's the key. I'm sure he is.'

Even though the forced air system worked better in the chief's office than anywhere else in the building, Rebecca still felt uncomfortably warm. The mounting evidence that Nkaba was behind the supposed insurgency didn't stop the impending attack on the forward base. Closer to home, they now knew he was also planning a major incident in the UK as well. They may be zeroing in on Nkaba's motive, but they were still no closer to identifying his means or his opportunity.

'At least we know whatever he's got planned is going to happen around midday on Sunday,' said Rebecca.

'True,' agreed Hilary. 'But that gives us less than forty-eight hours to stop it. I guess the obvious place to start is with the prime minister.' Hilary hit the intercom switch on her desk. 'Mary, do you have a copy of the prime minister's itinerary for Sunday?'

A minute later, Hilary's PA walked in carrying a single sheet of A4 paper, which she handed to her boss. Hilary scanned it quickly.

'There,' she said. 'Twelve hundred hours, Brownlow and the Indian prime minister arrive at the Anglo-Indian trade fair at the National Exhibition Centre.'

'How are they getting there?' asked Rebecca.

'Helicopter into Birmingham airport and then drive. If I recall, the NEC's just next door.'

In a second, Hilary had looked it up on google maps. Situated right on the outskirts of the city, the National Exhibition Centre was indeed located right next to the airport. It was also flanked to the east by the M42, beyond which was miles and miles of open farmland and countryside.

'Looks like a pretty good location for an assassination attempt to me. Plenty of open ground for a sniper to hide.' said Rebecca. 'And it certainly fits with the timings.'

'I agree,' said Hilary. 'But that's for the local police to worry about, with the Home Office and the Met. We still need to work out who's helping Nkaba. He certainly isn't doing this all on his own. What about the South African mercenary? Kruger, is it?'

'It is,' confirmed Rebecca, 'But I doubt if he's involved.'

'Why not?' asked Hilary.

'Well, a bit of troublemaking in a small African country is one thing. Assassinating the head of a first-world country is something else completely. Even though he can't resist getting his hands dirty every now and then, Kruger still runs a very profitable private security company. I don't think Nkaba could afford anywhere near enough money to put that in jeopardy.'

Rebecca paused to allow her brain to catch up.

'And think back to the video. Kruger didn't know about Nkaba's plans for a second spectacular. That came as a complete surprise. No, I think Nkaba will have roped in someone that he trusts completely. I'd better head back to my team and refocus on who that could be.'

Hilary checked her watch.

'The PM's VTC starts in five minutes. It's probably worth you sitting in. You'll need to stay off camera and keep quiet when I'm off mute, but it'll be good background for you. Who knows,' she smiled. 'One day, it might be you sitting here.'

Anthony Brownlow was tired and extremely bad tempered. He had drunk too much at last night's state banquet and was still paying for it. The quiet afternoon that his private secretary tried so hard to protect had been de-railed by the deteriorating situation in Free State and the repatriation event at Brize Norton. The press was having a field day. Brownlow was savvy enough to realise that he needed to invest some of his own political capital to get the situation back on the rails. Externally, he would do that with a discrete chat to a couple of well-trusted journalists. Internally, he needed to bang a few heads together.

Because of the new intelligence, the video conference had been expanded to include the home secretary, the Metropolitan Police commissioner, and her head of counter terrorism command. It would have been far better to get everyone together in the cabinet office briefing room, Brownlow grumbled to himself. He much preferred face-to-face meetings where he could look his subordinates in the eye. Video conferencing gave those that needed it a place to hide.

The meeting neatly broke down into the two separate problem areas. The impending attack on the forward base in Free State and the still-unknown threat within the UK. The home secretary and the Met commissioner supported the view that the prime minister was the obvious target for the Sunday attack. The timings for Brownlow's attendance at the trade fair in Birmingham had been in the public domain for weeks. Plenty of time to plan an assassination attempt. Tom Fletcher argued strongly that the prime minister should simply cancel his attendance, but Brownlow was having none of it.

'This visit by the Indian prime minister is vital to the economic future of the country,' he fumed. 'We're expecting more than ten-billion-pounds worth of business to be secured during the trade fair. There is no way I'm not going to be there. And before you suggest it,' he added, looking at the home secretary, 'I'm not changing my itinerary either. I will walk through the main entrance at midday as planned.'

The Met commissioner stepped in.

'Understood completely, prime minister,' she said. 'We're liaising with West Midlands police, and our security procedures for this week have also included the SAS's counter terrorism wing. I recommend we bring them into the planning loop for

Sunday straight away.' She looked for Admiral Bellis on her screen, who gave a thumbs up.

'Of course,' said Brownlow. 'Do what you have to.'

'The one thing we're still missing is any information on who the perpetrator might be,' continued the commissioner. 'Without any intelligence on that, our job is considerably more difficult.' The video link went embarrassingly quiet.

Hilary had no choice.

'Prime minister, perhaps I should come in here,' she said. 'We are chasing down everything we have on Simon Nkaba. As soon as we get anything useful, I'll make sure it's distributed out to everyone straight away.'

'Well, you'd better find something useful, and bloody quickly,' grumbled Brownlow. 'Everyone else is contributing. You're in danger of letting the side down ... again.' Hilary blanched at the second strike from the prime minister. The third one would surely be her last.

'Right, where are we with the situation in Free State?' Brownlow moved on quickly.

'Prime minister. If I can pick it up from here,' Admiral Bellis began. 'You'll have been briefed on the report from General Wilkinson earlier. We are still waiting for SIS to confirm the person in the video is Nkaba, but we believe the intelligence is actionable. In our opinion, there is an extremely high probability of an overwhelming attack on Hotel Fox, on or around 1200 hours on Sunday.' He broke off briefly, but no one offered a comment.

'In response, we have developed five courses of action. One, the high commissioner meets with President Kirrundi to outline the evidence we have and pressures him to arrest Nkaba. Two, the Free State army executes an attack on the insurgent fighters at the diamond mine, with our planning and logistical support. Three, we deploy UK force elements from Hotel Fox to the diamond mine to attack the insurgent fighters, supported by F-35s from HMS Prince of Wales. Four, we withdraw all personnel from Hotel Fox to Joseph Khalli barracks in New Devon before Sunday morning. And five, we reinforce Hotel Fox with the Royal

Engineer company and the training team. They dig in and defend the site together.

'Are you finished?' asked Brownlow tersely, his bad temper still very much in evidence.

'Yes, prime minister, I am,' replied Bellis.

'Because, in my view, most of what you're proposing aren't courses of action at all. For a start, how can the high commissioner take this to President Kirrundi if we can't prove it's Nkaba in the video in the first place? If we've got that wrong and it's not Nkaba, we'd never be trusted in Africa again. And the option of using British troops to attack the diamond mine is absolutely a non-starter. For a start, I thought they were all support troops and, if your intelligence summaries are to be believed, they'd be outnumbered over five to one.'

'Prime minister,' responded Bellis. 'The personnel manning Hotel Fox may not be front-line infantry, but they are still well-trained servicemen and women and would be more than capable of taking on the insurgents. You are correct in pointing out they'd be heavily outnumbered, but close air support from the F-35s would negate that.'

'And how do you think a British bombing raid on an African country is going to make us look around the world?' Brown challenged. 'We'd be ripped to shreds in the UN, not to mention the backlash across both the Commonwealth and the African Union. No, under no circumstances are you to use troops from the forward base or send in F-35s.' Brownlow looked around the various video screens, but no-one was keen to contribute. He continued.

'And do you really think we should abandon the forward base? What sort of message does that send? At the first sign of trouble, the British turn tail and run. In fact, of your five options there is only one that is even remotely doable. This is a local mess, and it must have a local solution. Just like I've said all along. The Free State army should be used. It's the only way. You can help them with planning and provide helicopter support, just like you've been doing since you first got there. But this is their opportunity to crush the insurgency once and for all. They should be chomping at the bit to get after them.' Brownlow paused again. 'Unless, of course, someone has a better idea?'

The question hung in the air for several seconds, but it was clear no-one was brave enough, or foolish enough, to challenge the prime minister.

'There you are then admiral,' said Brownlow. 'You have your orders. This is to be a Free State affair. No UK force elements are to be involved in the fighting. Do I make myself clear?'

'Perfectly, prime minister,' answered Admiral Bellis.

31.

The Final Week – Saturday

The heavy rain pounding on the hotel window woke Jelani far earlier than planned. He reached for his mobile phone. Not yet half past six. With a grunt, he climbed out of bed and pulled back the curtains. The rain was so heavy he could barely see out. The storm that the weathermen were predicting all week had finally arrived. Jelani flicked open an app on his phone that detailed the local weather. It forecast heavy rain all day with ninety-five per cent certainty. After making it through the last of the preliminary rounds yesterday, Jelani had checked with the event organisers at Bisley. They had obviously been tracking the bad weather too. Everyone agreed it would be far too dangerous for competitors to be out on the range if the storm was as bad as predicted. The final round was scheduled to commence at ten o'clock, and the Imperial Meeting coordinator had promised a go/no go decision at least two hours before that. There was nothing Jelani could do except shower and head down for breakfast.

The storm arrived over London no more than half an hour later, but Rebecca was already awake. She had spent the night crashed out on the tiny two-seater settee in her office and was already regretting it. Stretching uncomfortably, she headed off for a quick wash and teeth clean. On the way, her mobile rang. It was James.

'Hi darling,' she answered.

'Hey there,' he replied. 'Sorry to call so early, but I guessed you'd be up.'

'Up and in work,' confirmed Rebecca. 'Where are you?'

'That's why I'm calling. We're just about to redeploy northwards. It seems the plan to hold the team in London has been overtaken by events, which is a complete bugger because it means we can't see each other tonight.'

Rebecca hid her disappointment. 'Not to worry, there's always another time.'

'Of course,' agreed James. 'As soon as this is over, we'll spend some proper time together. I promise. And I was listening in to yesterday's "senior event", so understand where your focus will be today. If anything comes up that we should know about, give me a shout.'

Always cautious on insecure comms, Rebecca knew exactly what James meant.

'Small world,' she said. 'I was listening too. And of course, if we find anything, I'll make sure you're first to know. Take care.'

'You too,' Simon ended the call leaving Rebecca to her ablutions and a busy day ahead.

'Morning sir. Welcome to day forty-four in the big brother house,' Mr Jones offered his familiar greeting as he sat down next to Rob, breakfast tray in hand.

'Morning Mr Jones,' replied Rob. 'It's going to be another busy Saturday.'

'Aren't they all?' said Mr Jones. 'Have we had any more details on today's op?'

'No, nothing as yet,' said Rob. He had also been listening into yesterday's video conference, on a remote link from the Joint Force Headquarters. After it had finished, he'd got his command group together to discuss options. They all agreed that the chosen course of action was definitely the best, although both Dan and Pete were concerned that the prime minister had put all their eggs into one basket. Rob thought they had a point and after talking it through he decided they needed a backup plan. At the end of the day, if the Free State army failed to neutralise the threat from the diamond mine, Hotel Fox would still be right in the firing line.

'We should see the orders from JFHQ any time now. Given our proximity to the diamond mine, I'd expect the planners to use Hotel Fox as a jumping off point for the attack. I also want to see how our own contingency planning is shaping up. Let's go for a progress report straight after the morning brief please.'

Mr Jones acknowledged the request and hurried off to make sure everyone was prepared, leaving Rob to contemplate what might just be the most significant day of his career.

Less than twenty-five kilometres away, Sarah was waking up to a second day in the storeroom. She was already fully alert, long before the silence was broken by the door key being shovelled clumsily into the lock. She moved to the middle of the room and forced herself into a submissive stance, head down shoulders sagging. A second later, the first guard stepped through the door and with no more than a cursory glance inside, took his place against the wall. Without looking up, Sarah registered his movements through her peripheral vision. The second guard entered with a mess tin and plastic cup. Sarah shuffled forward slowly with her hands outstretched, just like a grateful beggar receiving alms. The guard grinned spitefully at Sarah's apparent subservience and handed them over. She gave the slightest of bows and shuffled backwards, still facing the guards. Without even looking at her, the two guards turned and left the room, laughing openly at the discomfort they thought they had caused.

With the door locked and the charade over, Sarah put down the food and water, and analysed carefully how the handover had gone. Much like yesterday, she concluded. The guards appeared to be completely taken in by her play acting and believed she was no threat at all. In which case, it was time to make her move.

Jelani finished his breakfast and headed back to his room. It was still raining hard. As usual, he had eaten alone and talked to no-one. He hadn't seen any of the other competitors at the Royal Berkshire. It seemed that most were either staying in accommodation at Bisley itself or were in more down-market hotels. That suited Jelani just fine. The last thing he wanted was to socialise with the competition. He felt his phone vibrate and saw it was a text message from the Imperial Meeting coordinators. They had decided to postpone the final shoot for twenty-four hours. Jelani swore aloud. Seeing the disapproving looks from the elderly couple walking towards him down the corridor, he swore again. Louder. He reached his own room and locked himself in.

Fuck, fuck, fuck! This was the worst possible outcome. But Jelani knew what had to be done. His uncle had made it very clear what the priority was. He reached for his day sack and threw in his waterproof jacket, some warm clothing, and the essential supplies he'd gathered during the week. Then he retrieved his gun case from under his bed. Checking he had his passport, he gave a last quick look around the hotel room and walked out.

Jamie Phillips couldn't remember the last time he'd worked so hard. Yesterday he'd pulled an all-nighter with no breaks to be sure today's plan was good to go. The staff officers in the Free State Army Headquarters were all extremely keen and generally hard working too. But their attention to detail was woeful. Time and time again Jamie had to go back over their work and fill in the gaps. He looked up at the large clock above the map table. Twelve fifteen. He knew the Chinooks had all left the carrier and were inbound to the barracks. With nothing immediately to occupy him, Jamie wandered out of the headquarters building. The bright sunlight caught him out again and he reached for his sunglasses. In front of him, the parade square was full of Free State soldiers all weighed down in full battle gear. They snaked away from him in lines of thirty or so. Each line represented one platoon and each platoon was a single Chinook load. All around him, officers and sergeants were shouting last minute orders to their troops. There was tension in the air, even though Jamie knew most of the soldiers had been told almost nothing about the impending operation.

Not the way the British army would have done it, he thought wryly, but he understood the reasons behind the Free State army's alternative approach.

Almost a mile away, Max Kruger was also waiting patiently for the British helicopters to arrive. Alongside him was one of his employees, a former sergeant from the South African Defence Force. Under his command was the mortar crew that had been blooded in the attack on the forward base. They had positioned the same two mortars in pits dug in a sheltered clearing, far away from the nearest road. Stacked alongside was a mountain of ammunition. Kruger would normally have left the oversight of a job like this to his more-than-capable lieutenant, but the man-mountain was busy overseeing preparations at the diamond mine. Kruger nervously checked his watch. He was no stranger to combat, but it had been a while since he'd been this close to the sharp end. After all, he thought to himself, soldiering is a young man's game. In a less obvious show of nerves, he cleared his throat.

'How sure are you of the range?' he asked.

The former sergeant had years of experience and knew exactly what he was doing.

'Don't worry boss,' he said. 'We'll be fine. Even with cold tubes these ladies will throw the first few rounds right onto the parade square. Once they've heated up, we'll walk them straight into the HQ.'

'Good, because I don't want to waste any time pissing around. This has to be a continuous fire mission.'

'Oh, it will be,' confirmed the former sergeant. 'The target is so fucking large we can't miss.' A minute later, they heard the unmistakable thump-thump of the approaching Chinooks.

'Okay,' said Kruger. 'Time to go to work.'

Away to his right, Jamie saw the lead two Chinooks inbound to his location. At the same time, his senses subconsciously picked up an incoming whistle. He'd first heard that sound over ten years ago as a young subaltern in a platoon house in Afghanistan, and he would never forget it. Without thinking, he threw himself onto the ground, a millisecond before the first rounds impacted. What little semblance of order existed among the waiting soldiers disappeared straight away. The crash of the exploding rounds was mixed with the agonising screams of those who'd been caught in the blast, followed immediately by the terrified shouting of those who feared they might be next. Panicked soldiers began running in every direction, but in the ten seconds it took for the next pair of rounds to arrive, none came close to reaching safety. Both rounds ripped right into the middle of a line of helpless soldiers, felling dozens. The screaming rose to an unimaginable level as the slaughter continued. Every one of the next six rounds landed smack in the middle of the parade square, each adding to the carnage. From the cockpit of the lead Chinook, Jim Farmer watched horrified as the destruction unfolded beneath him.

'Abort, abort,' he screamed into the radio. His pilots needed no encouragement. There was no way they could even contemplate landing in that meat grinder. As one, they whirled around and fled for the coast and the safety of the carrier.

Jamie raised his head a few inches above the ground. The rounds were still raining down. It seemed impossible that anyone could have survived the onslaught. But he could still hear the moaning of the wounded on the parade square in front of him. Again, his subconscious sensed danger. The explosions were getting closer.

Jamie had first-hand experience of indirect fire and knew if he didn't get the hell out of there real quick, he was in deep shit. Gritting his teeth, he hauled himself to his feet and ran for his life.

After a lung-busting hundred metres, he knew he had to be out of the kill zone. He threw himself back to the ground, heaving so hard he thought he would puke. Rolling over, he looked back in the direction of the army headquarters. The main entrance had just taken a direct hit. Bits of wood and shattered glass flew everywhere. Three rounds later and the explosions reached the operations room.

It didn't stand a chance.

Out of the corner of his eye, Jamie saw headquarters staff spilling out of the remaining buildings, their panic evident even from this distance. He had no way of telling how many of his colleagues had made it to safety before their building had been hit.

And then it was quiet, save for the low moans that could still be heard from the parade square and the crackle of the flames from the headquarters buildings that were all now alight. The fire was fast taking hold. Palls of smoke also rose from the now pockmarked ground and the stench of charred bodies was already overpowering. Amazingly, the wooden flagpole was still standing. It was blackened and charred, and on it the national flag still hung, as limply as before.

32.

It didn't take long for word of the disaster at Joseph Khalli barracks to spread over the military communication channels. Jim Farmer had relayed the barest details back to the carrier and from there the Joint Force Headquarters sent out a flash update to all UK force elements within Free State and back to Northwood. Fortunately, the bulk of the Royal Engineer company was dispersed across New Devon on infrastructure projects and the training team had been busy working in another part of the barracks. The consequences of the attack were most acutely felt at Hotel Fox where Rob and his command group had just finished reviewing their contingency plans for such an eventuality.

'Well, that moves the goalposts,' said Mr Jones, his voice heavy with understatement. 'I guess the Free State army won't be flying in to save the day anytime soon.'

'Just how many casualties did they take?' asked Pete.

Dan had the update in front of him.

'Still too early for exact figures, but they're estimating well over one hundred dead and many more injured. We've not been able to establish any comms with the Free State Army HQ, so we must assume that's no longer operational either. To my knowledge, they didn't have an alternative set up.'

'So, where does that leave us?' asked Rob, focusing the command group back on their own problems.

'I think we can safely assume the Free State army will be out of the game for the foreseeable future,' offered Dan. 'A tier one military would struggle to absorb what's just happened and crack on with no impact on operations. They've got no chance.'

'I agree,' said Mr Jones. 'Certainly in the timeline we're interested in. They'll be in no state to contribute.'

'Okay, so that narrows down the options,' said Rob grimly.

'Right,' confirmed Dan. 'We're on our own.'

'That puts us back to CDS's courses of action from yesterday,' said Rob. 'We can't influence the first one, and the enemy's vote has taken the second off the table. That leaves us with three, four and five. Effectively, run away, stand and fight, or go on the offensive. Thoughts?'

The question hung in the air for several seconds while everyone considered the options. Then Pete spoke up.

'To be honest boss, none look that appealing. I've never been one to run away, but we do have time to evacuate the site and it's potentially the safest option. Digging in and defending could work. Again, there's time to prepare and we know we'd put up a good fight. But the enemy would be calling the shots – they can attack when and where they choose, and they have an overwhelming advantage in numbers.'

'Dan, how do you think an attack would go down?' asked Rob.

'We know the bulk of the enemy's only had basic training, so they'll have to keep it simple. The obvious plan would be to divide their forces into two. Use one to fix us in place and then roll us up in a flanking attack with the other.' Dan's professional input made sense.

'And do we have the wherewithal to defend against that?' asked Rob.

Dan considered the question carefully.

'That depends. I could split the WMIKs and keep half back to counterattack any flanking move. It might work. But what really worries me are their mortars. They've used them twice now, to good effect. We would be fixed in defensive positions and unable to manoeuvre. They could just pick us off with indirect fire, until we're too weak to defend against a flank attack. That's what I'd do.'

Rob considered what his force protection specialist had just said.

'Okay. What about the other option?'

'What, go and attack the diamond mine?' Pete couldn't believe what he was hearing. 'Do we really think that's a viable option.' Silence descended again as they considered Rob's latest suggestion.

It was Dan who took up the challenge.

'We'd certainly have the element of surprise,' he began. 'Remember, they don't even know we know they're there. According to the intelligence, the attack on JK barracks was a risk mitigator for them – they didn't know the Free State army was preparing an attack on the diamond mine. Also, the SF team still has overwatch on the mine, so we've got nailed-on intelligence regarding numbers and locations. Finally, we know they're planning on moving out early tomorrow to attack us. That means they'll want their fighters to get a good night's kip. If we get our timing right, we could hit them when they're least prepared.'

'There's all the positives,' said Rob. 'What about the negatives?'

'Unfortunately, sir, there's plenty of those too,' said Dan. 'We don't have much time to plan and prepare because we'd have to move out from here straight after dark. Night attacks are notoriously difficult, especially if you've not trained for them – and none of your people have. Finally, numbers would still be against us. The only well-trained troops you have are my two flights of gunners. That's just sixty-four pax. Of the rest of the personnel here, more than half of them would be a liability.'

Mr Jones started to protest.

'Mr Jones, I mean no offence, but we've all been working together for a while now, and my training section has a really good sense of who's weapon handling skills are competent and who's are not. Many of your people are very proficient, we saw that when we did the additional training for the convoy teams. But others are not. I've spoken to my team at length, and we think the maximum size force we could deploy, including my gunners, is no more than one hundred.'

Rob didn't question Dan's judgement.

'Then what you're saying is we could muster an assault force of approximately one hundred to take on an unsuspecting opposition north of one thousand. That doesn't sound like good odds to me,' he admitted.

'No, they're not,' agreed Dan. 'The one thing that would level the playing field is close air support. Just a couple of F-35s would make all the difference. My flight sergeant is a qualified forward air controller and we've got all the ground-to-air comms fitted in my command vehicle. We'd be a bit rusty, but we'd certainly be able to call them in.'

But before they could get too enthusiastic, Mr Jones brought them all back down to earth.

'Let's not forget that the general was expressly forbidden from launching an air strike by the PM yesterday,' he warned.

'Leave that to me,' said Rob. 'Dan, work with Mr Jones to identify who you can use for your assault force. I want a simple plan. Something that we've got a reasonable chance of executing successfully when it's dark and the adrenaline is flowing. Pete, I'm sorry, but you're staying here. I need someone I can trust because if our plan doesn't work, Hotel Fox will still be a target. If that happens, it's down to you to get everyone safely back to New Devon. Right let's get cracking. There's a shed-load to do and very little time.'

As they started to break up, the ops controller came into the briefing tent.

'Sir, your sister's on the Brent for you.'

Rob hurried across to the ops room and picked up the phone.

'Hi Becca,' he greeted his sister a little abruptly. 'We need to make this quick, it's a bit busy here right now.'

'No, I know,' replied Rebecca. 'I've just heard about the attack on the barracks. The latest update confirmed over one hundred Free State soldiers have been killed. What does that mean for you?'

'It means that there'll be no one to stop the bad guys attacking here tomorrow morning,' said Rob. 'Unless we do.'

'That's your plan?' Rebecca asked disbelievingly. 'I was on the PM's VTC yesterday and he point blank ordered Admiral Bellis not to.'

'I know,' said Rob. 'I was dialled in too. He also refused to sanction a withdrawal from here, but I'm planning that as well.' Rob briefly outlined the conclusions his command group had just reached.

'Rob, you need to be careful. This is getting really serious now.'

'You're telling me. What's more, I can't believe Nkaba's behind all this. I mean, why does he need to start an insurgency in his own country?'

Rebecca realised that Rob still only knew half the story.

'Nkaba is behind all this, but it's got nothing to do with overthrowing President Kirrundi,' she explained. 'We think it's all about taking revenge on Anthony Brownlow.'

'What?'

'I know, it sounds impossible, but that's the most likely explanation. You must keep that to yourself. The chief didn't even brief the PM about the whole revenge thing yesterday. She doesn't think he would be able to act objectively if he knew. Brownlow humiliated Nkaba years ago at a student debate in Oxford and we think this is his payback. He hates Brownlow and plans to assassinate him at the same time as the attack on you tomorrow.'

'How can he assassinate Brownlow?' Rob asked, still struggling to take in all that his sister was telling him. 'Is Nkaba in England?'

'No, he's sent somebody else,' said Rebecca. 'It must be someone he really trusts, but we're still trying to work out who that could be.'

Rob went quiet for a second. Then it suddenly dawned on him.

'Achebe,' he said simply.

'What?'

'Achebe, his nephew. We know he hates us. And he disappeared the day after Sarah went missing. I knew he had something to do with that, the little shit.' Rebecca seldom heard her brother swear, but her mind was already racing.

'Wait a minute, I've seen that name somewhere.' She rummaged urgently through the mountain of paper on her desk. 'Here it is.' In her hand was a list of Free State nationals who had entered the UK in the last two weeks. Noah had shown her the computer print-out not more than an hour ago. Quickly she scanned down it. 'Achebe, J S. Came through Heathrow last Thursday. Hang on Rob,' she said.

'Noah.'

The young analyst responded immediately.

'Can you check to see if this Achebe character is still in the country?' As he went to take the list from her, something caught Rebecca's eye and she held onto her end, surprising Noah and ripping the paper almost in two. Ignoring his apologies, she pointed to the line entry for Achebe. 'What does "F-slash-C" mean in the comments column?'

'Er, "firearms carriage", I think,' said Noah. 'Let me call up the home office database.'

'Rob are you still there?' asked Rebecca down the secure phone. 'Good, bear with us, we're onto something here, I'm sure of it.'

Noah came straight back clutching his iPad.

'It is firearms carriage,' he confirmed. 'And if you tap here, it should take you to … there.' A new window opened on the screen displaying a PDF of Achebe's firearms carriage application form. 'It says here he temporarily imported an Anschütz Match 54.30 Precise Stock Target Rifle.'

'Why would he have been allowed to do that?' asked Rebecca.

Noah scrolled down further.

'It would appear he's competing in the Imperial Meeting,' he said. 'Whatever that is?'

'Becca,' Rob shouted down the phone. He had heard every word of their conversation. 'It's Bisley,' he shouted again.

'Achebe's shooting at Bisley. The Imperial Meeting is the marquee event. It's the final competition of the whole shoot and the winner is awarded the Queen's Prize.'

'When does the Imperial Meeting take place?' asked Rebecca. Noah jumped quickly from the home office database to a web browser.

'It looks like it's been going on this week,' he said. 'And the final shoot is today.'

We've got him! Rebeca thought.

'Rob, you're brilliant. We've got a name and we've got a location.'

'That's great,' said Rob. 'Best you get on and finish the job and I'll do my best at this end.' Rebecca put down the secure phone to Rob and immediately reached for the other one on her desk, which was languishing underneath Noah's laptop. Dialling from memory, she got straight through to the head of Scotland Yard's counter terrorism command.

Back at Hotel Fox, Rob was sat alone in the corner of the ops room. He knew that Dan and Mr Jones were busy working on the diamond mine assault and Pete was all over the withdrawal plan. He had a far harder job to do. Steeling himself, he reached for the Brent phone and called up General Wilkinson. After a short chat with the chief of staff, the general came on the line.

'You've heard the news from JK barracks, I take it,' he began, getting straight to the point as usual. Rob confirmed that he had. 'We've spent the last couple of hours trying to get some high-level direction from Northwood,' continued the general. 'So far, nothing.'

Rob was exasperated.

'General, they do understand the situation down here, don't they?'

'Yes Rob, they do. But this is strategically difficult. The PM gave very clear direction yesterday and no one in the chain of command is willing to go against that.'

'Just so I've got it straight then, sir. The prime minister has ruled out attacking the insurgents and he won't let us withdraw. That only leaves the do-nothing option, which is sit here and wait for the attack.'

'I know how it seems,' said the general. 'But we will get further direction shortly.'

'With respect sir. I don't have time to wait for "shortly". We've done our estimate down here and there is no way we can defend this site against what we know is coming. Do nothing is going to get us all killed.' Rob deliberately didn't continue, forcing the general to respond.

'What are you suggesting?' he asked finally.

'We're working up an assault plan on the diamond mine, in conjunction with Terry Willis and his team. We believe an attack at midnight tonight is our best option.'

'You know I don't have the authority to sanction that,' said the general.

'I know sir. And I also know that you don't have the authority to provide close air support, which we really need to have any chance of success.' The silence was painful.

'Look Rob, I can't stop you from planning what you're planning, but I am giving you a direct order. Remain at your location until we receive higher direction. Please acknowledge.'

At that moment, Rob truly understood what people meant when they talked about the loneliness of command.

'I acknowledge your order, general,' he replied quietly.

33.

Rebecca was still in her office as the clock on her wall clicked past seven. Since her call to Scotland Yard, she had not done much, except stand and watch the rain that continued to run down her windowpane. It had not let up all day. She couldn't help but feel a little deflated. After all the pressure of tracking down Nkaba and then identifying his nephew, doing nothing was difficult. It felt like days since she'd been out of the building. She'd exhausted the small stash of emergency clothes in her locker and desperately needed a long soak in the bath. She should go home but was waiting for a return call confirming that the police had Achebe in custody. The counter terrorism commander had promised. With nothing to focus on, her thoughts turned to Rob. She could only imagine the difficulties he was facing, literally life and death for those under his command.

The ringing of her landline broke Rebecca's train of thought. The digital display confirmed it was the call she was expecting. Unfortunately, the news was not what she wanted to hear.

'Because of the heavy rain, the final day's shoot at Bisley was postponed until tomorrow,' the police commander explained. 'But when we got there, there was no sign of Achebe. We raided his hotel room, but he was long gone. No sign of his rifle either. His phone is switched off so we can't track him that way, but we did get the details of his hire car from the valet service. Every police car from here to Birmingham is on the lookout for it. He won't get far. Especially seeing as we know where he's heading.'

Rebecca thanked the commander and hung up. It was finally time to go home and leave it to the police. That bottle of Cabernet Sauvignon was calling, but at the back of her mind, something nagged at her. Something she was missing. She didn't doubt that the net was closing fast around Achebe, but a sixth sense was telling her it wasn't closing fast enough.

Except for half a dozen gunners who continued to guard the main entrance to the site, Mr Jones had mustered every man and woman under Rob's command in the field kitchen. Most knew that something was up, but Rob still took the time to explain exactly what the situation was and his chosen course of action. Since his call with General Wilkinson, Rob had gone over and over the options in his mind. The general's intent was clear – the direct order was testament to that. But, Rob knew, that didn't make it the right thing to do. When he closed his eyes, he was straight back on that cold, forbidding mountainside in the Brecon Beacons, all those years ago. Then his gut had told him his orders were wrong, but he'd followed them and had been tormented by the outcome ever since. Now his gut was telling him again his orders were wrong, and this time two hundred lives were at stake. Lives he was directly responsible for. This time, he would follow his gut.

Rob finished the briefing and patiently answered the long list of questions that followed. He was asking a lot from his people, and they needed the confidence he'd made the right call. With the last question finally dealt with, Mr Jones stepped forward and dismissed everyone. There was just time for last minute checks of personal equipment before moving out.

Darkness fell quickly in Free State. No real time that you could really call dusk. Without her watch, Sarah could only guess the time. But it had to be between seven and eight. The light was disappearing from her prison's windows, and it was beginning to grow decidedly cooler. Sarah had spent the whole day stepping through the escape plan in her head, but the truth was she could only really be sure of the first part of it. Even if she successfully managed to deal with the two guards, everything beyond the storeroom door would be reactionary. It was hard not to admit being scared – fear of the unknown was a powerful thing. But she'd done it before, and she could do it again. Besides, Sarah knew that if she didn't make a move soon, her chance would be gone.

The familiar scraping of the key in the lock announced it was dinner time. Sarah stepped forward into the middle of the room as usual, only this time her heart was pumping wildly, and her hands were shaking. She forced herself to calm down as much as she could and adopt a subservient stance.

Even with her head down, she could see the first guard's routine hadn't changed. Leaning against the wall, weapon still slung lazily over his shoulder. The second guard entered, hands full with the mess tin and mug. Sarah took a deep breath and made her move.

A single stride replaced the shuffling steps the guard was expecting. Before he could react, she brought her knee up into his groin with all the force she could muster. The guard groaned sickeningly. He dropped the food and sank to the floor. Quick as a flash, Sarah advanced on the second guard who was struggling to unsling his rifle.

Too slow.

She extended her arm and with an open palm, struck him explosively on the nose. The power from her forward momentum was rewarded with a shattering of bone and the guard's head snapped back. Without hesitating, Sarah followed up the first blow with a sharp elbow, to the side of his head. The guard crumpled, dropping his rifle. In a flash, Sarah picked it up and delivered a mighty crack to the back of his head with the butt. He fell unconscious.

Sarah spun around. Her first victim was desperately clutching his groin while trying to get to his knees. He managed it, but as he looked up, he realised all he had done was present the perfect target. Like the leadoff hitter in a major league baseball team, Sarah's swing was true. The rifle butt connected heavily with the guard's temple, and he hit the ground with a thud.

Sarah stood for a second as the adrenalin coursed through her. She forced herself to breath slowly and control her heart rate. Stay focused, she admonished. This is just the first step.

Her next actions had been well thought through. She quickly removed the key from the outside lock and shut the door. Then she took the heavy combat knife from the belt of the first guard and began slicing away strips of his shirt. She bound both guards' hands and feet as tightly as she could and used the last two strips as gags. Satisfied that they were going nowhere, she quickly patted them down. Apart from an AK-47 magazine apiece, the search yielded nothing. She checked over both weapons and selected the less rusty one. Tossing the other one away, she scooped up the spare magazines and jammed them into the pocket of her combat trousers. With a deep breath, Sarah pulled open the door a few inches and peered outside. By now, the sun had set completely and there were few lights to be seen. She slipped out of the storeroom and locked the door behind her. Crouched low, she waited for her eyes to adjust to the darkness and considered her next move.

The assault force from Hotel Fox numbered exactly one hundred and two men and women. Spread between a dozen land rovers and two four-ton trucks, they moved out in two separate groups. It was dark and the air was heavy. They covered the distance between Hotel Fox and the diamond mine slowly and carefully. The SAS team had not reported seeing any enemy patrols, but nobody was taking any chances. The vehicles halted on an old dirt track that looped around the back of the hill where Captain Willis had established his observation post. They were still almost a kilometre away from the mine and completely out of sight. Rob and Dan doubled forward to where the SAS team were hidden. Rob checked his watch. Not yet nine o'clock. They slid into the hide, ignoring the disagreeable odour of the four troopers who had now been in the field for over a week. In hushed tones, Terry brought them up to speed with the comings and goings in the camp below.

The update did not include any information on Sarah's escape for the simple reason his team hadn't witnessed it. The small storeroom that had been her prison was completely hidden from their view by the large storage sheds. The dark shadow thrown off by the nearest shed was now providing Sarah some much needed cover. Twice she had gone to move and twice she had been forced to shrink back at the last second as fighters came into view. She held the AK-47 tightly, feeling a reassurance in the weight of the weapon. She knew that opening fire was a last resort as the noise would immediately betray her position. But if she had to, she would.

Time passed slowly, but eventually the numbers wandering around the site reduced to a trickle. She estimated it must be almost an hour since she had escaped the storeroom. How much longer would it be before her guards were missed? She readied herself again. This time there were no last-minute distractions. Crouching low, she broke cover and scurried across the open ground in front of her before flinging herself down next to a dark, single-storey building. There were no lights coming from any of its windows and Sarah hoped it was unoccupied. Cautiously she peered around the edge of the building. Parked in front of her were two G-Wagons. She recognised the dented tailgate of the nearer one.

A quick look right and left confirmed the coast was clear. She ran forward and tried the handle of the cargo door. It was unlocked and she clambered inside. Her spirits soared. In the far corner was her webbing vest and she could clearly see the personal locator beacon still clipped to the side pouch. She reached over and switched it on. The small screen immediately came to life, the low green glow casting a lurid shadow in the back of the vehicle. Sarah knew it would take the device a few minutes to hunt down the GPS satellites high above her. In the meantime, she had a decision to make. Should she leave the beacon where it was or take it with her? If she was re-captured with the beacon on her, they would know the diamond mine was compromised. Safely hidden away in the back of the G-Wagon, no-one would be any the wiser. She quickly keyed in her six-figure identification code and left the beacon where it was. As quietly as she could, she climbed back out of the G-Wagon. Still silent, she backed away around the side of the second vehicle.

Straight into the arms of the man-mountain.

Before she realised what was happening, he had grabbed her arm and ripped the AK-47 from her grasp.

'What have we got here?' he asked. Sarah struggled, but she was no match for him. He frisked her quickly, threw away the two magazines and tucked the knife in his belt. He also found the storeroom key. He spun her around and pushed her back towards captivity. Out of the shadows, a figure loomed up before them. Almost as tall as the man-mountain, she did not recognise the bulky shape of Simon Nkaba. But he knew exactly who she was.

'What's she doing out here?' he questioned angrily.

'Looks like she was just out for a late evening walk,' answered the man-mountain glibly. 'But don't you worry. She'll be back behind bars soon enough.' They reached the storeroom, and he unlocked the door.

'In.'

The two guards were both still trussed up but conscious. Using the knife he'd taken from Sarah, the man mountain cut them free. They shrank away from him terrified.

'Out.'

They ran for the door but before they could leave, Nkaba grabbed one by the scruff of his neck.

'Get a bucket of water,' he ordered. Turning to Sarah, he continued, 'Clean yourself up. You stink. I'll be back later.' The man-mountain retrieved the second AK-47 from the corner of the room.

'You won't be needing this,' he said to Sarah with a grim smile. He walked out, slamming the door behind him, and leaving Sarah feeling very much alone.

Rob checked his watch again, telling himself it wasn't a nervous reaction. There was plenty of time before they needed to get into position. Next to him in the hide Terry and Dan were still kicking around options for the forthcoming assault. Tempted as he was to join in, Rob reminded himself he was a logistics officer. He was competent enough at basic soldiering but what was being discussed was a level above him. He stayed silent, trusting the professionals to do their job.

Then from the back of the hide, he heard two quiet but urgent beeps. After a couple of seconds, he heard them again. Rob looked closer. The noise was coming from an olive-green container, about the size of a shoebox. It looked like some sort of communications device. On its front was a luminous screen, maybe twenty centimetres wide. Next to it was a small keypad and a short, stubby aerial. Something had remotely caused the device to fire up.

'What's that?' asked Rob as the screen filled with a tiny-scale map of the world.

Staff Sergeant Hayes crawled across the hide and picked it up.

'It's our personal locator beacon base set,' he said. 'Someone must have just activated their beacon.' Rob watched fascinated at the map reset to a larger scale and reset again. On the third iteration, the west of Africa was clearly visible, from Morocco in the north to Liberia in the south. Somewhere in the middle of the map, a blue dot was flashing. The map reset again.

'Is that the same system the JFHQ uses?' asked Rob, hardly daring to believe it could be.

'Of course,' confirmed Hayes. 'The army's only got one system.'

'Can you tell whose beacon it is?'

'Everyone registered on the system has their own, unique identifier,' Hayes explained. 'If they enter that into their PLB, we can tell who it is. If not, we just know the beacon's been activated.' Rob looked back down at the base set. The map continued to expand and there was now a second black dot just to the left of the first.

'That's us,' said Hayes before Rob had time to ask. 'And it's at maximum scale now, so the PLB is ... less than one click away.' At that moment, the base set beeped again. A small window appeared in the centre of the screen, displaying the numbers: two-six-four-seven-five-five. Hayes reached for a ruggedized iPad and started tapping.

'Two-six-four-seven-five-five is Major Grey,' he confirmed. Rob almost leapt in the air. Terry and Dan had stopped their conversation and were listening in intently.

'Jay, are we saying that Major Grey's PLB is definitely down there in the diamond mine?' asked Terry.

'Absolutely boss,' he confirmed. 'One hundred per cent certain.'

'We've got to call it in,' Terry said. 'Right away.'

'Hold on a second,' said Rob. 'Let's think this through a minute. Don't forget we're here against the express orders of General Wilkinson. He still thinks we're hunkered down at Hotel Fox awaiting direction from Northwood.'

'Oh, shit. You're right,' said Terry.

Just then the secure high frequency radio squawked into life.

'Blade zero-three, this is Weybourn one-one, message over.' Clearly someone in the Joint Force Headquarters had also been monitoring a PLB base set. Terry killed the speaker and reached for his headphones. Rob could no longer hear what was being received, but it was clear the exchange was somewhat one sided. After a couple of minutes, Terry peeled off the headphones and handed them to Rob.

'It's Weybourn six-actual,' he said. The general's personal call sign.

'Weybourn six-actual, this is Hotel Fox six-actual, receiving over.' Rob identified himself with his own personal call sign.

'Hotel Fox six-actual, just what the hell are you doing at Blade zero-three's location, over?'

The general's mix of formal communication language and cursing caught Rob off guard. What else could he say?

'Weybourn six-actual, I'm pursuing course of action three, over.' It was the general's turn to be caught off guard. The silence lasted for so long that Rob thought the communications link had dropped out. Eventually, he heard.

'Roger, Hotel Fox six-actual. How do you intend to accommodate the new information regarding the PLB, over?' Rob could not believe what he was hearing. He'd expected the general to give him the almightiest bollocking and order him to stand down immediately. Instead, he wanted to know how he was going to help Sarah.

'Weybourn six-actual, we're working up a plan now, over.'

Again, the pause seemed never ending.

'Roger, Hotel Fox six-actual. Can we help, over?' It appeared the general was all in.

'Weybourn six-actual, our likelihood of success increases greatly with the provision of close air support, over.'

What the heck, thought Rob. Don't ask, don't get.

'Hotel Fox six-actual, acknowledge … but can't promise that. Good luck. Weybourn six-actual out.'

34.

Rob pulled off the headset and turned to face the others. He was still struggling to process what he'd just heard from General Wilkinson.

'It would appear we have the tacit approval from the commander to proceed,' he said. Dan and Terry looked at one another. They couldn't believe what Rob had just said.

'What about close air support?' asked Dan.

'Well, he didn't commit to that,' Rob confessed. 'Plan for the worst and hope for the best.'

'Okay, I guess that's better than a flat no,' said Dan. 'What are we doing about Major Grey?'

'That's an easy one,' said Rob. 'I'm going down there right now to get her out before you launch the attack.'

'What?' exclaimed Dan. 'You can't do that.'

'Why not?'

'Because you're the CO,' said Dan. 'You need to lead the attack.'

'No, Dan. You need to lead it. You're the RAF Regiment officer. You're much more qualified than me.'

'That's crap sir and you know it.' replied Dan. 'You've brought us this far. We need you to see it through.'

Rob was secretly grateful for Dan's passionate argument, but held his ground.

'Seriously Dan. You've got this. Right now, Major Grey needs me more. I can't ask anyone else to go down there and bring her out. You know how it works.'

Dan and Terry looked at one another again. This time resigned. They could see Rob had made up his mind.

'Okay boss,' said Terry. 'Best we take a couple of minutes to plan how this works.'

Staff Sergeant Hayes stuffed a spare radio into an empty pouch on Rob's webbing vest and hooked him up to the throat mike and earpiece.

'We're on channel two,' he confirmed. 'It's all set.'

'Thanks staff,' said Rob. A quick radio check confirmed all was in working order.

'Right,' said Terry. 'We'll follow your approach through night vison goggles and give you a shout if you're heading into danger. The PLB is still transmitting, but we've not been able to locate Major Grey. I can only assume she's being held somewhere out of our line of sight. I'd start behind those storage sheds if I were you.'

Rob nodded. Terry's suggestion made sense. He looked down at the diamond mine. This far away, it was difficult to make out much detail with the naked eye, but as far as he could tell, all was quiet. He checked his watch. 2315 hours. Time to go.

He turned to Dan.

'Start the assault at midnight as planned. Regardless,' he commanded. 'If I haven't found Major Grey by then, the confusion you generate should make it easier for me to stay undetected.'

'That's true,' said Dan. 'But it'll make it a bloody-sight more dangerous for you too.'

'Possibly,' conceded Rob. 'But that's for me to worry about. Good luck.' With that, he slipped out of the hide and began his way down the slope towards the mine.

Sarah was mad at herself. Having done the hard work to escape, she'd screwed it all up by running straight into the man-mountain. Her only consolation was that at least she'd managed to activate her personal locater beacon before being recaptured. She'd expected a hard time from the mercenary, but he seemed content just to throw her back into the storeroom. Perhaps he had something more pressing on his mind.

Sarah definitely had something more pressing on her mind. The man who had threatened her had to be Simon Nkaba. And given the deference the mercenary had shown him, he also had to be running the show. That was not good. The guard without the broken face returned with a bucket of cold water and a rag. He hurled a torrent of abuse at her as he dumped it in the middle of the room, but was careful to keep his distance. Two other guards accompanied him, both of whom kept their weapons firmly pointed in her direction the whole time. Sarah noticed with some satisfaction that the guard was hobbling badly and clearly still in considerable pain.

Sarah ignored the bucket. It was only a day since she'd been relaxing in Monifa's bathtub. Her clothes might stink but she didn't. But that wasn't going to help her. Sooner or later Nkaba would be back, and he'd made his intentions extremely clear. Sarah estimated he must be a good seven or eight inches taller than her with a weight advantage of well over one hundred pounds. But she wasn't going down without a fight. Of that she was damn sure.

The stresses of the evening had taken their toll and Sarah found herself dozing. She was brought to her senses by the key scraping in the lock, then the door crashed open. The first thing Sarah saw was a fierce light coming from the large lamp that was advancing steadily into the storeroom. It was dazzling after the darkness and Sarah could see nothing beyond it. She got up cautiously. The door was kicked shut. As the light reached out to all corners of the storeroom, Sarah recognised the huge bulk of Simon Nkaba standing menacingly in front of her. Unhurriedly he placed the lamp on the floor beside him.

'So, you're the little bitch Jelani had to deal with.' It was a statement rather than a question. Nkaba's stare was piercing and full of hate. Sarah said nothing. Just stared right back.

'I think we'll start with you on your knees, bitch.' Nkaba's voice rose to a shout. 'I said on your knees.'

Sarah kept the same defiant stare and didn't move. She could practically see the anger rising in Nkaba. The clenched fists. The jutting jaw. The blazing eyes.

Nkaba took half a pace forward.

It was just what Sarah was waiting for. Quick as she could, she took a step forward of her own and feinted a left-handed punch upwards towards Nkaba's jaw. He instinctively swayed to his side, loading all his weight on his left leg. In response, she kicked out with her right boot as hard as she could, catching Nkaba squarely on his left kneecap. His leg buckled but he stayed upright.

'Aargh,' he roared. 'You'll pay for that.'

Faster than Sarah thought possible, he flung out a wild haymaker that connected solidly with the side of her head and sent her spinning to the floor. She cried out. But rather than follow it up straight away, Nkaba paused and reached down to massage his damaged knee.

He had all the time in the world.

The lights flashing in front of Sarah's eyes refused to subside, but she bloody-mindedly dragged herself back to her feet. Still unsteady, she limped forward again. Nkaba stepped towards her. Sarah tried another left-hand feint and was rewarded with the same response. Hardly able to believe he could be that stupid, she lashed out with her right boot again. Nkaba screamed in pain, and this time his knee collapsed under him. Seizing her chance, Sarah ran for the door, but Nkaba was too quick. He reached up as she passed and grabbed her ankle. She fell heavily to the floor. They both scrambled to their feet, but Nkaba was marginally quicker. He gripped her by the shoulder and flung her powerfully across the room. Sarah hit the far wall like a rag doll and collapsed. This time no amount of determination was going to get her back on her feet. Seeing the fight was over, Nkaba lumbered slowly towards her.

It had taken Rob half an hour to cover the distance from the observation post to the edge of the diamond mine. Moving carefully from one piece of cover to the next, he'd followed Terry's direction from above. He paused behind a low rocky outcrop to catch his breath.

'Boss, suggest you loop left around the perimeter,' directed Terry over the radio. 'It looks pretty quiet, but I'd still recommend the long way in.' Rob looked around him. Off to his left were the four large storage sheds, stretching away into the distance. Lined up like guardsmen on parade, they looked dark and menacing. Staff Sergeant Hayes estimated there were at least a couple of hundred fighters currently holed up in each one.

Hopefully all fast-asleep, dreaming about tomorrow's battle, Rob thought.

Terry's suggested route would take him behind the storage sheds out of view from the observation post where they all assumed Sarah was being held. The blind spot was minimal, so her prison could only be some kind of tiny outbuilding or storage facility.

'Roger,' confirmed Rob. 'Moving now.' Keeping low, he began working his way around the very edge of the site, pausing every thirty seconds to listen for any danger. Soon he disappeared behind the first shed. Terry's running commentary in his ear was reassuring and kept Rob moving at a fair pace. But it still took him a good five minutes to get to a point parallel with the end of the furthest shed.

'Right boss, your next move is out of cover and over to the far corner of the last shed. From about halfway, we'll lose visual on you, so keep talking. Note the time is 2350 hours exactly. Squadron Leader Dan reports his troops are all in place and he'll begin his attack in one-zero minutes, over.'

'Roger,' said Rob again. He paused for a second forcing himself to breathe deeply. This was not where he had expected to be on day forty-four in the big brother house. He squeezed his eyes tightly shut, summoning up every ounce of courage he had. He really hoped in a few hours he'd still be around for Mr Jones to welcome him to day forty-five. Giving a last glance round, he forced himself forward into the open towards the storage shed.

Back on the hill above the mine, Dan was standing in the back of his command land rover, looking around nervously. Aligned to his left and right were six of his eight WMIKs, with weapons pointing down into a kill zone he was planning to drive the enemy into. Hastily dug in on both flanks was the rest of his small force. The weight of their firepower would have little affect down in the diamond mine. Instead, they would guard against a possible counterattack. Waiting back at the observation post were the two remaining WMIKs and a dozen of his best gunners. They were his reserve, ready to be flung into the fray whenever and wherever they could be decisive. Worried that he had missed something, but sure that he hadn't, all Dan could do now was watch the second hand of his watch countdown to midnight.

Rob kept to the shadows and rounded the edge of the last storage shed. He gazed across at the blind spot behind it. Sure enough, there were two identical storerooms, standing side by side. They were small, no more than ten metres square. But the walls looked sturdy, even from fifty metres away. He could see a single window set high in the side wall of each. Looked like bars across them. Then he saw someone walking towards the storerooms, carrying a lamp. They stopped at the first door. Even with the lamplight, it was impossible to see who it was. Rob watched as the door was flung wide open and the person stepped inside. The space outside was plunged back into darkness as the door was kicked shut.

Rob was in a dilemma. Was Sarah in that storeroom? If not, going in could be a big mistake. For all Rob knew the room could be full of fighters, and that wouldn't end well. Alerting the whole camp only minutes before Dan was due to start the assault was a bad idea. But if Sarah was being held there, what business could that person have? It didn't take long to work out that whatever it was, it couldn't be good.

Then Rob heard a woman's scream. It was clearly a scream of pain. No need to think any more. He checked the safety on his assault rifle was clicked off and quickly worked a round into the chamber. Then he heard another shout of pain. This time a man's voice. Adrenalin pumping, he sprinted towards the storeroom. Without pausing, he aimed his boot at the door and kicked it open.

The lamp was lying on its side in the middle of the room. The huge shadows it threw were dark and disorienting. But that didn't stop Rob recognising the crumpled figure on the floor by the far wall. It was Sarah. The only other person in the room was standing over her, loosening his belt. Rob acted automatically. Not pausing to shout a warning, he raised his rifle and fired. Once, twice, three times into the back of Sarah's assailant. Nkaba pitched forward and fell to the ground. Rob rushed up and kicked him to one side. Nkaba rolled onto his back, groaned, and died.

Ignoring him completely, Rob knelt down beside Sarah. He reached out and touched her face gently.

'Hey there,' he whispered. 'Are you okay?'

Sarah opened her eyes slowly, the pain clearly visible. She blinked a couple of times before recognising Rob.

'Cut that a bit fine, didn't you?' she croaked.

35.

The Final Day

'Boss, are you good?' the voice in Rob's ear was insistent. 'Are you good?'

'We're good,' responded Rob. 'Shots fired were mine. And jackpot, I say again, jackpot.'

Jackpot was the codeword to confirm Sarah had been rescued.

Terry turned to his staff sergeant punching the air.

'He's got her.'

'Yeah, but it looks like he's woken up the whole place in the process,' said Hayes drily. He pointed down to the mine where they could see definite signs of movement.

Terry keyed his radio mike again.

'Boss, looks like your efforts have been noticed. We now have multiple tangos up and about near your location.'

Bugger, Rob thought to himself. A single random gunshot may well have been ignored as a negligent discharge from a bored guard. Three in quick succession sent an altogether different message. He checked his watch. Still five minutes before the assault was due to begin.

'Roger. Find gunner six-actual and request he launches the assault immediately.' Rob knew that the next few minutes would be vital. If whoever was in charge at the mine had time to take control and bring their overwhelming numbers to bear, it could spell disaster for the assault. Judging by the swiftness of Terry's acknowledgement, he knew it too.

Rob turned his attention back to Sarah. She had managed to sit up but was still looking extremely groggy. He ripped the water bottle from his webbing vest and handed it over. Sarah drank deeply. Rob followed up that success by producing a chocolate bar that Sarah snatched from his hand hungrily.

'So is the cavalry on its way, or is it just you?' Sarah manged to ask through grateful mouthfuls.

'A bit of both,' answered Rob. He quickly brought Sarah up to speed on the events of the last week. Before he could finish, his voice was drowned out by the sound of half a dozen machine guns opening up. The assault had started. Even inside the storeroom, it got their attention. The gunners were firing in short, disciplined bursts, as they were trained to do. The overlapping chatter of the heavy weapons was unrelenting. Wave after wave creating a continuous wall of sound, as magnificent as it was deadly.

Rob ran over to the storeroom door and nudged it open a few inches. The ammunition belts were loaded four-to-one with tracer rounds that lit up in spectacular shades of green as they sped towards their target. Dan had spread out his vehicles far enough along the hillside to achieve a defilading effect across the front of all four storage sheds and that was where all his gunners were concentrating their fire. From above, the effect was mesmerising, and it must have seemed impossible that anyone could survive such an onslaught.

Tucked outside the immediate line of fire, Rob's vantage point looked like a safe place to be. From it, he could see the maelstrom of tracer rounds spitting up from the hard-packed earth in front of the storage sheds and spinning away crazily in all directions. One pinged off the door frame only inches from his head. Maybe not such a safe place, after all. Opposite him in the lee of the nearest shed, a growing number of fighters were sheltering from the certain death on offer beyond. Fortunately, they were all too busy concentrating on their own survival to be looking his way. Not wanting to change that, Rob carefully reached out and removed the key that Nkaba had left in the lock. He then quietly shut the door and secured it from the inside. Smiling at Sarah, he said:

'How about we just stay here for a bit and let the cavalry do their thing?'

Dan stood in the back of his command vehicle and surveyed the scene below him with growing anxiety. To the untrained eye, everything looked fine. There was very little movement in front of the storage sheds and the enemy appeared to be pinned down. But Dan knew better. He had gambled that the weight of fire from his patrol vehicles would leave the poorly trained fighters frightened and disoriented and they would be drawn into the kill zone. But that hadn't happened. The couple of minutes reaction time from Rob's shots had been used by someone down there to do the opposite. Instead of streaming out towards the open ground in front of the storage sheds and into his ambush, most of the enemy fighters had been diverted out of the buildings through other exits well away from the kill zone. Although he couldn't see them, Dan was sure they were preparing for a counterattack on his position, almost certainly against both flanks. And that spelled danger. Even though he had chosen his ground well, Dan knew that an attacking force with the numerical advantage he was facing would eventually overwhelm even the best prepared defensive position. Terry appeared at his side, and it was obvious that he had reached the same conclusion.

'Not looking good,' Terry said grimly.

'No,' agreed Dan, 'It's not.' Both men knew the correct tactical decision was to withdraw now, before it was too late. But that would then leave the enemy force intact and free to carry out its attack on a completely undefended Hotel Fox. No, they knew that their job was to stand and fight. To force the enemy to commit its entire force to defeat them, and to inflict as many casualties as they possibly could, in order to leave it too weak to mount a second attack on the forward base. If necessary, they had to go down fighting.

'There!' shouted Terry. He pointed down to the mine where a large group of enemy fighters could be seen running from behind the storage sheds and into the undergrowth. They were quickly out of sight. It was obvious they planned to loop the long way around behind the mine and then advance on the right flank of the British position. A second group followed soon after, but this time the gunners were ready. Withering fire rained down and as many as half were cut down before reaching the cover of the surrounding savanna. At the same time, more fighters broke cover, heading in the opposite direction. Another group followed shortly after. The gunners' fire chased them into the undergrowth, but most made it safely away. Seconds later, Dan heard a cry of pain from the nearest patrol vehicle as one of his men went down injured. In addition to advancing on both of his flanks, the enemy had also started to lay down a strengthening counter-fire to his front. Dan ducked down instinctively. He knew they were in real trouble now.

From the relative quiet of the storeroom, Rob and Sarah sat frustrated as the battle developed around them. They couldn't see but could hear as the growing band of fighters were pulled together from the shelter of the storage shed and sent on their way to outflank the British position. Rob knew he had to leave Dan to control the fight, but he couldn't just sit there and do nothing. He radioed Terry for an update.

'Not good, boss. Not good at all,' was the disturbing feedback. 'We're taking casualties from strong counter-fire coming from the mine and we're about to be outflanked.' Rob listened. He could hear the outgoing small-arms fire that confirmed Terry's assessment.

'What is gunner six-actual's intent?' he asked.

'He's deployed the reserve and we're consolidating our position to meet the flanking attacks. After that, we've no more cards to play,' Terry added unnecessarily. Rob needed to respond but he genuinely didn't know what to say. No stirring words from him were going to make a difference now.

Terry listened as the static from the radio crackled in his ear. He also knew there was nothing Rob could say that would make a difference. They'd done everything they could. It was time to fight for their lives.

At that moment, the ground to air radio in Dan's land rover burst into life.

'Gunner zero-one, this is buster zero-one. Two-ship inbound your location from the west providing show of force, over.' Dan's flight sergeant, and acting forward air controller, grabbed the mike instinctively.

'Roger, buster zero-one. Be advised that following show of force we have urgent kinetic tasking for you. Multiple tangos advancing on both the north and south of my location. Target coordinates to follow. We will outline fox-lima-oscar tango with green, repeat green markers, over.'

'Roger, gunner zero-one. Ack green markers. Standing by for uplift of target coordinates.'

Dan reached for the tactical radio. 'All callsigns, this is gunner six-actual. Deploy green glowsticks, I say again, deploy green glowsticks.' As one, each soldier dug in at the forward edge of the British position reached for a green glowstick, cracked it open and hurled it out in front of them. Then the world above exploded as two F-35 Lightning jets roared over their heads, low enough to touch.

Pushing six hundred knots, the jets flashed by and screamed over the diamond mine barely a heartbeat later.

'What the hell was that?' shouted Sarah as the noise of the jets began to fade.

'That was the RAF finally coming to the party,' answered Rob, unable to keep the grin from his face. 'We need to get going.' He handed her his Glock.

'Why?' asked Sarah. 'In case you hadn't noticed, there's still a major firefight going on outside. Not sure we need to be part of that.'

'I agree,' replied Rob. 'But you can be sure those F-35s are going to start dropping ordnance really soon and we don't want to be anywhere near this place when they do.'

Recognising the lesser of two evils, Sarah agreed.

'What's the plan then?'

The pilot in the lead jet was working hard. Having hurtled over the diamond mine at less than one hundred feet, he swiftly pulled up to a safe height and banked sharply back round towards the fight. Looking down, he could see pinpricks of light from the green glowsticks making a faint but clearly discernible u-shape on the ground below. That u-shape marked the forward line of his own troops. Then two GPS coordinates flashed up on his screen. He punched a button, and they appeared as target indicators over a map on a second screen. When the indicators turned to red, he knew that two of his five hundred-pound bombs had locked on. Another quick look down and he mentally superimposed the real time image below him with the target data on the screen. It was all very tight.

'Gunner zero-one, I calculate both your targets are danger close, over.'

The forward air controller replied immediately.

'Roger, buster zero-one. Concur, but we have no alternative.' As always, the final decision to fire rested with the pilot. He made it quickly.

'Roger, releasing in three, two one. Bombs gone.'

As soon as he heard that, the forward air controller gave a thumbs up to his squadron leader. Dan keyed the tactical mike again.

'All callsigns, this is gunner six-actual. Friendly ordnance inbound. Danger close. Take cover, take cover, take cover!' He threw away the microphone and hunkered down inside the vehicle as securely as he could.

The two bombs landed within less than a second of each other and the explosions sounded like one. Huge heaves of earth were thrown up perilously close to the dug-in troops, but warned in advance, they were all hugging the ground in safety. The insurgent fighters were not so fortunate. Tightly bunched, they were advancing slowly and quietly towards the British position.

They had no warning and never knew what hit them. Unbelievably, the explosions didn't kill them all, and a number clawed their way back to their feet as the blast wave passed.

'Open fire!' Dan's troops could see little of what they were shooting at, but it didn't matter. As they unleashed a wall of lead into the devastation left by the bombs, the insurgent fighters still standing took the only realistic choice available to them. They turned and ran for their lives.

The two bombs provided Rob and Sarah the cover they needed to exit the storeroom. The plan was simple. They would retrace Rob's route into the diamond mine, at least until they reached a safe place in the undergrowth where they could shelter until the fight was over. Unfortunately, as soon as Rob looked out from the storeroom, he could see that plan wasn't going to survive the first fifty metres. Three fighters had taken up firing positions alongside the front edge of the nearest storage shed. Right now, they were staring in awe at the two huge plumes of fire and smoke caused by the F-35's bomb run, but Rob knew that distraction wouldn't last. They needed to be removed.

Rob motioned Sarah to stay in the doorway. He ran forward a few paces to give himself a clear line to the fighters, then he brought his rifle up to his shoulder. Taking careful aim, he gently squeezed the trigger and watched the first fighter fall. He squeezed again. Two down. The third fighter ran. Rob followed him with his rifle, firing again, once, twice. The fighter pitched forward. Rob lowered his rifle. Then, to his right, he sensed rather than saw movement. Within touching distance. Turning quickly, his eye caught a flash of light as it glanced off the blade of a heavy combat knife held high in the air. A moment later, it was arcing down toward him. His own weapon remained pointing uselessly away in the direction of the downed fighters. He was defenceless.

Without even realising it, Rob tensed up waiting for the knife to strike. But instead of pain, the next thing his senses registered was the sharp crack of a handgun. And again. A body fell heavily onto him. It slithered down his side like an erotic dancer, ending in a lifeless heap at his feet. Rob looked up to see Sarah walking towards him, right arm still extended. A wisp of smoke escaped from the barrel of the Glock.

'Cut that a bit fine, didn't you?' was all he could manage.

Knowing that it wouldn't take the F-35 pilots long to turn their attention to the diamond mine, Rob and Sarah swiftly retreated to the far edge of the storage shed and then back into the undergrowth. As fast as they could, they scrambled up and away from the mine. Once they'd reached a safe distance, Rob confirmed over the radio that they were no longer in the target area. It took the F-35s less than a minute and four more five hundred pounders to remove any remaining threat to the British troops. Job done, they wheeled away and headed back to the carrier.

Rob and Sarah approached the British position cautiously. The last thing they needed now was a blue-on-blue. They needn't have worried. Terry was at the top of the hill waiting for them. He escorted them back to the observation post where the wounded were being treated. Rob counted a dozen casualties but only one serious. The doc was busy doing his thing and assured Rob the soldier would live.

Dawn was fast approaching, and Rob stood looking down on what was left of the diamond mine below him. The first streaks of orange light glimmered tantalisingly on the eastern horizon. The dark smudges of smoke that rose from the still smouldering buildings threatened to spoil the view, but he didn't care. All the one hundred and one men and women he'd led into battle had survived the night and Sarah was safe as well. The African sunrise was impressive, but it didn't come close to beating that. All around him preparations were being finalised for the recovery back to Hotel Fox, under the ever-watchful eye of the regimental sergeant major.

A few minutes later, Mr Jones appeared at his side.

'All set, sir,' he reported.

'Thanks, Mr Jones.'

'Oh, and just one other thing, sir.'

'Yes.'

'Congratulations on making it to day forty-five in the big brother house!'

36.

It could have been any other Sunday morning in July when Rebecca awoke. The bright sunshine streaming in through the bedroom window of her small, south London flat confirmed it was going to be a gorgeous summer's day. But Rebecca wasn't interested in the weather. Although she understood the tactical oversight of the day's events was strictly a matter for the police, she also knew she couldn't avoid somehow being part of it. And that meant heading back into Vauxhall Cross.

She dressed quickly, ignored breakfast, and headed to her local tube station at a run. The Sunday underground schedule forced her to wait ten minutes for a train. She had another delay at Stockwell before making the one-station hop up the Victoria line into Vauxhall. At least the main entrance at Vauxhall Cross was twenty-four hour manned, and there was no queue at the entry tubes. Two minutes after showing her pass to one of the bored-looking security guards, Rebecca was in her office, firing up her computer.

Jelani Achebe was cold and stiff. It had been almost dark the previous evening when he abandoned his hire car in a small car park on the edge of town and trudged the mile and a half to his lay-up point. He'd been here before, of course. He'd checked out half a dozen potential firing positions before finally selecting this one. Located to the southeast of his target, he knew it was a good one. By midday, the sun would be almost directly behind him, so he'd have no problems with shadows, nor did he have to worry about the sunshine giving him away by reflecting off his scope, the only piece of his equipment he couldn't camouflage. He was a good hundred metres above his target and almost seven hundred metres from it. A long shot, but well within his ability. To his front and right was farmland. Crops of some kind. He had no idea what but was confident they wouldn't need much tending on a Sunday morning. To his left he could hear noise from the motorway he'd driven up in the pouring rain the previous afternoon. That had been a challenge, but he'd been careful, kept to the speed limit and made it without incident.

The ground beneath him was still wet from yesterday's rain and the undergrowth around him was heavy with early morning dew. He ate the last of his energy bars and drank another bottle of water. Then he crawled forward the final few metres from the lay-up point into his firing position. He'd left the heavy gun case in the boot of the SUV and had carried his rifle up in a light, waterproof slip. It was now time to break it out and get set up. Jelani took his time. He knew almost to the minute what time his target would appear. He also knew he'd have no problem making a positive identification from the many photographs he'd studied on the internet. He assembled his weapon calmly and methodically, just like he would have if he'd been preparing to shoot in the final of the Imperial Meeting. He felt a quick pang of regret that the chance to win the Queen's Prize had been taken from him but consoled himself with the thought that this was the reason he'd really come to the UK. He checked his watch, still two hours before show time. The sun was getting stronger by the minute and even though he was hunkered down, he could still feel its warmth on his back and legs. It would never be West Africa warm, but what could you expect from this shitty country, he thought fiercely to himself. He re-arranged the floppy green hat that hung generously over the back of his neck and settled in to wait.

The first report of the previous night's action in Free State appeared in Rebecca's inbox shortly after eleven. It was extremely succinct and even she could tell a stack of detail had been left out. Hardly surprising as most of the actions of the British forces appeared to have directly contravened the prime minister's specific direction. Nevertheless, she was relieved that at least someone had been strong enough to make the tough decisions, and that Rob and his troops were safe. She was reading the report through a second time, when she heard a light tap on her office door. The chief was also working on Sunday.

Rebecca started to stand but Hilary waved her to sit back down. She stepped into the office and took one of the small easy chairs in front of Rebecca's desk.

'I take it you've seen the latest SITREP?' she asked. Rebecca held up the piece of paper she'd been reading.

'I have. It doesn't say much.'

'No, I know, but I've just had a long chat with Admiral Bellis' military assistant. She also an old Somervillian, although a few years after me of course. It would appear the decision to attack the diamond mine was taken by your brother and against the express orders of General Wilkinson.'

'Oh shit.' said Rebecca.

'Well maybe under normal circumstances,' agreed Hilary. 'But given the fact that the Free State army had been so thoroughly defeated earlier, and he also managed to rescue Major Grey, I'd say he's every chance of getting away with it.' Rebecca's sigh of relief was audible. 'It might take the Ministry of Defence a few goes to get its story straight, but Admiral Bellis will definitely want some heroes to come out of this, and both Major Grey and your brother are likely to be at the front of the queue.'

'What's going to happen to Simon Nkaba?' asked Rebecca.

'Nothing,' said Hilary. 'Not now.'

Rebecca's face darkened, her anger showing.

'After what he's done. Why not?' she demanded.

'Because he's dead. Your brother killed him.' That hadn't been in the report. 'All we need now is for the police to pick up that nephew of his and it's all over. What did you say his name was?'

Achebe,' replied Rebecca. 'Jelani Achebe.'

'Yes, I thought so,' said Hilary. 'I'm sure Achebe was the name of the third Free State boy at Oxford.'

'But if Nkaba is … was,' Rebecca corrected, 'Achebe's uncle, that means the Achebe you knew must be married to Nkaba's sister.'

'I didn't even know he had a sister,' said Hilary.

'It came up in the background checks my team did on Nkaba, but I didn't think anything of it.'

The two of them looked at each other.

'Does that mean he's part of it?' asked Rebecca.

'Peter. I think his name was Peter,' said Hilary. 'And who knows. Does it change anything?'

For a while neither spoke. Both trying to think through where this new piece of the jigsaw might fit. Rebecca was first to break the silence.

'I still don't buy it,' she said. 'Something doesn't feel right.'

'What do you mean?' asked her boss.

'Well, you said yourself revenge is a dish best served cold.'

'I did.'

'So, I get the political devastation facing Brownlow if Hotel Fox had been overrun and stacks of British troops had been killed. At the very least, he'd have had to resign. But whatever the reason for getting back at Brownlow, you'd want him to be haunted by what you'd done for years to come, wouldn't you? You wouldn't want to just kill him straight away.'

The silence returned.

'Are you suggesting that Brownlow isn't the target then?' said Hilary eventually.

'What if you wanted to break him personally as well as humiliate him politically?' Rebecca let the question hang.

'You'd kill the person closest to him,' suggested Hilary.

'His wife.'

'Of course,' said Hilary. 'Disgrace him publicly and destroy him privately. The perfect combination. Achebe's nowhere near the NEC, is he?'

'No, he's not. He's wherever Brownlow's wife is. Where will she be on a Sunday morning?'

'In church,' said Hilary immediately. 'I sat next to her at a dinner party in Downing Street last year. She's very religious.'

'So where does she go to church. Somewhere in Whitehall? Chequers?' Rebecca was clutching at straws.

'No, she goes to her local church. In the village where the family home is. Great Bourton.'

Rebecca was straight onto google maps.

'That's over thirty miles away from Birmingham. They'll never redeploy assets in time,' she looked at the clock. It was already quarter to twelve.

'We need to get onto the Met's protection command. She must have a close protection officer assigned.' said Hilary getting to her feet.

'Not fast enough,' responded Rebecca. 'There is another option.' She grabbed her mobile and hit the last number redial.

'Come On! Come On!'

The mobile phone clipped to James' black tactical vest buzzed insistently. He looked down at the screen and saw it was Rebecca. For a second his finger hovered over the red button. Then he stopped. Rebecca knew exactly what was going on. She wouldn't call unless it was urgent. He answered it.

'Rebecca.'

'James, look I haven't got time to explain,' gabbled Rebecca hurriedly. 'But Anthony Brownlow is not the target.'

'OPSEC.' said James automatically.

'Bugger operational security,' replied Rebecca. 'This is too urgent for that. Achebe isn't about to shoot the prime minister, he's about to shoot the prime minister's wife. She'll be leaving the parish church in Great Bourton in less than fifteen minutes and you're the only person who can get to her in time.'

James worked the problem over in his mind for no more than five seconds.

'Okay, but I can't just pull our chopper off task and head down to Great Bourton. The police are calling the shots up here and at the very least I'll have to convince the bronze commander.'

'But there's no time for that,' urged Rebecca.

'Leave this to me,' said Hilary to Rebecca quietly. 'Major Wilberforce,' she raised her voice. 'It's Hilary Blythe, chief of the Secret Intelligence Service.'

'I know who you are ma'am,' said James.

'What Rebecca's just said is one hundred per cent true. And you are our only possible response. I'll speak with the gold commander at Scotland Yard. In the meantime, I comfortably outrank the police commander on the ground, and I authorise you to redeploy to Great Bourton immediately to protect the prime minister's wife.'

'Good enough for me ma'am,' said James. 'We're on our way.'

The helicopter pilot flew the thirty-five miles from Birmingham to Great Bourton with the throttle at maximum all the way. Even so, it still took twelve minutes. Coming in from the north, he wheeled round the edge of the village and brought the Puma to a hover above what looked like a primary school. The seventeenth century church was right on the nose.

'What now?' he yelled at James over the intercom.

'Get us close to the church as possible, we'll rope down.'

Nudging the cyclic, the pilot manoeuvred forward until he was directly over the small churchyard. Avoiding the trees blowing about wildly in the helicopter's downdraft, he held steady as a crewman threw a thirty-foot line out of each cabin door. Before the ropes had even hit the ground, James and one of his troopers were sliding down at breakneck speed. Below, the vicar was at the church door bidding farewell to his congregation after his eleven o'clock service. He watched flabbergasted as the two SAS men dodged the headstones as they ran towards him.

From his firing point, Jelani saw the helicopter appear over the village. He cursed. Someone had worked it out.

But there was still time.

The old wooden doors to the church were opening and through his scope he could see the vicar in his black cassock and white surplice slowly walking out into the sunshine. He moved the crosshairs onto the first female member of the congregation out after him. Not her. A second lady came into view. Not her either. Jelani forced himself to stay calm. He could hear the Puma overhead and knew very soon his opportunity would be lost. More people were leaving the church and his target zone was getting congested. A clean shot now would not be easy. Then he saw her. Yellow dress. White hat. Head down, face in shadow. Jelani needed to be sure. She looked up as someone spoke to her. It was definitely her. He already had the shot calculated. Crosshairs settled, yellow filled his scope. Jelani breathed in slowly. Exhaled half a breath. Paused.

Then he squeezed the trigger.

Dressed head to toe in black, including Kevlar helmet and goggles, James knew he must be frightening the life out of the mainly elderly churchgoers as he sped through the graveyard towards them. The Heckler & Kock G3 assault rifle in his arms probably didn't help much either. But he only had one thing on his mind. Find the prime minister's wife.

The entrance to the church faced south, so as the congregation spilled out many had their heads lowered or were holding up their hands to avoid the glare of the sun. That didn't help. Then James saw a yellow dress advancing down the path. The face beneath the wide-brimmed hat looked familiar and he cut that way. The crowd parted and he was directly in front of her. Instantaneously, he was smashed in the back with the force of a freight train. He stumbled forward but kept his footing. Something deep inside his brain noted that his body armour had just performed exactly as the manufacturer said it would. And just as well. James straightened up.

'Mrs Brownlow,' he said holding his arms wide to appear as non-aggressive as possible. 'I'm Major Wilberforce of the Special Air Service regiment. Please could I ask you to step back inside the church.'

Seven hundred metres away, Jelani saw the black-clad figure step straight into his line of sight a fraction after he pulled the trigger. He knew the bullet would take almost a second to reach its target and watched helplessly as the soldier caught it square in the middle of his back. Straight away, he worked the bolt open, ejected the spend cartridge and reached for a new round. But when he looked through his sight again, the yellow dress was already disappearing back into the church. He fired again but knew immediately the shot wasn't good. A second later, he saw it impact harmlessly on the stone arch over the church door.

Mrs Brownlow was old school. In her time as the prime minister's wife, she had seen practically everything and although James' gallant introduction had been a first, it hadn't phased her one bit. Without raising an eyebrow, she had turned around and did as she had been asked. Behind her, James saw a puff of stone as the second round hit the wall above him. A second later, he heard in his earpiece.

'Got eyes on the shooter. To the southeast.'

'Right, you bastard,' said James. 'You're mine.' He called up the pilot and in a second, the helicopter was back in the hover over the churchyard. James signalled to his wingman and together they leapt onto the ropes. Without waiting for them to climb up, the pilot banked away towards the source of the shots.

Jelani knew his chance had gone. All he could do now was get out of there. He pulled his rifle back into the hide and snapped closed its bipod legs. As he hastily shovelled it back into the slip, he was aware that the noise of the helicopter was getting louder. He looked up. The Puma was advancing rapidly with two soldiers swaying perilously thirty feet below. It dipped, almost driving the soldiers into the ground. At the last second, they let go of the ropes and threw themselves forward, like two circus acrobats. They rolled over and, in a flash, were both back on their feet, weapons up, running towards him. Jelani knew there could only be one outcome. He tossed his rifle to one side and slowly raised his hands.

37.

After receiving further orders, the Puma pilot headed for London. He flew fast and half an hour after Jelani had been bundled aboard, the helicopter was touching down on the helipad at Vauxhall Cross. An SIS security team was waiting to greet them, but James insisted on staying with his prisoner. Jelani was thoroughly searched, and his belt and bootlaces were removed. He was secured in an interview room in the basement of the building.

Standing in the adjoining viewing room, Hilary and Rebecca studied Jelani through a large one-way mirror. He was sat on a grey metal chair in front of a grey metal table. Both were bolted to the floor. He stared impassively at the mirror, obviously knowing he was being watched.

'Did he say anything on the flight down?' asked Hilary.

'Not a word,' replied James. 'Once he was in the back of the chopper and we got the plasticuffs on him, he clammed up completely. And no sign of nerves whatsoever. He either doesn't realise how much shit he's in, or he thinks he's got a way out.'

They stared back at Jelani. It was true. He looked like he didn't have a care in the world.

'Right,' said Hilary. 'I think it's time we changed that.'

A minute later, all three were in the interview room. Hilary and Rebecca took the two metal chairs bolted down on the other side of the desk. James stood by the door, looking menacing.

'I want a lawyer,' said Jelani straight away. 'I know how this works. I don't have to answer any questions from you. I want to see a lawyer.'

'All in good time,' said Hilary calmly. 'And we're not here to ask you questions. I just want to bring you up to date with everything that's been going on in your country.'

Jelani looked surprised but said nothing.

'As I'm sure you know,' continued Hilary. 'A large group of insurgent fighters have been gathering in the Free State hinterland to attack the British forward base at Harris Field.'

Jelani still said nothing, but Hilary didn't miss the flicker of recognition in his eyes. He knew exactly what had been planned.

'Anyway. Last night that group was attacked and defeated. It is no longer a threat to the forward base or any other British or Free State army forces in your country.'

That did get a reaction.

'You're lying,' he snarled.

'No. No I'm not,' replied Hilary. Her voice so low that Jelani almost had to lean forward to hear. 'We know all about your uncle's plans. The supposed insurgency created to hide his true intentions. But that's all over now. The South African mercenaries have fled and now they've gone, there's nothing to keep the insurgency together. Those fighters that survived will melt away back to their villages as soon as they can.'

'My uncle will never give up,' shot back Jelani, his anger rising. 'You'll see. Even if what you say is true, he'll come back stronger.'

'No, Jelani. He won't,' interrupted Rebecca. 'He won't come back stronger. In fact, he won't come back at all. Your uncle died in the fighting last night.'

'You're lying,' Jelani shouted again.

'No, we're not,' answered Rebecca quietly. 'Your uncle is gone. That just leaves your father. Why don't you do yourself a favour and tell us all about him.'

'What?' said Jelani, his anger turning to confusion.

'Your father,' pressed Rebecca. 'What part did he have in all this?'

'What are you talking about? My father is the reason all this happened in the first place.'

Hilary and Rebecca exchanged glances. So, Peter Achebe was involved.

'Okay, Jelani.' said Hilary. 'Was it Peter Achebe calling the shots? Was he the one pulling your uncle's strings?'

Jelani shook his head, perplexed.

'What do you mean, Peter Achebe pulling the strings?'

'Peter Achebe, your father.'

'Peter Achebe hasn't been pulling any strings. He's dead. He died in a helicopter crash fifteen years ago. And he's not my father.'

Jelani's bombshell dropped like a rock in a fishpond. Suddenly it was Hilary and Rebecca on the back foot.

'Peter Achebe married your mother, Afia Nkaba. We know that. Why do you say he's not your father?'

'Because he isn't,' shot Jelani, his voice rising again. 'You people. You don't know anything, do you?'

'Well, if we don't know, why don't you tell us?'

Jelani paused, looking at Hilary and then at Rebecca.

'When my mother was just eighteen, she went to England to see her brother in Oxford. He was studying there with President Korrundi and Peter Achebe.'

Hilary nodded.

'I know. I was there too,' she said.

'There was a debate. My uncle was a speaker. So was Anthony Brownlow, your prime minister. Afterwards, there was a big party. The President and my uncle didn't go, but Peter Achebe took my mother.'

Jelani stopped talking and stared across the table, his eyes blazing with anger.

'Go on,' encouraged Hilary.

'Peter Achebe promised to look after my mother, but he got in a fight. It was all a set-up. Brownlow's mates arranged the whole thing. But the police came and arrested him anyway. That left my mother all alone.'

He stopped again.

'Do you know what roofies are?' he asked bitterly.

'What, you mean Rohypnol?' asked Rebecca. 'The date-rape drug?'

Jelani nodded.

'Brownlow gave it to my mother. In her drink. Then he took her back to his place and he raped her.' Jelani was screaming. 'Anthony Brownlow raped my mother!'

Oh my God, thought Rebecca.

'And you're the result,' she blurted out.

'Yes. I'm the fucking result,' Jelani leapt to his feet. 'I'm the fucking result. Anthony Brownlow is my father!'

James stepped forward quickly and grabbed Jelani. The noise had alerted the security team and a second later they rushed into the room.

'Get him out of here,' ordered Hilary. 'Take him to the holding cells until we can hand him over to the police.' The security team dragged Jelani from the room.

Ten minutes later, Hilary and Rebecca were back in the chief's office. Hilary headed straight for the drinks cabinet and poured two large measures of something strong. She handed a glass to Rebecca.

'Wow,' she said. 'I was not expecting that.'

'Did you believe him?' asked Rebecca.

'Why not? As I said, Brownlow was a real shit at Oxford. So much privilege. If he wanted something, he just took it. I think he genuinely believed he could do whatever he wanted.'

'But rape?'

'I know. Not many people knew about Rohypnol back then. And who would believe a visiting African teenager over someone like Brownlow. All he had to do was get Peter Achebe out of the way, and that didn't prove too difficult.'

'And when she found out she was pregnant, Peter Achebe did the decent thing and married her?'

'I guess it was the least he could do, after failing to protect her in Oxford,' said Hilary.

'Well, it certainly confirms Nkaba's motive,' said Rebecca. 'I mean, who wouldn't want to get back at Brownlow after that?

'It was clearly more than just a grudge about the debate. And I bet when Peter Achebe died, Nkaba took in his sister and nephew. Seeing Jelani growing up in his own house must have driven him crazy. An everyday reminder of what Brownlow did to his sister.'

'I wonder when Jelani found out who his real father was,'

'Fairly early on, I'm guessing. I mean he doesn't exactly look like your typical West African, does he? The lighter skin tone and the slim nose are a bit of a giveaway. A DNA test will confirm it of course, but when you think about it, the evidence is all there.'

'What happens now?' asked Rebecca.

'Well, Achebe doesn't have diplomatic immunity. It'll be down to the CPS of course, but he should be tried for attempted murder.'

'No, what happens to Anthony Brownlow?'

'What do you mean?' replied Hilary.

'You know. All this plotting against him. He is the prime minister, and that night in Oxford was over twenty years ago ...'

Hilary got up from the desk and looked out of the window. The sun was shining, and London was calm and serene. She shook her head. Not for long.

'It makes no odds who he is,' she said firmly, turning back to face Rebecca. 'Rape is rape and no-one's above the law.'

She reached for the phone and punched the button for her PA.

'Mary, get me the Metropolitan police commissioner please.'

Hotel Fox

A Sarah Grey Thriller

This is the first novel featuring the indomitable Sarah Grey. There will be more. If you enjoyed it, or even if you didn't, I'd love to hear your comments. You can contact me via any of the following:

fredsmithauthor@gmail.com

@fredsmithauthor

Fred Smith Author

Also

Please leave a review on Amazon